"A spray of white French lilac was in Horace Harvey's hand," F.O.P.P.'s representative informed them, smirking as she did. "Maybe you have good reason to worry about Tillie Greenleaf."

"White lilac won't be blooming in Connecticut for another month or two," Kathleen said.

Susan thought the statement was irrelevant. "So what?" she asked.

"So I think I'd better look more closely at that body," Kathleen said. "Watch Tillie, won't you? Just don't let her say anything stupid. I'll be back as soon as I can!"

And Susan found herself responsible for Tillie Greenleaf, lover of flowers, the environment, and especially, it seemed, white French lilacs.

A GOOD YEAR FOR A CORPSE

VALERIE WOLZIEN

FAWCETT GOLD MEDAL • NEW YORK

For my two Judys—
Judy Armstrong and
Judy Ryan.
For all their support.

A Fawcett Gold Medal Book
Published by Ballantine Books
Copyright © 1994 by Valerie Wolzien

All rights reserved under International and Pan-American Copyright Conventions. Published in the United States of America by
Ballantine Books, a division of Random House, Inc., New York,
and simultaneously in Canada by Random House of Canada Limited, Toronto.

Library of Congress Catalog Card Number: 93-90868

ISBN 0-449-14833-5

Manufactured in the United States of America

First Edition: April 1994

10 9 8 7 6 5 4

ONE

Horace Harvey was unusually busy the week before he died.

He checked into his hotel late Saturday night.

Early Sunday morning, he treated the president, vice president, and secretary of the Hancock, Connecticut, chamber of commerce to brunch at the Hancock Inn. His appetite apparently unsatisfied, he proceeded on to afternoon tea in the home of the town's mayor, followed by a wine tasting and meeting of Parks Are People, better known as P.A.P.

Monday he got an early start and was seen at the breakfast meeting of the F.O.P.P. (Friends of Potted Plants), where his Savile Row chalk stripe stood out among the loden green uniforms the group had tailored at great expense so they would be appropriately dressed while working. That afternoon he strolled through the extensive system of parks maintained immaculately by the H.E.C. (Hancock Environmental Committee), where specimen flowers bloomed among ecologically correct, water-retentive ground covers, where wildflowers blossomed, where pesticides were unknown, and where good bugs feasted on bad bugs. It was excellent exercise, and that night he dozed off during an awards dinner given by the board of the local historical society.

Sixty-seven-year-old men tire easily, and Horace Harvey was spied yawning more than once Tuesday during lunch with the organizer of the town's amateur theater group. But later in the day, he attended an open hearing on noise pollution and development in Connecticut, enjoying a spirited debate between the chairman of Q.U.I.E.T. and the leader of H.O.P.E.

Wednesday, Horace Harvey was seen following the mayor around town hall, speaking with the professional gardening staff of Hancock, arguing with the custodian of the building where the theater group in town performed, leaning over a computer screen with the reference librarian in the historic files of the library, and, finally, sharing coffee and doughnuts with the acting chief of police.

He spent Thursday morning on the phone, arranging for the big meeting that he planned for that evening. No one knows what he did in the afternoon.

TWO

THAT AFTERNOON SUSAN HENSHAW WAS IN HER KITCHEN trying to grind coffee beans, talk on the phone, and figure out why the family's new puppy seemed to prefer dirty paper towels to the expensive food their veterinarian had recommended. "Well, I guess I'll have to drive over to your office before we leave. Thanks anyway," she said into the receiver. Hanging up the phone, she noticed that the papers covering her large pine kitchen table were shifting in the wind.

It was a beautiful spring day, one of the first of the year, and the windows were open to catch the fresh breezes. "Hi!" Susan called out, seeing her friend Kathleen crossing the Henshaws' mossy brick patio outside their back door.

"Hi, yourself," Kathleen responded, entering the room and dumping three large paper bags on the tile countertop next to the door. "Fabulous day. I thought you'd be outside walking the dog."

They both turned and looked at the mound of fur lying in the corner of the room. One light beige ear was soaking in a large personalized ceramic water bowl.

"I see you decided on a name," Kathleen commented. "Does she really look like 'Spike' to you?"

"No. Jed didn't notice that the bowl was printed when he bought it—you know how husbands get in unfamiliar stores. And the poor animal still doesn't have a name. Chrissy wants to call her Chelsea—which is definitely not politically correct. Chad keeps thinking of clever names

3

like Dammit and Fart Face. Jed says we should call her Spot."

"Why?" Kathleen asked, looking down on the eight-week-old golden retriever bitch. "There's not a mark on her that I can see."

"She makes them on the rug. Do you believe this? I think we're going to have to start family therapy to get this thing resolved. It's ridiculous."

"What do you call her in the meantime?"

"Almost anything. She seems to respond more to tone of voice than any particular word. Maybe we should name her Sleepy—she drops off the second she walks in the door. She loves being outside, but I can't leave her there. She keeps eating crocus—mostly the yellow ones. Do you think they taste different than the purple and white?"

"Lemon, grape, and coconut?"

"Sounds silly, doesn't it?" Susan admitted. "But she's so tired. Do you think they're poisonous?"

"I have no idea, but I'll ask Tillie the next time I see her. She knows the most amazing things about plants. And spring bulbs are one of her specialties. You wouldn't believe . . ."

Susan chuckled as her friend continued. Kathleen had recently discovered the joys of gardening, and in Hancock, Connecticut, Tillie Greenleaf was the guru of the garden. Kathleen had removed the barrette that was stylishly confining her thick blond hair, and sat down, massaging the small of her back.

"Are you okay?"

"Between picking up Bananas and all this cultivating, my spine is getting more of a workout than it's used to," Kathleen answered, referring to her three-year-old son, Alexander Brandon Colin Gordon, by his nickname. "What are you doing?" she asked, peering over Susan's shoulder.

"Trying to map out two short trips—to Boston and Washington, D.C."

"Sounds like fun. When are you planning to get away?"

"Soon. Early next week. And it's not going to be fun. I'm taking Chrissy to look at colleges. I'm not looking forward to spending all this time with her. . . ." She frowned at the papers in front of her.

"You two still feuding?" Kathleen was well aware of her friend's anxiety over her daughter's choice of boyfriend—as was everyone who knew Susan. For over a month, she had been loudly bemoaning her daughter's infatuation with a young man whom she considered unsuitable.

" 'Feuding' is not the word. She's now talking about not going to college at all. She wants to stay here with Brian. She says that an artist doesn't need a formal education—an artist needs to live. Of course, that's Brian talking. He doesn't want her to leave and stop buying gas for that dreadful Mustang he drives. . . . I just can't believe this is happening to Chrissy. She has so much going for her. There's no reason for her to ruin her life like this."

"She's not going to ruin her life. She just has a crush on someone you don't like." Kathleen repeated the same thing all Susan's friends had been saying.

"I suppose so, but, you know, probably someone thinks that about every teenager who does something so stupid that it really does affect the rest of their lives." Susan bit her lip and shuffled the papers in front of her. "Well, maybe she'll see something at one of these schools that will make her forget Brian."

"Of course. She's such a talented artist, and once she gets to college, she'll find out how much she has in common with the other students." Kathleen went on, "You might actually enjoy the trips, you know. Boston and Washington are both beautiful in the spring. You'll be right on time for the cherry blossoms in D.C., won't you?"

"Maybe. Of course, there might still be frost in Boston. But this is silly. What's in those sacks?"

Kathleen smiled and patted the top bag. "Thank goodness you asked. I was wondering how I was going to bring it up. It's a complete set of the records of H.E.C.—Hancock's Environmental Committee, you know. It's the oldest ecological group in town—it's been around since the beginning of the movement. H.E.C. was founded on the first Earth Day in 1970," she said with pride, then frowned and continued, "and I don't think anyone has done anything since then except take notes and stuff them into one of these three bags."

Susan stared at the Bloomingdale's, Saks Fifth Avenue, and Grand Union bags, the contents of which were bursting over her kitchen counters. "It all looks very biodegradable," she commented.

"I wouldn't mind adding it to the compost pile myself," Kathleen admitted. "But I have to organize the entire mess. It's my job," she explained further. "I'm the new secretary of H.E.C."

"And what have the previous secretaries been doing?"

"Apparently storing the bags," Kathleen answered with a shrug. "But I'm supposed to go through this stuff before the meeting tonight."

"You're kidding."

"No. It's important. We want to be able to reply intelligently to any questions Horace Harvey asks about the history of H.E.C." Kathleen was emptying the Saks bag as she spoke. Handwritten notes, typed sheets, crumpled receipts, a half dozen spiral notebooks, glossy black-and-white publicity photographs, color snapshots, and a large bulging manila envelope were distributed across the table. "I think this is the first bag—chronologically. I hope some of the stuff is dated."

"How did you get to be secretary of H.E.C.?" Susan asked, flipping through one of the notebooks.

"I was asked." Kathleen opened one of the notebooks and glanced at the first page, frowning. "I haven't been a member very long, and I don't go to many business meetings, so I didn't know about this mess. Usually I just help out in the parks since I can take Bananas along with me—in fact, that's why I joined in the first place."

"I remember you telling me about it last October."

Susan had watched for a half dozen years while Kathleen adjusted to life as the wife of a widower in the suburbs. Not naturally domestic, Kathleen had often found it difficult to connect with the community. Capitalizing on her experience as police detective in the city, Kathleen had run a security business until the birth of her son. She had then tried out various service organizations before joining the fall bulb-planting parties that H.E.C. held in the town's elaborate park system. "And I guess I was so flattered that anyone would think of me as an officer of the group that I didn't stop to consider what I was getting into," Kathleen explained.

"H.E.C. is a fine organization, you know. There have been hundreds of flowers and trees planted in the last twenty years by H.E.C. And because of H.E.C., Hancock had a professional recycling center functioning fifteen years ago. H.E.C. sponsors dozens of speakers and projects in the public schools. Hancock's park system would be almost half the size it is presently if H.E.C. hadn't been so active. . . . You probably know all this, don't you?" she interrupted herself.

Susan had lived in Hancock for fifteen years. "I know some of it," she admitted. "And I know that you all must have green thumbs. The parks are looking fabulous. I was just admiring those urns of pansies at the municipal center yesterday."

"H.E.C. has nothing to do with any plants in pots."

Susan looked up, surprised to hear the change of tone in her friend's voice.

"I know what you're thinking," Kathleen added quickly. "I've picked up the prejudices of the group I belong to, I guess. You see, F.O.P.P. is our competitor."

Susan blinked. "Fop?"

"F.O.P.P. Friends of Potted Plants. It's a much smaller group than H.E.C.: they do nothing except plant and maintain the potted plants located in public spaces in town."

"And the two groups are in competition? Isn't Hancock large enough for everyone to carve out their own space?"

"We compete for financial resources. In this case, Mr. Horace Harvey's financial resources, to be specific," Kathleen explained.

"Oh." Susan paused and thought for a minute. "I think I heard him mentioned recently. There were two women talking about him in the puppy socialization class that we're taking at the high school. He's planning on leaving a large sum of money to some civic organization, right? But I thought they were referring to something historical."

"That probably would be S.O.D. It's an organization that wants to save an old dump in town."

"What old dump?"

"A colonial dump from pre–revolutionary war days. I don't know very much about it. Apparently someone who lives down by the river was having an addition put on their house, and this thing was discovered when their backyard was being excavated. At least that's the story I was told."

"It must be huge. Hancock was a thriving community even in those days."

Kathleen answered slowly. "I don't think it's that big. From what I heard, it's just a small pile of buried rubbish. Tillie thinks that this is a case of much ado about nothing. She says it won't cost a lot to excavate the dump site, and there really isn't much general interest in town about it." She frowned. "I mean, I think it's interesting, but I was a history major in college."

"So what is H.E.C. going to do with the money if Mr. Harvey gives it to you?" Susan was slightly amused at the conflict her friend seemed to be feeling.

"We'll redo everything," Kathleen replied enthusiastically, grabbing a pile of her papers before they tumbled to the floor. "There'll be water gardens and wildflower meadows. The entire north section of Toad Hill Park will be turned into a walled rose garden with rare heirloom varieties. We'll build an herb garden along the banks of the river, with a special section of aromatic plants for blind people to enjoy. And greenhouses will keep the parks open in the middle of winter. . . ."

"Heavens. How much money is this man giving away?"

"I don't know. Apparently he has at least a million, and he plans on leaving it all to one organization. He grew up here, although he made his fortune somewhere else. But for some reason, he decided that he wanted to do something for Hancock. I suppose he was grateful to the town for the outstanding beginning it provided for his life or something like that." Kathleen picked up the Grand Union bag and peeked inside. "This seems to be correspondence. Maybe there's a letter from Mr. Harvey explaining it all."

"Why don't I look for it while you sort through that stuff?" Susan offered. She found herself intrigued by the situation as well as the man. The conversation she had overheard in her puppy-training class had convinced her that H.E.C. wasn't the only organization that believed it deserved to be the recipient of Mr. Harvey's largesse. In fact, two young women had seemed convinced that something called P.A.P. was very likely, if not certainly, the organization he had chosen to endow, so she was surprised by Kathleen's next words.

"There's very little doubt that Mr. Harvey has decided to give H.E.C. his money."

"Really?"

"Yes. He came to a meeting a few days ago, and he was very enthusiastic. He spoke with Tillie privately after the group broke up and assured her that he was going to leave his entire fortune to H.E.C."

" 'Leave his entire fortune'? You mean he's talking about writing a will in favor of H.E.C.? He's not going to give away the money immediately?"

"Exactly. It should all be explained in the letter. Have you found it?"

"Not yet." Susan had been sorting the correspondence into a half dozen piles while they chatted. "How are you doing?"

"I don't even know where to begin. There are maps of all the parks in town here, lists of plants bought, records of plants planted, tables of planting times, freeze dates. . . . It's fascinating. When I have more time to look at it all, I'm going to enjoy it." She got up and headed toward the coffee machine on a nearby counter. "Who would have thought that a city person like me would love gardening? Even Jerry has gotten involved. We're going to have a vegetable garden in the backyard this summer, and he spent all day Saturday rototilling the spot. It will be so good for Bananas.

Tillie believes that children should be exposed to plants at an early age.

"Want some coffee?"

Susan nodded, and Kathleen filled two mugs with the steaming brew and carried them back to the table. "I sure wish I knew what questions Mr. Harvey might ask. It would make everything easier."

"Is he interested in gardening in a technical way? Will he want to see your plant lists? Or do you think he just wants to see the plans of what H.E.C. has accomplished in the parks?" Susan asked, trying to pin it down.

"Maybe the layouts of the parks," Kathleen answered slowly. "Tillie didn't say anything specific, but I got the idea that Mr. Harvey is less interested in what we do than in getting his name on it."

"I don't understand."

"He will only give us the money if we agree to put his name on a park. I think that might be the reason that he chose H.E.C. rather than a different organization. Wouldn't you rather have your name on a park than on a dump—no matter how historical?"

In one of those coincidences that make life interesting as well as confusing, Susan was to hear more about Horace Harvey almost immediately after Kathleen departed to pick up her son. Sorting through the papers that her friend had promised to collect before dinner, Susan was still searching for the philanthropic letter when her phone rang.

The caller, Alissa Anthony, was the main force behind the local amateur theater group. Susan, like many citizens of Hancock, had come to dread getting one of her begging phone calls. Thus far this month, Susan had been talked into donating her wedding dress, dozens of white sheets, and a few bolts of fabric that were to be used for backdrops in the coming production of *Waiting for Godot*. Alissa had already explained her unique interpretation of the classic to Susan; apparently the two bums were women left at the altar, waiting hopelessly for a man who would change their lives for the better. The Henshaws were planning to be out of town the evening of the performance.

"Susan . . ." Alissa began in her habitually breathless voice.

"I don't have anything else that's white," Susan lied, hoping to preserve her linen closet full of thick white towels.

Alissa's voice laughed up and down the entire scale. "Oh, I wouldn't ask you for more," she lied more musically than Susan. "It's just that you've been so generous that I was hoping for a small favor, something that won't take more than a minute. . . ."

"What?" Susan was abrupt, knowing that Alissa loved a soliloquy more than a dialogue.

"A phone call. I just want you to make one phone call. You wouldn't mind doing that so live theater can thrive in our little burb, would you?"

"Who—"

"I knew I could count on you!"

"I didn't say—" Susan tried again.

"You are so articulate, so forceful. I've often wondered why, with your gifts, you don't run for public office. . . ."

"Who do you want me to call and why?" Susan insisted on sticking to the point before she was overwhelmed by all the flattery and began imagining herself as Mayoress Henshaw—or maybe Congresswoman Henshaw. A political career would certainly keep her busy and give her something to worry about other than her daughter. . . .

". . . Horace Harvey."

"What?" The familiar name jerked Susan back to reality.

"I'd like you to call Horace Harvey. Of course, I've already spoken to him. Every member of the group has spoken with him, but I think maybe the opinion of an outsider, so to speak, would carry more weight. You know what Shakespeare said—"

"Yes." In fact, she knew more than a few things he had said. But she also knew that encouraging Alissa to quote a line or two was dangerous. A couple of lines could quickly grow into the entire play, complete with hand motions, pregnant pauses, and plenty of time allowed for applause. "I don't know Horace Harvey," Susan said quickly.

"That doesn't matter. I've told him all about you."

"Why?" Susan asked, completely mystified.

"Don't tell me you haven't heard what that man is doing!"

"Kathleen said something about giving his money to the H.E.C.—"

"H.E.C.! Absolutely absurd! They have control over every park in town already—as well as most of the men and women on the city council. You don't believe that stuff about volunteer labor, do you? Hancock spends a small fortune on professional gardeners and equipment to keep those parks looking so good. And H.E.C. keeps begging for more money for more plants. Connecticut was a beautiful state before all these so-called horticultural experts started mucking around. I have terrible hay fever every spring and fall, and I think it has a lot to do with all these damn parks. All that gaudy flowering. It does nothing to nourish the soul the way theater does. And it's your job to explain that to Horace Harvey. You're a mother. Think of the children!"

Susan resisted an urge to hang up. "The children?" she repeated, hoping that she understood the explanation. Maybe she should rearrange her schedule and renew her acquaintance with that play. She was beginning to feel a growing empathy for those two tramps and their dreary wait.

"The children deserve the best we have."

Susan could envision the movement Alissa would make as she threw her long red braid over her shoulder and narrowed her green eyes. She had often wondered if Alissa acted dramatic because of her inherited looks, or if her appearance was the result of much work attempting to match her personality.

"Alissa, I don't think I can do something like this. . . ." Susan tried to interrupt the flow.

"Never, never say anything like that! We all have more influence than we think we do. . . ."

Susan heard an abrupt change of tone and started to speak. "I—"

"You know, you owe more loyalty to Hancock than to Kathleen and her organization," Alissa insisted. "Think what it has done for your family. This town has educated your children, provided a place for them to swim, playing fields, parks. . . ." She seemed to realize that she was defeating her own argument. "Look, if you feel uncomfortable calling someone you don't know, why don't you just go to the meeting tonight? I'm sure you'll support us once you hear all the arguments."

Susan was confused, but grateful that it seemed she was going to escape committing herself. "What meeting?"

"Kathleen didn't tell you? I heard H.E.C. was trying to pack the room."

"What meeting?" Susan repeated.

"Horace Harvey has invited the officers of all the groups that he is investigating to the Hancock Inn for coffee and dessert. Some people think that he is going to be asking questions that will lead him to decide exactly which group deserves his money. Although—" and Susan heard a rare touch of insecurity in Alissa's voice "—he may have made up his mind already and be planning to announce his choice."

Susan decided that she didn't have to mention what Kathleen had told her about Tillie Greenleaf's belief that her group had already been chosen. "I'm not an officer in any group that's being considered," she protested.

"But you're a community leader, and except for your friendship with Kathleen, you're probably as fair as anyone else in town. And you've been so generous to the production of the play and everything. . . ."

Susan, who had donated everything Alissa requested hoping that she wouldn't be asked to act (before realizing that Alissa had absolutely no intention of allowing her to step on stage), felt she had done more than enough for her. She wasn't even sure that she believed a little theater group was necessary in a town so close to Broadway and which already provided plenty of opportunities for theatrical expe-

rience in the schools. Of course, if the choice was between
amateur theater, parks, potted plants, or a colonial dump,
she, for one, would have a difficult time making up her
mind. And she was beginning to be interested in just what
Mr. Harvey would decide. "You know," she interrupted
Alissa's persuasive tones, "I think maybe I *will* go to that
meeting."

The Hancock Inn was Susan's favorite local restaurant.
Charm and good food attracted many of her friends as well,
and she had decided that, if she ever had an affair, the Inn
was the last place she'd choose to go. But tonight she could
walk in naked between virile twenty-one-year-old twins and
she wasn't sure anyone would notice.

A lot had happened after Alissa hung up. Kathleen had
returned to pick up H.E.C.'s documents, bringing her son.
Bananas had crawled under the kitchen table while his
mother was once again searching for correspondence from
Horace Harvey, and when she was ready to go home, he
had declared his intention of never leaving the puppy he
had found. Kathleen had looked so tired, and it had been so
many years since Susan spent any time trying to calm a
temper tantrum, that she had foolishly volunteered to take
care of Bananas, bringing him home after dinner. Everything would have been fine if she hadn't forgotten that she
had promised her daughter that she would meet her at the
mall. And if Chad's shop teacher hadn't called up and explained that Chad had cut himself with a mat knife and had
been taken to Hancock Hospital accompanied by the school
nurse and the guidance counselor. And if Jed hadn't been
late for dinner for the third night in a row.

The puppy had, once again, not been taken outside
enough. Over dinner, Chrissy had explained that her mother
was sabotaging her only chance for happiness in life, and
Chad announced that he was probably going to die from
blood poisoning. Susan decided that an evening out was
just what she needed. She could take Bananas home on her
way to the restaurant.

When Susan finally arrived at the Hancock Inn, she was

tired—tired of her family, tired of Kathleen's family, tired of puppies and hospital personnel. In the best of all possible worlds, she would have found the opportunity to slip into a booth at the rear of the Inn's cheerful plant-filled bar and sip a glass of chilled Chablis. Instead, she couldn't even find a spot at the counter.

Charles, the tall, distinguished man who had been greeting guests at the Inn for as long as Susan had been coming, was standing near the front door, talking on a portable phone and waving mute directions to his staff at the same time. The lobby was filled with groups of people, each one speaking a bit louder than those nearby in an attempt to be heard. Susan spied a few friends, dozens of neighbors, and many women with whom, over the years, she had shared a line at the local grocery store. The crowd was mainly female. Most of them were middle-aged, well dressed, well coiffed, and well made up. But there was a universal expression of intense seriousness on their faces that the combined efforts of Elizabeth Arden, Estée Lauder, and Christian Dior couldn't tame.

And the noise! Many of the town's most articulate people were here, competing to be heard. Susan hiked her purse up on her shoulder and entered the room.

"Susan. Yoo-hoo! Susan! Over here!"

Just her luck that the first person she saw was Alissa Anthony. Susan put a smile on her face and was turning in the direction of the caller when she was grabbed from behind.

"Susan. Thank God, you're here. Come with me." Susan spun around and discovered Kathleen a few feet (and a couple of people) behind her. She intended to join her, but Kathleen hurried away, around the corner and out of sight before Susan could push through the crowd. The best she could do was run in the same direction and hope Alissa didn't follow.

Alissa didn't. Instead, Susan found herself squashed between two men she had known slightly and disliked intensely for years. But her feelings for them couldn't be matched by the way they felt about each other. Bob Arnold and Ralph Spinoza coached competing Little League teams—teams that were the finalists in the play-offs. (Ralph Spinoza's A&E Mitsubishi had won with a record-setting double play in the last inning.) They were both runners, but Ralph Spinoza had won the annual Hancock Halloween Marathon—four years in a row. But Susan thought that the final blow had been when Ralph Spinoza had beaten Bob Arnold for a coveted position on the Hancock Town Council last November—and his slogan (still plastered all over town on posters that turned out to be impervious to the Connecticut winter) was "Don't Vote for a Loser." The posters displayed a photograph of Ralph victoriously crossing the finish line at the marathon. People who looked closely enough at the background could make out Bob Arnold panting in the distance.

"This is just some sort of ego trip for you, Bob." Susan recognized the supercilious tone that was Ralph Spinoza's usual speaking voice. "You didn't give a damn about all this until I started H.O.P.E."

"I happen to have been very involved in these same issues when I was in college. . . ."

"You mean students were politically active all the way out there in Idaho? I would have thought just fitting the class time in between digging up potatoes—"

"The University of Idaho is an excellent institution of higher learning. You would be surprised—"

Susan cringed, hearing Bob Arnold become more and more pompous as he became more and more stressed, and knowing that smooth and glib Ralph Spinoza was going to win this argument the way he won them all.

"I certainly would be. At Berkeley we didn't hear much about the activism of students in the potato belt. I guess we were just too busy with the Free Speech movement, S.D.S., the Vietnam moratorium. You might remember. They were some of the smaller issues of the time. Certainly not as important as keeping the sky safe for little birdies."

Susan was glad Bob Arnold was a runner. Even if he didn't win marathons, the exercise was probably good for his heart—and the color of his face indicated that particular organ was under a lot of strain. "Q.U.I.E.T.—" he began his rebuttal through clenched teeth "—is about more than birds. It's also about pollution and the quality of life here in Hancock. We need—"

"We need to get seats at the front of the room before Horace Harvey arrives. Of course, you may want to sit at the back. It's going to be embarrassing when H.O.P.E. wins all that money. Embarrassing for you and Q.U.I.E.T., that is." Ralph Spinoza pushed his way through the crowd, ostentatiously ignoring Bob Arnold while loudly greeting his friends and acquaintances.

Susan opened her mouth to console Bob, but he hurried off in the opposite direction. She shrugged. First Alissa and Kathleen and now Bob and Ralph—everyone was vanishing. She headed for the bar. Maybe the people in there would be a little more mellow than everyone else. And maybe she would become a little more so herself. She spied a friendly face.

The family's pediatrician had found a stool next to the bar and offered to buy her a drink. Susan gratefully accepted, and in a few moments they were sitting together in one of the small window seats that rimmed the back of the room.

"I saw Chad's name on a chart near the nurses' station at the emergency room," Dr. Sarah Carlson said, tasting her own glass of wine. "That boy certainly does keep you busy, doesn't he?"

"Actually, not as much as he used to. I didn't even take him to the hospital—the school took care of that," Susan admitted. "These days he doesn't seem to need me very much. And Chrissy . . ."

"I'm sure that's what they think," the doctor laughed. "But you hang in there. Teenagers frequently . . . What was that?"

Susan stood on tiptoes to identify who was screaming for a doctor. Sarah Carlson was more direct; she pushed through the crowd, running toward the sound. The person screaming had been joined by others of a like mind and voice, and most of the people in the room were heading in the same direction.

THREE

Horace Harvey's body was found beside six cases of 1990 California Chardonnay in the wine cellar of the Hancock Inn. There was a lizard money belt pulled tight around his neck and a wad of bills stuffed into his open mouth.

Thinking about it later, Susan couldn't recall exactly how she traveled from the nook in the bar to the basement of the Inn. She didn't remember walking through the halls. She didn't have any idea how she passed through the crowd. She only remembered looking down at Horace Harvey's body and then up into Tillie Greenleaf's blank, expressionless face.

"What—?" Susan's question was interrupted by Kathleen, who had appeared next to her.

"We have to get Tillie out of here," Kathleen insisted quietly. "If only there weren't such a crowd. You try going to the right and I'll barge through to the left. The first one to reach her can convince her to go upstairs."

"What do you mean? Why shouldn't she be here?"

"Just help me. I'll explain when we get upstairs."

Susan decided to trust her friend and began to push through the crowd. "Excuse me. Excuse me." Her politeness was wasted on the shocked people around her. Most of them shifted automatically as she shoved by.

Heavy wooden wine racks formed a barrier between Kathleen and Tillie, and Susan was the first to reach H.E.C.'s guiding light. "Tillie, why don't you come with me?" she asked gently, tugging on the heavy wool sweater that, despite the warmth of the day, Tillie Greenleaf wore wrapped tightly around her shoulders. "We can wait upstairs for all this to get . . . to get cleaned up."

It took a combination of nagging, pleading, and even some actual pushing, but Tillie finally allowed herself to be coaxed from the cellar. Susan could only hope that Kathleen had seen them depart and was following. It was easy to leave the wine cellar. Most of the people in the Inn were trying to get downstairs to see what all the commotion was about and were happy to move out of their way.

Susan led Tillie to the main dining room. It looked to her like most of the Inn's uniformed staff were congregated there. Apparently unwilling to sit at tables reserved for guests, they were standing in groups around the room and near the doorway. Charles was comforting a sobbing young waitress, but he hurried over to Susan as soon as he noticed her.

"Mrs. Henshaw, I'm so glad to see you. What are the police saying?"

"I . . . I don't know." But Susan did know that the question wasn't all that unusual. She had worked with the police during previous murder investigations. "Actually, I haven't seen anyone official," she added, glancing around the large and now inappropriately cheerful room.

"I called the police immediately," Charles said.

Susan was afraid she had offended him. "I'm sure you did just the right thing," she assured him. "And they've arrived?"

"I escorted them downstairs myself." Charles stood a little straighter.

"Brett . . . ?" Susan thought about Hancock's chief of police, a man she had known for years.

"Chief Fortesque isn't in town. He is out in California at a training seminar of some sort for the entire month. We had a burglary at the Inn a few nights ago, and this new man came," he explained further.

"A new man?" Susan wondered if she was imagining the disdain she heard in his voice.

"His name is James Malarkey. He's on loan from the state police department." Charles frowned and looked around. The waitress he had been comforting had moved across the room and was sitting at a table speaking earnestly to Kathleen and Tillie. Other members of the staff were scattered around, but no one was near enough to overhear them. "James Malarkey is not Brett Fortesque," he muttered ominously.

"You don't think he's competent?" Susan asked.

"He hasn't found our burglar, but I don't suppose that means he's incompetent. He's certainly energetic and enthusiastic, but he doesn't seem very open."

" 'Open'?" Susan thought it was an unusual choice of words.

"You'll understand when you meet him. And I could be wrong. I've only spoken with him a few times, but he didn't strike me as very professional. Maybe you could help him out, Mrs. Henshaw? A burglary is one thing, but a murder could ruin the Inn. People don't want to be reminded of dead bodies while they're dining."

"I really don't think—" Susan was commencing on her standard disclaimer when, once again, Kathleen commanded her attention.

"Mrs. Gordon is calling you," Charles announced needlessly. Everyone in the room had heard the summons. "Perhaps you should join her. I myself will head downstairs. If you will just remember what this could mean to the Inn . . ."

Susan heard the unasked question. "You know I always do whatever I can." She'd committed herself. She'd done it before and she would do it again. Her only salvation was that someday someone would forget, she thought as Kathleen joined her.

"I'm worried, Susan. Tillie may be accused of this murder, and she's not the type of person who should be involved in a situation like this. She's not careful. She'll be misunderstood."

"Why would anyone think she killed Horace Harvey?"

"I told you. Horace Harvey was going to leave his money to H.E.C."

Susan wasn't so sure about that, but this wasn't the time

to argue. "Surely Tillie Greenleaf wouldn't kill him to get the money!"

"I know that, but other people don't."

"It's not as though the money is going to be her own," Susan continued her thought.

"Susan! What a thing to say!"

"I know. I—"

"And it's not even relevant. People who know Tillie know that she cares about H.E.C. as much as she cares about anything. She is a very passionate woman—some people call her a fanatic, in fact," she added, lowering her voice. "That's why I had to get her up here."

"Why? Did she do something before I got downstairs?"

"Nothing much. She just announced to anyone who would listen that she was glad that Horace Harvey was dead."

Susan turned and looked at Tillie Greenleaf. Tillie was intently picking dried mud off the bottom of her sweater, a scowl on her face. "She doesn't seem out of control," she commented mildly.

"But look over there." Kathleen directed her attention to three women standing together in the doorway.

"Winkin, Blinkin, and Nod? The Three Stooges in drag? Three escapees from a school for delinquent women where they are punished for their sins by being forced to wear silly uniforms?" Susan had noticed at least a half dozen women around the Inn costumed in identical clothing. It was hard to miss middle-aged adults garbed in forest green Ultrasuede culottes and vests over creamy lisle turtlenecks, golden knee-high suede boots, and Hermès scarves patterned with leaves. They looked a little like overgrown Girl Scouts, and Susan wondered if there was a shelf around somewhere piled high with perky green berets.

Kathleen didn't even smile. "That's F.O.P.P."

"The potted-plant people." Susan nodded, trying to match her serious look. Absurdity usually amused her.

"They seem to be out in force. They'll be anxious to blame this on us."

"You mean on H.E.C.?"

"Yes. Those uniforms may be ugly, but they're a good idea," Kathleen continued to muse out loud. "They make F.O.P.P. look like a very large group."

"And they aren't?" Susan tried not to realize that she was already asking questions, already investigating.

"Heavens no! How many people could it possibly take to maintain the planters in public places in Hancock? There aren't all that many of them, and F.O.P.P. just buys flats of annuals and sets them out in the spring and fall. It isn't even real gardening. Tillie says that gardening is lots of dirt and lots of weeds and a few perfect flowers." She frowned at the women across the way. "I usually wear jeans, holey Keds, and Jerry's old Antioch sweatshirt."

Susan didn't bother to assure her of her own good looks. Certainly Kathleen had been beautiful long enough to expect compliments no matter what she chose to wear. She had another thought. "Who runs F.O.P.P.?"

"Honey Bradshaw."

Susan stopped and thought for a moment. She knew Honey slightly—enough not to like her, but not enough to know exactly why. Although she knew a lot about her. It was hard not to; Honey was always telling stories about herself. When vacations were mentioned, Honey would regale everyone with tales from her latest. Say something about education and one would hear reminiscences of Honey's years at Bryn Mawr. Politics brought forth Honey's agonizing over the recent election. Food inspired either diet stories, a compendium of Honey's favorite restaurants in the area, or, possibly, lists of what Honey (a woman with many allergies) could and couldn't eat and how it must all be prepared if anyone was foolish enough to invite her to dinner. But, in fact, Honey didn't lack for invitations. She frequently gave large dinner parties, and even if her guests thought the reason for their entertainment was to show off her chef's cooking skills and her marvelous collection of inherited Minton, they had to return the invitations, didn't they? Honey had, in fact, either impressed or irritated a large segment of the population of Hancock for years. "Is Honey here tonight?"

"Well . . ." Kathleen paused to look around. "I haven't seen her, but in this crowd, that doesn't mean much. I'm sure she was invited. Everyone involved in any of the groups Horace Harvey was considering was invited."

"Then you don't have to worry about Tillie. She wasn't the only person with a motive to kill him, right?"

"But what is Tillie's favorite flower?" The voice that asked the question wavered ominously and, startled, the two friends turned to the speaker.

Susan found herself face-to-face with a woman wearing F.O.P.P.'s distinctive uniform. Susan didn't know who she was, but apparently Kathleen did. That she took the question seriously was seen in her careful answer. "Tillie always says that white French lilacs are her favorites, but she loves them all. Even flowers that other people think of as weeds—"

"A spray of white French lilac was found in Horace Harvey's hand," F.O.P.P.'s representative informed them, smirking as she did. "Maybe you have good reason to worry about Tillie Greenleaf." She threw the words over her shoulder as she left the room.

"White lilac won't be blooming in Connecticut for another month or two," Kathleen said.

Susan thought the statement was irrelevant. "So what?" she asked.

"So I think I'd better look more closely at that body," Kathleen said. "Watch Tillie, won't you? Just don't let her say anything stupid. I'll be back as soon as I can!"

And Susan found herself responsible for Tillie Greenleaf, lover of flowers, the environment, and especially, it seemed, white French lilacs.

"Why don't we go for a walk? I'm sure no one would mind if we wandered around down by the pond for a while. No one seems to need us for anything." Susan made the suggestion after spending fifteen minutes watching Tillie Greenleaf stare off into space.

"I . . . I don't know where my purse is."

As these were the first words Tillie had spoken, Susan

thought she had made some progress. "The place is full of police; no one is going to run off with your purse. I could use some fresh air, couldn't you?"

At Tillie's nod, Susan stood up and, to her surprise, discovered that Tillie was willing to follow her from the building. There was a policeman at the door, a man Susan recognized, and he stood back to let the women pass. Apparently they weren't the only people who had left. The elegant, well-lit gardens that surrounded the Inn were filled with people taking the air. Couples strolled slowly, speaking in low voices. Small groups gathered on stone benches placed under large elm trees, just beginning to bud. The stone wall that surrounded the property was the correct height for sitting on, and half a dozen individuals had taken advantage of that fact. If Jane Austen could have ignored the clothing and benefits of electricity, she would have felt right at home.

"It's a little chilly," Susan said, realizing that they seemed to be the only people outside without coats. Tillie, despite her sweater, was rubbing her hands together. "I have ski jackets in my car. They've been used all winter. In fact, they were on their way to the cleaners—"

"Let's go get them before we freeze," Tillie suggested in a no-nonsense manner. "I certainly don't think they're going to let us back inside to get our coats—at least they're not going to let us out again."

Susan looked around and saw what she meant. These people hadn't left the Inn after the murder. They had been out here a while; possibly they hadn't even been inside all evening. They were warmly cloaked from the evening chill in coats, gloves, hats, and scarves.

"We wouldn't be here without your friend in the police force," Tillie continued.

"My friend . . ." Susan started, realizing what had happened as that same policeman hurried up behind them.

"Mrs. Henshaw," he said quietly but urgently. "I thought you had permission to leave or I wouldn't have let you pass. I had orders, but I thought, knowing your relationship with Chief Fortesque, that you were different, but . . ." The young man stopped, removed his hat, and smoothed back his hair before replacing it. "I'm going to get in a lot of trouble, Mrs. Henshaw. If anyone discovers that I let you out here, I'm going to be in a whole lot of trouble."

"Then why don't we just head back in before anyone notices us?" Tillie said. Once again, Susan was impressed with the woman's quiet logic.

The front hall of the Inn was still crowded with confused and anxious people. The only person who noticed their entrance was a tall, thin man in a gray Burberry with a red silk scarf slung across his shoulders. Later, Susan was to curse their luck; it was no way to meet the visiting police chief.

James Malarkey's glance took in Susan and her companions, and then, as a smile crossed his face, he turned his back on them. Susan wondered if he wished to appear enigmatic. Tillie shivered slightly, and Susan decided to head for the fireplace that blazed in the barroom.

Kathleen joined them. People were beginning to return to the main floor of the building, their curiosity either satisfied or thwarted permanently by the police, who had now cordoned off the wine cellar. "You two look cold," she commented, sitting down between the women.

"We were outside," Tillie stated flatly, not looking up from the table before them.

Susan nodded. "I think we did something pretty stupid. We left the building. It's my fault. I just wasn't thinking. I thought the fresh air might do us all some good, and suggested we walk around outside. The officer guarding the door recognized me and let us pass without any questions— and we came back inside as soon as we realized what we'd done—but James Malarkey saw us return. I don't know what he thought. I should have known better," she added sadly.

"I don't know why you keep saying that," Tillie Greenleaf spoke up. "I went with you of my own free will. If that police officer at the door had been doing his job, he wouldn't have let us pass. This isn't just your fault."

Susan opened her mouth and then shut it again. Tillie

was right and she knew it; Susan was entirely too inclined to accept responsibility unnecessarily. Despite the seriousness of the situation, Kathleen was grinning broadly; Susan's friends were well aware of this failing. "Well, it might cause problems, no matter whose fault it is," Susan said. "What about the lilac? Could you see anything?"

"No one is allowed near the body and no one is answering any questions," Kathleen answered.

"Lilacs?"

"We were told that a bunch of white French lilacs were clasped in Horace Harvey's hand."

"How very strange," Tillie said flatly. "I would imagine that the only blooming lilacs in Hancock at this time of the year are in my greenhouse. Of course," she continued, apparently unaware of the looks Kathleen and Susan were exchanging, "they probably could be found in one of the better florists in the city. Madderlakes, perhaps, or that place near the Polo Lounge . . ."

"Tillie, if it turns out that this rumor is true, you would be smart to say absolutely nothing about lilacs in your greenhouse or any other place unless you are asked a direct question about them."

Tillie responded with a broad smile. "Why, Kathleen, you really don't think anyone is going to accuse me of murder, do you? I hated the man, but I wouldn't have killed him."

"Why?"

"Why did I hate him?" Tillie mused a moment. "I suppose because he was a self-important person who used what other people cared about for his own advantage."

"But he was going to give away all his money," Susan protested. "Or maybe he signed his will already, and now that he's dead, all of his money is going to a good cause."

"That may be true, but he certainly didn't care about the causes," Tillie said forcefully. "Horace Harvey was only interested in getting his name on the largest monument he could find. He wouldn't have cared whether little children starved or oceans covered the earth if he could be sure of getting perpetual bold type for his name. Personal immortality was his good cause—his only cause as far as I could tell."

"So H.E.C. wouldn't have accepted his money if it had been offered?"

"Oh, yes, we would have." Tillie surprised Susan with the firmness of her answer. "And we would have displayed his name just as prominently as he wished. Don't be shocked. The world's environment is critical—and it's killing people. Lack of water in some places is causing serious famine. Global warming . . . Don't get me started. Besides, you know all about it. Hancock can only do so much, but H.E.C. was going to be able to see that it was doing all it could. And it takes money to accomplish anything. Believe me, I would have done just about anything for that money." For the first time, Susan saw signs of a sense of humor in Tillie as she smiled at her own last words. "But I wouldn't have killed him. Not even if I had seen his famous will signed and notarized and promising H.E.C. millions of dollars. I'm dedicated to my cause, but I'm not a fanatic. My personal values are still intact."

"That's the trouble with H.E.C.—they're always talking about values, acting as though they're going to save the world. We're only talking about plants, Tillie. Just plain, ordinary plants. And you know what Shakespeare said about plants—" Alissa Anthony had suddenly appeared.

"Yes, we do, we do." Susan rushed in to stem the tide of quotations that she feared imminent. "You know, Alissa, I'm glad to see you. I wanted to ask you some questions." Susan took Alissa by the elbow and tried to urge her away. She had noticed tears in the corners of Tillie Greenleaf's eyes and thought Kathleen would be more of a comfort if the two of them were left alone. "Tell me what you think about all this."

"Chills. I don't think; I feel. Chills. Deep chills in the depth of my soul." Alissa's voice was at about the same depth as she claimed her emotions to be. She reached back and tugged on the green velvet bow that was tied around her hair, and red curls exploded over her shoulders and around her cheeks. "Murder. Murder." Alissa continued to repeat what seemed to be her key themes. "The greatest crime one man can commit against another. The final crime," she ended, leaning close so Susan could stare into her dilating pupils and speculate on possible medication. "We have witnessed the ultimate tragedy."

"You saw it . . . ?"

"We have felt the emanations of hatred, the shock, the horror, the final fears, the return of peace after the deed was done. . . ."

"You didn't actually see the murder take place, did you?" Susan asked with some certainty of what the answer would be.

"I didn't need to see it. I could feel it. The very second I walked into the Inn tonight, I knew the danger. . . ."

"Alissa is very sensitive." One of her acolytes appeared and added her own opinion. Susan knew that the woman had had a major part in the theater group's last production of *Woman and Superwoman*, in which all the main characters had been female, of course.

"I think we're all feeling pretty upset about this," Susan answered.

Certainly no one was going to argue with that. And no one had a chance to; the evening was coming to an abrupt end. James Malarkey announced that the Inn and the surrounding area was to be cleared. Uniformed police officers would be at the entrance to the parking lots and record the names, addresses, and telephone numbers of everyone present.

FOUR

SUSAN WAS TENSE, AND SHE KNEW IT WOULD BE A LONG time before she relaxed enough to fall asleep. It was just after nine o'clock when she dropped Kathleen off, and she entered her own garage a few minutes later. She was, in fact, hoping to chat with her children, take a warm bath, and join her husband for a nightcap and a cozy discussion about the evening. Instead, she discovered that her children were still out and Jed was sitting in the living room with Honey Bradshaw. He leapt up when Susan appeared in the doorway, and Susan guessed that entertaining this guest had been just a little too much for him. After over twenty years of marriage, he was rarely so thrilled by her presence.

"Hi, dear. Honey is here to see you," he announced strangely. "And I guess I'd better walk the dog. It's been quite a few hours, and you know how puppies are." Jed made this second announcement with a smile at their guest. Susan knew how puppies were, too, and usually she was the only family member who was terribly concerned with the eight-week-old ball of fluff. Before possessing a family pet, she had envisioned hours of healthy exercise. But at this stage in the animal's life, more time was spent standing than walking. Of course, she did bend and stoop to pick up after the animal. That should be good for her figure.

"Of course, I understand. You know how I love dogs. Unlike some people." Honey Bradshaw added this ominous note before continuing, "But, then, I suppose the entire town has heard about my lawsuit." She sighed loudly.

Susan figured she'd hear whether or not she asked, so

she decided to be polite. (Okay, it's not what she had taught her children, and she sincerely hoped they had better manners than she did, but after all . . .) "What lawsuit?"

"We're suing the Fiske Home."

The Henshaws had lived in Hancock long enough to recognize the name of an old mansion on the highest hill in town. Five years ago, it had been converted into a retirement home for women with careers in the early airline industry by a man named Jonathan Fiske; Mr. Fiske's mother had been one of the first stewardesses. "Why on earth are you suing them?" Jed stopped in the doorway long enough to ask.

"Well, you know I live over there," Honey began by announcing her neighborhood—certainly the most expensive in town. "And, of course, we have a very large lawn."

"Of course." Susan smiled as politely as she would have wished one of her children to.

"But the trouble with living on a corner lot is that there are so many cars passing, and I worry so about Isabell and Aubrey. . . ."

"Isabell and Audrey?"

"Aubrey. Aubrey is a little boy." Honey spoke slowly and distinctly, possibly thinking Susan had some sort of hearing problem.

"Your children." Jed jumped into the conversation, never having been in the position of hearing Honey Bradshaw regale the women's sauna at the Hancock Field Club with tales of her uterus and what she called its "tragic inability" to do the job it was designed to do.

"Honey doesn't have any children," Susan quickly informed him.

Honey nodded solemnly. "The great misfortune of my life," she admitted proudly.

"I'm sor—" Jed began, looking embarrassed.

"Don't be sorry for me," Honey protested, throwing her hands in the air, simultaneously warding off any unwanted sympathy and displaying perfectly manicured nails. "I have my Isabell and my Aubrey."

"Your poodles!" Jed exclaimed, and Susan knew he was

remembering the two large dark brown animals that thoroughly sniffed all guests entering the Bradshaw home; this was called "giving kisses" by their owners.

"My Irish water spaniels."

"Of course. Beautiful animals. I'd better take care of our puppy," Jed insisted, hurrying from the room before he made another mistake.

"We're just beginning to learn about dogs," Susan tried to explain. "I'm afraid we don't recognize the more distinguished breeds."

Her careful choice of adjective worked. Honey Bradshaw smiled and continued her tale. "Well, Isabell and Aubrey are very well trained. I started them with the best professional trainer in the state at six months, and they still attend class at least once a week. Isabell got her C.D. before any other bitch in her age group, and Aubrey has really come along splendidly since his operation and should qualify any day now."

"How nice," Susan commented, having no idea what was being talked about.

"So you know that there's nothing for anybody to complain about. Between their breeding and their training, my dogs are champions. Most people would be proud to be associated with them."

"What does this have to do with a lawsuit or the Fiske Home?"

"They have refused to allow Isabell and Aubrey on their land. I couldn't believe it. There they are right next door, with this large property being used for absolutely nothing. None of their residents do more than sit outside on the benches next to their front door—and that's only in the spring or fall; otherwise it's either too warm or too cold. That huge lawn is completely wasted while poor Isabell and Aubrey are risking death by exercising too near the road. . . . You just can't imagine how insensitive and inflexible these people turned out to be. Is this any way to treat your next-door neighbor? And to think that I supported their petition to move into the house! Do you believe it?"

She asked, but Susan was too smart to answer. Now that

she thought about it, she seemed to remember that Honey had supported Jonathan Fiske's use of the property. Of course, at the time, the town council was deciding whether to allow the forty-six-room mansion to be converted into a retirement residence or expanded into a development of more than twenty-five condominiums. Honey had, in fact, spearheaded a petition drive to keep the condo developers out, claiming to be concerned with the resources of the town's water, sewers, and recycling services rather than the value of her own adjoining property. She had convinced enough citizens of this to overwhelm the town council with names, forcing them to vote in her favor. But it seemed that things weren't working out quite as she had wished.

"I did so much for them," Honey continued her lament. "And they won't even let me exercise Isabell and Aubrey there—so I sued."

"You sued them for the right to take your dogs on their property?" Susan was getting interested in spite of herself.

"No, I sued them because they attempted to poison my darlings. But my lawyer would be very unhappy if he knew that I was discussing this. We're still preparing my case. And anyway, that's not what I came here to talk about. F.O.P.P. needs your help. This murder could destroy us."

"I—"

"I know you're good friends with Kathleen and I know she was just named to the board at H.E.C., but this issue is more important than personal loyalties. The future of Hancock depends on you."

Susan had actually been present at the town council meeting when Honey had convinced the group that the Bradshaw interests were identical with Hancock's interests. Susan had a feeling that she was going to hear that speech again. "I don't see how," she began her protest, determined to be more resolute than Hancock's elected officials.

"You know what was found in Horace Harvey's jacket pocket, don't you? Someone from H.E.C. was spreading it all over the Inn before the police even had time to clear out the public."

Susan, thinking of white French lilacs, didn't answer immediately.

"And it didn't necessarily have anything to do with us, you know," Honey continued. "There are lots of possible explanations. A police plant. Or maybe H.E.C. decided to frame F.O.P.P. for the murder and put it there. . . ."

Susan couldn't remain quiet indefinitely. "Why would anyone belonging to H.E.C. plant white French lilacs on Horace Harvey to incriminate F.O.P.P.? Don't tell me they're your favorite flower, too?"

Honey appeared stunned. "No, of course not," she said slowly. "Everyone knows that they're Tillie's favorites. She celebrated her fiftieth birthday last Thanksgiving, and her husband had huge boxes of them flown in from some nursery in Hawaii for the party. I didn't realize . . ." There was a long pause, and Susan waited silently for further revelations.

But Jed and puppy had returned. Though they entered through the back door, Jed had apparently forgotten to replace the gate that kept the animal confined in the kitchen. A very damp lump of beige fluff, delighted at the unexpected opportunity to explore, ran wildly in figure eights around the matching living room couches.

"Jed! She's getting everything soaking wet. Where did all this water come from?" Susan cried, managing to clasp the animal to her chest.

"I'll take her," Jed offered. "I'm already soaked," he added. "The Murrays over on Dogwood Lane turned their sprinkler system on early this year. I had to dash after the dog through their lawn. The collar slipped over her head."

"Doesn't he have a name yet?"

"She." Susan was glad to correct the only thing she knew about her dog. "We're working on it. Getting everyone to agree isn't easy."

"Oh. My husband just leaves all that to me."

"Well, the children are really more of a problem than Jed," Susan said, startled to see that Honey was gathering her things together. "Are you leaving? I still don't understand—"

"You really should figure out a name for that dog. She's

not going to learn anything until she has a name." Honey stood up, clasping her suede bag under one arm. "I really must go."

"But I thought you wanted—"

"It's getting late and I'd better get home to my own babies. They need their walkies, too, you know."

Susan, completely mystified at this change, hurriedly got up to accompany her guest to the door. And she really did have to hurry.

Honey Bradshaw was moving as quickly as possible without breaking into a run. There was no small talk at the doorway, and the lights of her Jaguar had barely come on as she pulled the car out of the drive.

"Well, she certainly changed her mind," Susan commented, reentering her home and pulling the door closed behind her.

"Maybe she was afraid we'd ask her to help clean up," Jed suggested, appearing in the hall with a pail of soapy water and two large sponges.

Susan looked down at the paw prints on her new wool carpet. "And to think I waited until the children were older to have light carpeting," she said, reaching out for a sponge. "I should have picked out a pattern. Does Karastan make something with brown paw prints?"

Susan hadn't been sleeping well since her children became teenagers. It seemed like either Chad or Chrissy was out late, or their phones were ringing, or some new problem had appeared that could only be sorted out in the middle of the night. Recently, of course, she spent a lot of time thinking about her daughter's decision to date someone her parents didn't like. The dog didn't help much either. Though it was perfectly content to be locked in the kitchen when the house was quiet, a footstep on the stairs, the sound of a Grateful Dead tape being played, the slightest noise, convinced the animal that someone was heading downstairs solely to take a short trip outside. Luckily, the house had a large lawn; not as large as the Bradshaws', but large enough to keep road noises from turning into disturbances.

Usually. Tonight Susan was startled from her sleep by what appeared to be military maneuvers on the lawn. Loud engines and flashing strobe lights appeared at the windows. The dog yelped. Jed muttered and rolled over in his sleep. Susan got up.

She pulled a long coat over her nightgown and hurried downstairs, waiting to slip into the boots that stood by the kitchen door, and hoping to reach the dog while the animal's bladder was still full.

Success. Susan grabbed the long nylon leash hanging over the wire barrier to the kitchen and connected it to the animal's collar. The puppy knew the direction it was to take, and they were out the back door in record time. They hurried to the bed of ivy beneath the large blue spruce, and the dog paused for a moment before Susan led her around the corner to the front lawn. The puppy, unaccustomed to these late night excursions, was thrilled until one of the line of cars going down the road backfired, sending the animal into hiding behind Susan's chilly legs.

There were four police cars, a rescue van, and a couple of dark sedans still visible in the distance when she had finally coaxed the dog to the curb. They were moving slowly up the street, lights flashing, one low siren moaning. Susan was wondering what, exactly, was going on when Kathleen's classic Jaguar XKE roared up.

The window was already rolled down, and Kathleen thrust her head out as the car stopped. "Get in. We have to go down to the police station," she ordered.

"I can't do that!" Susan protested. "I have the dog here."

"She's just a puppy, she can sit on your lap," Kathleen insisted.

"I—"

"Get in!" Kathleen repeated. "They've arrested Tillie, and you may be the only person who can help."

Susan didn't see that she had any choice. She picked up the puppy, ran around to the passenger's door, and did what Kathleen had ordered. Kathleen accelerated and they were hurrying after the police procession before she had a chance to wonder what Jed would think if he woke up and discovered her absence. Oh, well, she could always call him, she decided, turning her attention to the more important problem.

"Tillie's been accused of murdering Horace Harvey?"

"Arrested," Kathleen corrected briefly. "They let her make one phone call before leaving the house, and she called me. She said that her husband was going to call their attorney, but she remembered that I had been a police officer and . . . and so she thought I could help. They're taking her to the holding cell at the police station."

"And you think they'll let you talk with her there?" Susan asked.

"I don't know. All I know is that she said they were arresting her because they found the murder weapon outside the Inn. . . ."

"And they think she dropped it there when we went outside!"

"I guess so," Kathleen agreed. They had caught up with the procession, and she had slowed her car down to match its solemn pace. "So if you just tell them that—"

"Wait a second. He was strangled. I saw the belt around his neck," Susan protested, trying to ignore the puppy's paws in her face.

"No. Well, maybe. There's no way that there's been enough time for an autopsy. But apparently before or after someone put a belt around his neck, someone hit him very hard with a jeroboam of Mumm's. The bottle was found outside with pieces of skin, blood, and hair on it."

"And the police think she was carrying that when I went outside with her?"

"We spoke for maybe three minutes. All Tillie said is that she had been arrested for the murder, that the bottle had been found outside, that she was being taken to the municipal center and that her husband would find her a lawyer. I told her I'd get down there as soon as possible, and she seemed relieved. And then, as I was backing out of the driveway, I thought of you. I met up with them—" she nodded out the windshield at the cars they were following "—on the way to your house."

"So you think we can just walk into the police station, explain that Tillie didn't hide the murder weapon outside when she was with me, and then they'll let her go?"

"We can't just leave her there alone. She needs us," Kathleen answered.

"Then we'll do what we can," Susan replied sensibly. There was a moment of silence before she continued. "What do they think they're doing? It looks like a funeral procession for someone famous."

"Odd, isn't it?" Kathleen commented.

"I suppose I'd better leave the puppy in the car," Susan mused.

"You'd better not," Kathleen said. "The window to the driver's seat tends to slip down—she might climb out." She looked at Susan and shrugged. "The complications of falling in love with an antique car."

Susan looked down at the puppy, drooling happily in her lap, and realized what she looked like. "I'm wearing my nightgown," she announced.

"There's no time to change now," Kathleen said, steering the car into one of the parking spots marked "visitors." "Just keep your coat closed." She opened the car door, the lights went on, and she took a closer look at her companion. "Why are you wearing boots? It isn't raining."

"It's safer to walk through our backyard in the dark if you're wearing something that can be rinsed off." Susan got out of the car and placed her puppy on the ground.

Kathleen shook her head, and the two women walked into the police station with the puppy trotting between them.

Directly inside the door a clock hung over the large desk piled high with papers and books. Susan blinked under the bright fluorescent lights flooding the room. What she'd thought she'd seen was true: It was only 12:14 A.M. She had slept for less than half an hour. She glanced down at the puppy; there had been no need for the animal to go out. The dog cocked her head, and Susan reminded herself that all the books insisted that dogs didn't smile.

"May I help you?" A blond head appeared over the mounds of reading material, and Susan and Kathleen were confronted by a woman in her early twenties with hair held straight up on her head by an orange silk band, bright purple glasses slipping down her nose, and shoulder-touching earrings. "I'm the night dispatcher," the woman explained. "Well, I'm the substitute. It's my aunt's job, but she needed emergency surgery last week, and I needed a quiet place to study for my finals—anyway, I'm helping out until she gets back. And you don't want to know all about that, do you?" she interrupted herself to ask, apparently seeing the scowls on Susan's and Kathleen's faces.

"We need to speak with Tillie Greenleaf," Kathleen explained.

"Tillie . . . ?"

"The woman who was just brought in here," Susan added. "The woman who was arrested for the murder of Horace Harvey."

"Oh. I didn't know that he was the one who died. . . ." The young woman pushed her glasses up on her nose and stopped speaking.

"We need to see her," Kathleen prodded.

"I can't help you there. You'll have to speak with Detective Malarkey. Every time I do anything without asking him first, I get in trouble, and this is sure more important than anything else that's come up—he could fire me if I do something wrong now." She frowned. "Do you think that means my aunt would be fired?"

"I—"

"I don't think we have to worry about that now," Kathleen said, not giving Susan time to finish her sentence. "We must see Mrs. Greenleaf immediately. There's no reason that we shouldn't be allowed to do so. I was an officer with the state police, so—"

"So when we need an ex-officer in the state police, we'll be sure to call you." The deep voice came from behind the women, and both Kathleen and Susan turned to look at the speaker.

"Excuse me?"

Kathleen's voice was as cold as the look on her face, and Susan realized she didn't recognize James Malarkey. "I know Kathleen will do anything she can to help Hancock's acting chief of police." Susan quickly jumped into the conversation. No use making more enemies than absolutely necessary.

"And just what is Kathleen offering to do?" the policeman asked sarcastically.

"There's been a murder—" Susan began.

"There's been a person arrested for that murder," James Malarkey responded.

"The wrong person!" Kathleen burst out.

"So that's what the ex-officer of the Connecticut State Police is here to do—to let us know that we've arrested the wrong person."

Susan glanced at Kathleen. There was a smirk on James Malarkey's handsome face, and she wondered how her friend was taking it. Not well, she decided. In fact, Kathleen looked like she was ready to explode.

"You're not a lawyer, are you?" the man asked. "Because Mrs. Greenleaf could sure use one right now."

"Her husband is contacting a lawyer, and I'm sure they'll be here soon," Kathleen answered through gritted teeth.

"Good. Why are you here?"

"Because she's my friend. Because I know you arrested the wrong person. Because Tillie called me and asked me to help."

Susan decided it was time to speak up. She started by introducing herself and then continued, "Kathleen is only trying to help out a friend. If you would just let her see Tillie Greenleaf for a few minutes. What harm could it do?"

"That is a point." James Malarkey's response surprised them both. He reached out and placed one well-manicured hand on Kathleen's arm. "Then maybe you'd like to see her right away?" he suggested gently.

"I . . ." Kathleen was thrown off track by the change of attitude, but she regrouped quickly. "Yes," she answered loudly. "Yes, I definitely would."

"She's back in my office." He turned and waved at a uniformed officer coming in the front door. "This man will show you the way."

"Oh. Thank you." Kathleen said nothing more, starting to follow the man indicated.

"Where are you going, Mrs. Henshaw?"

Susan, who had begun to follow Kathleen, stopped immediately.

"I was hoping for a chance to speak to you," the man continued politely.

"I . . ."

"Go ahead. There are some things that you wanted to clear up. Remember?" Kathleen flung the words over her shoulder as the door she was passing through swung shut behind her.

"Why don't we go in here?" James Malarkey suggested, nodding to a door on the other side of the room. "It's the kitchen, and frankly, I could stand a cup of coffee. How about you?" he added, holding the door open for her.

"I'm fine. Thank you, but . . ." She suddenly remembered something. "But I have my dog with me."

"Well, the sign on the front door of the municipal center says that only Seeing Eye dogs are allowed, so you'll have to pretend to be blind." He chuckled at his own joke. "But aside from that, he'll probably be better off in there. There's linoleum on the floor," he added, noticing the quizzical look on Susan's face.

Susan frowned at the puppy, who was pulling on her leash, apparently thinking that Kathleen's direction was more interesting. "He's a she," Susan responded. "Come on, sweetie," she added, tugging on the leash.

"I assume you're speaking to the dog," he said with a wink, following her into the brightly lit room.

"Yes." This man was making Susan very uncomfortable, and she decided that the only thing to do was sit down and shut up—which she did.

"Coffee?"

Susan nodded. "Black."

"You don't have to hold on to the leash like that. As long as the door is closed, she can't get out. And she seems to want to check out that corner."

Susan released the dog, who immediately scurried toward

the corner indicated, sniffed around the cupboards that lined both sides of the angle, turned around a couple of times, lay down, and fell asleep. "Little late for someone that young."

"It's late for me," Susan admitted, stifling a yawn. "And it's been a very eventful evening."

"I heard you have a lot of experience with murders. I guess it's something that no one gets used to, though." He handed her a Styrofoam cup of steaming liquid and sat down across the table from her.

Susan felt a ridiculous urge to ask how much "experience" *he* had with murders, but merely smiled and sipped her coffee. Then winced.

"Awful, isn't it?" James Malarkey smiled. "I've never understood it. The machine is good. I bought the coffee from the same store where I get mine and I ground it myself, but it's always bad. For some reason, coffee in an office is never like it is at home. Do you find that?"

"I don't really know. I don't work," Susan admitted. "I mean, I do a lot of volunteer work and I take care of my house and kids, but . . ."

"But you've managed to avoid office coffee. Smart."

Susan appreciated his tact.

"We'll give your friends a few minutes to be together. I suppose Mr. Greenleaf will show up soon with a lawyer."

"Dr. Greenleaf. He's a retired professor." Susan took a deep breath and plunged in. "You probably want to know why you saw Tillie and me coming in from the parking lot at the Inn tonight."

"I thought you'd probably gone out for some air. Was there anything else I should know about that?"

Susan was confused. "No," she answered slowly, remembering that Kathleen felt it important that this man understand just that point. "It was stuffy in the Inn," she lied. "And I thought Tillie needed to get away. Seeing the body upset her quite a bit."

"Naturally."

"Why are you being so nice to me?" Susan blurted out the question that had been on her mind for the last few minutes.

"Don't you deserve it?"

It was late, it had been a long day, Susan certainly was not so accustomed to murder that she could view a dead man without getting emotional, and suddenly she was tired of this man's cloying kindness. "I think you're buttering me up for something," she said bluntly.

The temperature in the room dropped about fifty degrees. "I thought I was being polite. Maybe we should see what's happened to Dr. Greenleaf. . . ." He was on his feet and had left the room before Susan could regret her impulsive statement. She had other things to worry about now. The puppy was awake and busy doing the first thing she thought of when she opened her eyes. By the time Susan had finished with paper towels and a bottle of disinfectant she'd found in a cupboard, Kathleen was waiting to drive her home.

"Tillie was in pretty good spirits when I left. Her husband has one of the best criminal attorneys in the state on his way here. Tillie will be out in no time—at least on bail if no one realizes how foolish these accusations are. And I got the impression that almost everyone thinks this arrest is a mistake. There were two men talking about it in one of the offices—there are so many suspects that James Malarkey is ignoring right now. It doesn't make sense." She turned to Susan. "I hope you explained to him that Tillie didn't spend any time hiding champagne bottles on the property."

"He didn't ask me about that."

"Then what did you say to him? Why else would he want to talk to you?" Kathleen asked, pulling up in Susan's driveway.

"I have no idea. It was a very confusing conversation. But you know," Susan added, lifting the puppy from the car, "I think James Malarkey is trying very hard to be all things to all people."

"I wonder why," Kathleen said as her Jaguar roared out of the drive.

FIVE

The puppy (Susan had awakened at dawn with the perfect name for her, but had promptly fallen back to sleep and forgotten it) was getting an extra long walk this morning. The day was sunny, warm, and smelled of daffodils. And Susan had a lot to think about.

She had been involved in murder investigations before—a body had even turned up in her garage—but never had it been her fault that an innocent person was sitting in a jail cell arrested for murder. She had to get involved in the investigation.

On the other hand, her family needed her attention right now, and the new police chief certainly didn't appear anxious for her to help out. A lot of people in town, some of them close friends, were concerned about who had killed Horace Harvey; she could end up making some permanent enemies.

Of course, Kathleen was a good friend of Tillie Greenleaf. No matter how popular a person is, he or she certainly shouldn't be allowed to, literally, get away with murder. Was it her civic duty to look around a little? "And, let's be honest, dog. I don't trust that man to make the right decision."

The puppy looked up and growled. Susan decided that the animal shared her feelings about James Malarkey—and dogs were known for their good instincts, weren't they? She continued around the next corner, deep in thought.

So deep, in fact, that she didn't notice the massive Rottweiler until it was almost nose to nose with her puppy. A braided leather lead was hanging from the strange animal's neck, and Susan looked around anxiously for the owner. So much for her puppy's good instincts: The animal was leaping around, yelping and sniffing and generally acting as though she had just discovered her heart's desire. Susan wrapped the red nylon lead more tightly around her wrist and wondered if the large beast was going to attack her or her dog first.

"Down, Clancy!"

The miracle occurred. The animal sprawled on the walk, impervious to the puppy's demands for attention. Susan swung around to find the owner of the loud bass voice.

Ralph Spinoza was jogging along, casually approaching the animals. Susan was about to call out a greeting when she noticed that her animal was contentedly chewing on the Rottweiler's left ear. She jerked on the leash, and puppy, ear, and ear's owner all slid across the ground.

"Maybe I can help." Ralph Spinoza squatted down and pried open the puppy's mouth.

Susan hoped he wouldn't hurt her dog, but she could see that it had to be done. "She's just a puppy. She hasn't had any training yet. . . . But your dog is fabulous. Where did you have him trained?" she added quickly.

"Trained him myself. I told him to get down and stay, and he'll stay even if a truck runs over him."

Susan gagged a little at the image, but Ralph didn't seem to notice.

"A trained dog is a dog whose will is subjugated to your own. It takes constant attention, work, and discipline. Clancy! Sit!"

Susan wondered if it also took a loud, deep voice. Whatever, it certainly was working. Clancy came as close to leaping into a sitting position as it was possible for a dog to do. Susan's puppy started with surprise at the sudden activity and then crawled under the adult dog's gigantic chest and lay down with a sigh of contentment.

"You should start training right away. She's housebroken, isn't she?"

"She's only eight weeks old," Susan protested. A fleeting

memory reappeared of the chagrin she had felt upon discovering that every other member of Chrissy's play group was dry at night. "She usually goes on the paper, though." She didn't add that there was no place on her kitchen floor that wasn't paper.

"Well, there are some reliable people who believe in paper training." It was said begrudgingly. "You keep her in a crate when she's in the house, don't you?"

"We have one." Susan didn't admit that she was incapable of locking up her wonderful animal, although they had spent a minor fortune on the wire wonder that filled her laundry room.

"Keep her in that crate whenever she's not outside. Animals hate messing up their own space. She'll learn right away, and you won't have to bother with all that foolish paper." His manner indicated that he had solved all her problems and that was that. "So what does Hancock's most famous amateur detective think of the murder last night? Selected a suspect yet?"

Susan bristled at the tinge of condescension in his voice. "The police have already done that for me," she stated flatly.

"They have? Good for them. I thought James Malarkey was a real professional the first time we met. Glad to see that my opinion was valid. Who've they arrested?"

"They're holding Tillie Greenleaf, but I don't think—"

"Tillie Greenleaf! If that's not the stupidest thing I've ever heard. That woman's incapable of hurting a flea. Whatever made them think she did it? I'd better talk with that James Malarkey right away. The man's a fool. Clancy! Heel!"

Susan just had time to note that the Rottweiler leapt to its feet and circled its owner, coming to sit at his left side as she began to plead for more of Ralph's time. "Wait! Don't go! I don't think Tillie did it either, but I need to know more to make a case. Tell me what you know about all this."

"I know Tillie Greenleaf. Why do you think I have to know more than that?"

His voice was indignant, and Susan rushed to appease him. "You've been so involved in Hancock—you know all the people who run things in town—and you were there last night. I . . . We have to get Tillie released. You're the only person I can think of who might be able to help me do it!" At least the only person I've met out dog-walking this morning, she added to herself, plastering a pleading look on her face.

She didn't get the impression that she was totally convincing. Ralph Spinoza looked like he was ready to order his dog to follow him off at any minute. "After all, how many suspects are there?" Susan added desperately.

Strangely enough, it seemed to be the right thing to say. "That's a very good point. We should think it over," Ralph mused quietly before making another suggestion. "Why don't you come over to my house and we can have some coffee and make a few lists. I find that list making is very efficient, don't you?"

Susan was surprised at the turn of events, but more than willing to follow her neighbor's lead; besides that, she loved making lists. "If there's someplace that we can tie up my puppy . . ."

"No problem. I have two runs in the backyard. Clancy. Heel."

Susan and her puppy trotted obediently behind.

Susan had been to the Spinozas' home a few times—for the type of event that she always thought of as "social, sort of." Invitations read "come for cocktails and visit with the candidates for town council" (it being understood that guests were expected to support the same people the Spinozas supported in return for this hospitality), or dinner invitations to meet one of Ralph or Olive's favorite couples ("We knew you should get together—you all have so much in common") and then finding out that what you had in common was a dislike of the local elementary school's gym teacher, so why wouldn't you help circulate a petition to have the woman replaced—and, incidentally, destroy her career? Olive Spinoza was involved in state politics—and a party supporter of the worst kind. Susan was always afraid to accept one of her numerous invitations to tea (a sure sign of political intentions in the suburbs—certainly no one gave tea parties for any other reason) for fear that she would discover overwhelming guilt in the voting booth if she made up her own mind about the candidates.

She had, however, never been in the large split level's backyard. Since Ralph had mentioned his dog runs, she wasn't surprised by them, although they were bigger and more professional-looking than she would have expected. And in the middle of the lawn stood a circle of wooden fences.

Her host noticed where she was looking. "We're working on Utility," he said.

"Oh. Do you think we should put her in one of those runs?" Susan asked.

"You are an overprotective mommy, aren't you? Why don't we just tie your baby to that redwood chair? She'll be fine there, but if there's any problem, we can see her through the door." He nodded at the sliding glass doors. Susan could see a large oak kitchen table surrounded by a half dozen Windsor chairs.

"Great." She did as he suggested while the Rottweiler joined his twin in one of the long runs. The retriever immediately crawled under the chair and closed her eyes. Susan followed her host into the kitchen.

"I'll just be gone a second. I need some things from my study. There's a powder room right there, if you want to clean up a little."

Susan, sure her pet was okay, headed to the bathroom. It didn't take much time to complete her tasks, but she didn't return to the kitchen for almost ten minutes. And then she didn't know what to say.

But Ralph Spinoza didn't display any false modesty. "I was going to hang them upstairs, but my wife insisted on the guest bathroom. She's proud of what I've done. And I'm glad that I've been able to help out this town."

"I had no idea how many committees you'd been on or how many awards you'd won," Susan said honestly. They were both referring to the large powder room, which had been papered, literally, from floor to ceiling with certificates and letters of appreciation for what most of them, with an alarming lack of originality, referred to as Ralph Spinoza's "selfless contribution" to one local organization or another.

"I just like to do my part," he said modestly, putting a gray laptop computer down on the table. "So let's get busy. I think we should start with a list of suspects, don't you? Now, I have all the organizations in town that have requested and received a tax exemption for their nonprofit status. I think we should start there, don't you?"

"Ah . . ."

"And then you can add the other organizations that you know about, and we can put our heads together to remember exactly who was present last night, and then we'll just take it from there. Okay?"

Susan, unable to find an opportunity to express an opinion, just nodded her head. She had no idea whether or not Horace Harvey had been killed at the Inn or earlier in the day, but it would be interesting to see just what sort of results Ralph's approach might have. She watched his hands fly across the keys of his computer and wondered if it would be rude of her to ask for something to drink.

"Why don't you make us some coffee?" Ralph surprised her by suggesting.

"Sure." At least it showed that they were on the same wavelength, Susan thought, getting up and looking around the ultraneat kitchen. The Spinozas had four children, but you'd have a hard time knowing it in this room if it weren't for the flock of photographs on the Sub-Zero. They showed the children on their respective teams: junior and senior soccer teams, and midget league and senior league basketball. It showed the two girls in their Brownie uniforms and the two boys in their Boy Scout uniforms. In one snapshot the entire family was dressed in black velvet with white trim in front of the family's Christmas tree, and in another they were running down a beach in Bermuda, all in navy swimsuits with green and navy striped towels tossed around their necks. Susan made coffee thinking of her own very different children and wondering how the Spinozas managed to produce these clones. Could it have anything to do with the matching Rottweilers? she wondered, pouring milk into the small pitcher she'd found next to the Krups automatic.

"So look at this list."

Susan noticed that Ralph had not desired her attention until she'd finished making the coffee, but that could be coincidence, she reminded herself. Maybe. She placed the refreshments on the table and sat down, reaching out to adjust the computer screen so she could read it. "I don't understand," she began when she had spent a few minutes staring at the screen uncomprehendingly.

"It's a list of the organizations that might have benefited from Horace Harvey's will."

"Oh. They're all initials! I was trying to read the words. I wondered what 'Hope hec sod' meant."

"Hancock's Open Plan Employment, Hancock Environmental Committee, Save the Old Dump."

"What was that last one?" Susan asked before remembering her conversation with Kathleen yesterday morning. "Oh, that's the historic group, isn't it?"

"That's one way of thinking of it. You know what Olive and I call it? Save the Odd Dowager. The woman's delusional. She wasn't satisfied with the county historical society's response to her find, so last week she contacted the Smithsonian. Insane, isn't it?"

Susan didn't know who or what he was talking about, so she just sipped her coffee and tried to look intelligent.

"But I didn't see her there last night. Did you?"

Susan had no choice but to admit her ignorance.

"Martha Trumbull," he elaborated, and Susan heard the impatience in his voice. "Our very own local historian—or the woman who would like to be our historian, I should say."

Susan vaguely remembered hearing about an argument that had raged in the town council meetings last fall, something about whether or not the town of Hancock actually needed an official historian, she recalled. From the frown on Ralph's face, she gathered that he had not supported the notion, or at least Martha Trumbull's appointment. She also thought she remembered what the outcome of the discussion had been. "We don't have a historian, do we?"

"Not yet. And not as long as I have enough friends on the council to keep it from happening. The woman is a certified flake! She's claimed for years that we should give her an official position because she's a direct descendant of John Trumbull! Do you believe it!"

"I don't know who—" Susan began, but Ralph interrupted, and it looked like she wasn't going to be forced to admit that she didn't know this illustrious personage—she just hoped he didn't turn out to be the first vice president of the United States.

"A famous revolutionary war portrait painter! As though that was something to be proud of. You know the morals of painters. Look at that Marplethorp person."

"I don't think—"

"Okay. We're exaggerating." Ralph Spinoza displayed the winning smile that had been captured on his election posters. "And Martha is a charming, if slightly fey, woman. But we don't need a historian. We have a historical society made up of lovely women, every single one of whom would take it personally if the town council decided to choose an official historian."

And Susan suspected that he envisioned all these women voting for someone else the next time local elections came along. "But if she wasn't at the Inn last night, is she a suspect?" Susan asked, reminding him of his own stipulation.

"No. Come to think of it, she's been in the hospital for the last week or so."

"Why? Is she ill?"

"Hip replacement. I think that's what Olive told me." He shrugged and continued. "So I guess we don't have to worry about Martha Trumbull, do we?"

Susan, a little astonished by his lack of concern, just pulled the computer closer to her side of the table. She had decided to visit Martha Trumbull this very afternoon. "So what are our other options?"

"You know, maybe we shouldn't discount Martha so quickly. Maybe she got that nephew of hers to kill Harvey. I'll write his name down at the top of the list, shall I? We don't want to leave anyone out."

"No, of course not," Susan said slowly, watching as Ralph returned the computer to his side of the table and, if she wasn't mistaken, erased more than a few words before typing in "Ethan Trumbull."

"In fact, I've never trusted that young man. He struck me as a little strange the first time I met him."

"Strange?" Susan thought that Ethan would have to be very strange indeed if he killed a man so his aunt could afford to excavate an old well in her backyard.

Ralph nodded slowly, and Susan got the impression that he was trying to impress her with his thoughtfulness. "I gather you haven't met Ethan Trumbull."

"I don't think so."

"Don't be fooled by his prep-school polish. The man is living a lie. My nephew goes to Yale, too, and it's a little strange that he isn't on vacation this month, don't you think?"

Susan was surprised by this accusation, but Ralph was continuing, and she needed to focus.

"Do you have any idea why Malarkey arrested Tillie instead of Honey Bradshaw?"

"Honey Bradshaw?"

"They run competing garden groups. Why would one be more likely to kill Harvey than the other?"

"There was white French lilac found in Horace Harvey's hand," Susan said. The words were hardly out of her mouth when she was regretting her indiscretion. But apparently it didn't matter.

"And what about the marijuana found in his lapel pocket?"

"What?"

"Doesn't that incriminate Honey Bradshaw as much as those flowers incriminate Tillie?"

Susan was stunned. "What does that have to do with anything? Are you . . . Has anyone accused Honey of having a substance-abuse problem? I don't think . . ." She stopped speaking, completely confused.

Ralph Spinoza started to chuckle in a superior manner. "Don't tell me you're the only person in town who hasn't heard about the pot in the pots last fall?"

"I have no idea what you're talking about," Susan admitted.

"I heard it had been hushed up, but I didn't know how successful they'd been."

Susan had a feeling that she'd just lost a lot of status in this man's eyes. "Can you tell me about it?" she asked humbly.

"Sure. You know those ugly Grecian urns that ring the sidewalk around the municipal center? I think they have some sort of purple flower in them right now. Crocus or something . . ."

Susan had seen them. "Yes."

"Well, last fall it was noticed that among the chrysanthemums was a fairly large group of marijuana plants." He chuckled. "They'd apparently been growing there all summer, and anyone who noticed these lush green plants just thought they were part of the selection of foliage. Until a visit from the local representative of the D.E.A. He identified them right away. They were hard to miss, being right next to the police station. I understood that your friend the police chief had some fancy explaining to do."

"And those pots were maintained by Honey's group?"

"By F.O.P.P. Yes."

"Who planted pot in them." Susan had a difficult time keeping the doubt out of her voice.

"Probably not. Most of the people I spoke with assumed that some kids thought it would be a good joke, threw in the seeds, and just got lucky when no one noticed until the plants were full-grown."

"But what about the people who were taking care of the urns? They're watered and weeded by members of F.O.P.P., aren't they?"

"I think weeded, but not watered."

Ralph was chuckling as he spoke, and Susan could only guess how much enjoyment people had gotten from this particular event. Then something significant struck her. "How many people knew about all this?"

"Everyone on the city council . . . all of the police . . . everyone who worked at the municipal center . . . and everyone they told. As well as whoever planted the stuff."

"A large number of people."

"You could say that. Probably a couple of hundred. It's not going to be easy to narrow down the suspects from this, is it?"

"That's always true at the beginning of a murder investigation," Susan insisted. That was only the truth sometimes, but she was getting tired of the supercilious look on her host's face. "So who else do you have on the computer?"

"Alissa Anthony and that theater of hers. Do you remember when they put on *Medea*?"

"Not really."

"It was their first or second play. Alissa was Medea." He chuckled. "She was terrible. So terrible that I find it hard to imagine her as the killer."

"If she did kill someone, she'd probably want an audience—and call up all her friends at the local papers to review the act." They had been joined by Olive Spinoza. She threw her suede blazer jacket over the back of a chair and sat down. "The woman is an egomaniac."

Olive, Susan thought, was the perfect politician's wife. Good-looking, but conservative enough not to threaten any woman who might imagine herself a femme fatale; charming, but not inclined to gush; glib, but able to talk for at least a few minutes on almost all subjects without offending the most sensitive person. So Olive's comment about Alissa was uncharacteristic, to say the least. Susan looked at her curiously. "Alissa does get a little carried away," she agreed, and noted that the Spinozas exchanged glances.

"So maybe we should put a star beside her name here," Ralph Spinoza suggested slowly. "Myself, I wouldn't have thought that Alissa was a serious suspect, but after listening to you two, I've changed my mind."

Oh really? Susan didn't believe that for a moment. In fact, she was slowly coming to the conclusion that the reason she had been invited was just so Ralph could have a moment like this one—a moment that he had discussed in advance with his wife, she'd bet. She sipped her coffee and thought it out. She was tempted to argue about Alissa's inclusion on the list, but then she thought better of it. Why not follow where the Spinozas led? She glanced out in the backyard. Her puppy was still asleep; she had time.

"Good idea," she encouraged. "Do you mind if I get myself another cup of coffee?"

"Let me!" Olive jumped up as Susan had known she would. "I can't believe that my husband didn't offer you something to go with it. I bought some lovely chocolate croissants, just yesterday."

"No, thanks," Susan protested politely, hoping she would be ignored. "Who else do you have on that list?" she continued.

"Patty Taylor's next. She's running P.A.P., isn't she?" Ralph asked, watching the names scroll across his computer screen.

"Parks Are People," Susan mused, remembering what the acronym meant. "I've heard it mentioned, but I have no idea what it is."

"I can't say that I do either, but Patty is—"

Olive placed a tray of pastry down on the table and interrupted her husband. "Parks Are People is an interesting organization. The group is trying to make the parks in Hancock more user-friendly. At least I think that's how they put it. They want the parks equipped for multi-use activities. For instance, I think they raised the money for that new exercise equipment down by the fire station. And they're working now on getting money and permission for an outdoor theater near the pond down by the library."

"Then Alissa is in it?" Susan asked, thinking that she knew where all this was leading.

"Definitely not." Olive sat down while talking. "The

whole point is for the theater to be used by different groups in town—students, church groups, anyone who wants to perform, for all I know. Alissa wants to run a circle of thespians. P.A.P. is only to provide opportunities and equipment."

"How does Tillie Greenleaf feel about that?" Susan asked.

"My understanding is that she supports it," Olive surprised her by answering. "Why not? Thanks to some smart thinking on the part of the original town planner, Hancock has lots of parks, and Patty has some pretty good ideas and lots of youthful enthusiasm. Do you know her?"

"No." But Susan thought the named sounded familiar.

"She's a guidance counselor down at the high school. This is her first year in town, and she's really thrown herself into the life of the community. You'll probably meet her at the club this summer."

"She started P.A.P. and got all that done in just seven months?" Susan asked, impressed.

Olive nodded. "She probably has a lot of energy."

"I'll say."

"So who else is on your list, darling?" Olive asked her husband.

"Just Bob. Bob Arnold," her husband answered, looking slightly sheepish. "Everyone in town is going to think that I suspect him, I'm afraid."

Susan agreed, but didn't say anything.

"And, in fact, I don't."

"You don't think Bob is capable of murder, dear?"

Susan wondered if Olive was aware of just how strange that question sounded.

"Oh, I suppose everyone is capable of murder under the right circumstances. I just don't think that Bob would murder anyone so that Q.U.I.E.T. can survive. He only started that organization to compete with H.O.P.E. If you find me dead someday, you'd better look to see if Bob is holding the smoking gun. Competing with me is the only thing that motivates him."

"Which brings us to someone else who should be on

your list, Ralph," Olive spoke up. "You should be on the list, shouldn't you? After all, you organized and run H.O.P.E., and you were as anxious as anyone that Horace Harvey would leave his money to H.O.P.E. Ralph? Ralph, you're not listening to me."

"I think your puppy is eating our lounge." Ralph announced, standing up.

SIX

SUSAN HAD DROPPED HER PUPPY OFF AT HOME AND, AFTER covering her kitchen floor with a thick layer of newspapers, had driven to the greenhouse of her favorite florist. The Spinozas had both protested that the damage to their artisan-created adirondack lounge was completely unimportant to them, but Susan thought the least she could do was send a gift—an expensive gift, she decided, circling a large calamondin orange tree in a porcelain urn. The small weeds growing at the base of the plant reminded her of F.O.P.P.'s problem.

One of the store's young employees approached her. "It's a beautiful plant, isn't it? The fruit is bitter, but completely edible. Some people make marmalade from them. And we have a customer who swears by them in his Manhattans— he grows two plants under lights right next to the bar."

"Then you think this would make a good gift?"

"Well, it's a bit too large to send someone in the hospital—"

"What a good idea," Susan interrupted, glancing around while she considered her new idea. "Why don't you send the orange tree over to Mr. and Mrs. Ralph Spinoza—I have the address here in my purse—and I'll take that lovely gloxinia in the gray basket with me."

Addresses and credit cards were exchanged, and Susan was on her way to the Hancock Hospital with a minimum of fuss. Clouds were beginning to appear in the sky, reminding the hopelessly optimistic that winter still had its hold on Connecticut, and she appreciated the cheerfulness of the plant on the seat next to her. She only hoped Martha Trumbull would enjoy it, too, she thought, finding a spot in the hospital parking lot and pointing her car into it.

The information desk was immediately inside the door, and Susan headed there first. The hospital had liberal visiting hours, and she was hoping to see Martha immediately. The volunteer manning the desk informed her that Martha Trumbull was in room 418 and could have visitors at any time. Susan hurried to the closest elevator. The door was just sliding shut, and a handsome, blond man in his early twenties reached out and kept it open for her. Susan smiled her thanks, noticing that he had already pressed the button for the fourth floor.

Upon her arrival, Susan paused to ask directions to the room she was searching for, so she was surprised to find her companion for the ride up sitting on the end of Martha Trumbull's bed.

"Susan Henshaw! How lovely to see a new face. And what beautiful flowers!" The elderly lady lying in bed was wearing a white cotton peignoir with what looked like hand-crocheted lace around its high neck. Her cheeks were pink and her eyes were blue. Except for the medical equipment, the room looked like a Tasha Tutor illustration. "If you can stay awhile, maybe I can talk Ethan into going downstairs to the coffee shop and having some breakfast."

"My aunt has been trying to feed me since I was four years old. It's some sort of obsession." He beamed at his elderly relative as he stood up and took the flowers from Susan. "I'll put these on the shelf right there and leave you two ladies alone to chat. But I will return, Aunt Mattie, so don't get up and waltz off down the hall with that orderly who keeps flirting with you."

"Charming young man, isn't he?" Martha Trumbull said as the door swung closed behind her relative.

"Very." Susan sat down on the chair the hospital had provided for visitors. "Does he live in Hancock?"

"No. He's a graduate student. At Yale," she added proudly. "But he's staying in Hancock for a few weeks. They're on some sort of vacation there. So when I found out that I was going to have this operation, Ethan offered to stay in my house and take care of my darling pussies. And he's spent almost every minute of the day here with me. He's such a lovely boy."

Susan remembered Ralph's accusation, but said nothing. "How lucky for you that he's free right now. When did you find out that you were going to need this operation? I heard it was hip-replacement surgery."

"Last month," Martha answered, and went on to explain the history of her problem as well as details about the surgery and her recovery thus far.

Susan listened, happy that she was doing something useful and more than willing to wait to ask questions about S.O.D. and the historic site. But she didn't know exactly how she was going to introduce the subject. She was thinking about it when a perky young student nurse arrived carrying pills and juice.

"More guests, Mrs. Trumbull? You're definitely our most popular patient," the young woman said in a voice determined to be cheerful no matter how overtired or overworked. "Mrs. Trumbull's nephew is one of our regular visitors, and every member of the historical society has been in at least once," she added, handing her patient the medication and taking over the conversation. "Such interesting things you all talk about. I was telling my boyfriend last night about how back in revolutionary times, people used their dried-out wells for dumps. He thought we might try the same thing today in the reservoirs during droughts."

"And what would happen when the drought ended and the reservoirs filled again?" Martha Trumbull asked seriously.

"Then all that garbage would be covered up," the young nurse answered.

"That's one solution," Susan agreed politely as the nurse, stopping to straighten a blanket, started toward the door.

"The man who died came in to visit yesterday morning, didn't he? It gave me the creeps when I heard about it. Thank goodness they've arrested the person who did it. Otherwise I'd never be able to sleep! Just buzz if you want something," she added, closing the door behind her.

Some of the pink faded from Martha Trumbull's face, but she didn't speak until they were alone again. "Horace Harvey was murdered? When was this? What happened?"

Susan explained carefully, answering as completely as possible with Martha interrupting with questions, and she had just gotten to Tillie's midnight arrest when Ethan returned to the room, newspapers falling from his arms. "Aunt Martha, you won't believe what happened. That boorish man who visited you was murdered last night!"

"Mrs. Henshaw was just telling me all about it. Sit down and listen."

"Tillie Greenleaf was arrested almost immediately," Susan continued.

"Outrageous. The man who arrested her must have less brains than my charming illogical nurse," Martha insisted, moving around in an impatient manner that made Susan nervous. "Tillie Greenleaf won't allow anyone to pull a weed without placing it in a compost pile. She won't use pesticides because she believes in the balance of nature. She certainly wouldn't take a life with her own hand. Pure foolishness. What is that Fortesque man thinking of?"

"He's out of town. There's an acting police chief on loan from somewhere—"

"His name's James Malarkey," Ethan interrupted. "There's something about his background here in the paper. . . ."

"I'll read it later. Let's let Susan finish. She knows a lot about murder," his aunt insisted.

Ethan gave Susan a curious glance, but he did as his aunt wished, and it took Susan just a few more minutes to relate everything she knew about last night. She explained why Tillie was the prime suspect and she didn't mention any others, but Martha Trumbull was smart, and it didn't take her more than a moment to see what was going on.

"There's no reason to even consider that lilac—if Tillie had killed the man, she wouldn't have tucked a clue into his hand. If anything, that proves someone else is trying to frame her—probably the murderer. And why would Tillie kill him for the money instead of one of the other half dozen or so people he promised it to?"

"He promised to leave his money to more than one person?"

"Now, Aunt Martha, you don't know that's true," her nephew protested.

"I'll bet anything it is, and it's not going to be that hard to prove now that he's dead. There's no need for anyone to keep Horace Harvey's artificial benevolence a secret anymore."

"What do you mean? Why do you call it artificial? You don't think he was going to actually leave his money to one of the groups he was looking at?" Susan asked, startled.

Martha pursed her lips and fumbled around with the buttons on the control pad that hung over the bed's rails. "I can do it," she insisted when Susan reached out to help. "I'm just trying to get more comfortable—which I will be as soon as the pain medication starts to work. Moving the bed a few inches in one direction or another gives me a feeling of control, I suppose. But you wanted to know why I'm suspicious of Horace Harvey's generosity, and I should explain. It's not fair to slander a dead man, is it?" She paused for a moment, and Susan wondered just how much pain the other woman was feeling. She glanced at Ethan and read concern on his face.

But Martha Trumbull was determined to continue. "I didn't trust him when I first met him," she announced. "A man who would rather give his money to an individual than to the county historical society is not to be trusted." She nodded at her own judgment of the situation.

"But you've been complaining about the historical society for years," her nephew protested.

"And I have a right to. I know them," his aunt insisted. "I know them very well, in fact. But Horace Harvey didn't know them at all. I believe that I'm the only member of the group that he went out of his way to meet."

"Why was that?" Susan asked quickly, seeing that Ethan was about to interrupt again.

"Because I'm looking for funds to organize a dig of the historical site that was recently uncovered on my property. You've heard about it, haven't you?"

"Just a mention here and there." Susan's answer was intentionally vague. "What I've heard sounds awfully interesting, though. Colonial, isn't it?"

"I believe it to be from the time of the Revolutionary War. Possibly even pre-revolutionary. That is still to be determined. I've allowed no one onto the site with the exception of a small team of archaeologists from the University of Connecticut. They found it fascinating, but like the rest of us, they need financing before they can commit to the work. I certainly will not allow those amateurs from the historical society to get in there and muck things up. They destroyed most of the cemetery on Cemetery Hill, and what they didn't destroy they misinterpreted. Dreadfully irresponsible. I can't allow that to happen."

Susan, familiar with the town's historical graveyard only from chaperoning a fifth grade class trip, was surprised to hear anything negative about the place. A small group of thirty or forty old white tombstones stood on the south side of Cemetery Hill, their names, dates, and charmingly ghoulish inscriptions intact. The hill was dotted with dogwood and birch on a deep green lawn. Benches were provided for visitors, and the day of her visit, a guide from the historical society had worn colonial mourning clothes while conducting a fascinating tour of the area. There had been no sign of excavating at the time. But perhaps she should hear about that from someone less angry about it. She waited for Martha to continue her story.

"I had mentioned my concerns about this to the mayor a few weeks ago, and he, in turn, spoke of it when Horace Harvey questioned him about exactly what needed doing in Hancock. And that's how Mr. Harvey came to visit me yesterday morning."

"He was interested in financing your archaeological site," Susan said.

"So he claimed. I had spoken to him earlier in the week, actually. He called one afternoon three or four days after my operation. I'm a little shaky about time—there's something about being here and all this medication that makes everything blur—but I think he called again around dinnertime two days ago. Anyway, he explained that he was interested in leaving a legacy to Hancock and suggested that my site might be the type of thing he was interested in financing. Of course, I knew right away that he was lying. . . ."

"Why?" Susan asked.

"How?" Ethan asked at the same time.

"I've had a lot of visitors this past week, and Mr. Harvey is the talk of the town right now. Everyone seemed to think that he was going to leave his money to their favorite charity—and everyone knew that he was going to put his name on whatever charity he chose. What was he going to do? Insist on a sign mounted over my driveway announcing the entrance to the Horace Harvey Historical Site like something on a ranch in the Southwest?" She smiled, and Susan hoped the pain medication was finally working. "I think Mr. Horace Harvey just wanted my attention."

"Why?" Ethan asked before realizing that it was a tactless question. "Not that your attention isn't—"

"Don't flatter me. I look like hell, and the pain and the medication are doing nothing for my personality—or attention span, for that matter. You haven't seen Mr. Harvey, Ethan, but Susan has and—"

"Only dead," Susan interrupted.

"Excuse me?"

"He was dead when I saw him," Susan explained further. "So I'd really like to hear about your visit as well as your impression of what he was like."

"Well, first I should explain that he walked in here like he was Rockefeller and I was a kid standing on a street corner holding out my hand for a dime. I don't mean to take advantage of my situation, but I am lying in a hospital bed connected to all these machines. He could have assumed that I wasn't feeling my best. He could have at least pretended some concern. I don't expect presents from strangers, but a comment or two would have been nice. He marched in here with his trench coat flung over his shoulders and sat down as though this was his office and I was waiting for him. He barely said hello before announcing that he would fund my project if I could convince him that it was worth his while—or his money. He explained that he was going to be writing his will and that he wanted to leave his considerable estate to some deserving project in Hancock, Connecticut."

"Did he say why?" Susan asked.

"I've been wondering about that, too," Ethan said. "The paper says that he felt he owed a lot to the town, but there was no explanation of why he felt that way."

"That is a very interesting question," Martha agreed, forgetting her pain and starting to lean toward her guests. "Oh . . . No, I'm all right. Let me go on. I asked that very question. I mean, Hancock is a lovely town, but that doesn't explain much. After all, there are a lot of lovely towns. So I asked him. It wasn't easy either. I had to interrupt his spiel, and it was obvious that he didn't like it. I suppose most people are more polite to someone who has just suggested that they might give him thousands of dollars."

"Millions is what the paper said."

Susan nodded at Ethan's words.

"Really? He didn't strike me as a person accustomed to having a lot of money. Not that I'm terribly reliable right now. I really feel as though the surgeons not only replaced my hip with metal, but my brain with a large lump of cotton."

"You're telling us more than you think," Susan said, urging her to continue. "You said you asked him some questions. . . ."

"Yes. He mentioned how much the city had meant to him in his childhood—which I believe he referred to as his youth—and being an old schoolteacher, I asked him if it was the schools to which he referred."

"But it wasn't," Susan suggested.

"I gather not. He appeared rather startled that I had asked the question. I mentioned church and started to say something about other organizations. 4-H or the Boy Scouts were the ones I mentioned, I think. He acted as though I was screaming at him under bright lights and threatening with a rubber hose. He really became rather nasty, saying that I had no business to question him. But then one of the orderlies or nurses interrupted us for some reason or another, and by the time I got back to the whole discussion, he had calmed down and answered very civilly that he didn't care to single out one event or organization in his past."

"So he didn't want to talk about his past."

"He adored talking about his past. But only his recent past. I heard a version of his business adventures that made prospecting for gold in 1849 sound dreadfully dull. And, to be quite honest, I don't remember very much of it," she added, seeing that her nephew was about to ask another question. "I've heard little boys bragging about their conquests and adventures for years and years. Frankly, I don't believe very many of the stories, and I stopped listening closely about my fifth year in the classroom. I find that most boys and young men accept a smile and eye contact as proof of intense interest." She chuckled, and Susan joined her. Ethan looked vaguely startled by the admission. "And he was bragging so terribly. I didn't need to listen."

"Did you think he was lying?" Susan asked.

"I wouldn't be surprised. No, that's not fair. I think he was probably exaggerating his own importance. Apparently he did become rich in whatever he did, but that could have been luck as likely as not."

"Like winning the lottery?" her nephew asked.

"I hadn't considered that. I haven't given it a lot of thought, in fact, but people do become very wealthy from making the right investment, putting their money in with the right people, doing something as accidental as buying a poor piece of land and then discovering oil. . . . There are many ways for the fool to become a rich man."

Susan had limited experience with rich fools, or rich anybodies for that matter, but she nodded wisely.

"But I had no idea that we were talking about millions of dollars," the patient admitted. "Though I probably would have been even more skeptical about the money coming to my little project if I had known—the most wasteful person in the world couldn't expect to use more than a hundred thousand to dig up my little dump spot. Anyway, after he finished this story of how he had made his money doing something or other up in Boston, he sat back and waited for me to tell him how smart he had been."

"And you didn't."

"I've never believed in throwing around compliments, as you well know, Ethan. But I did make what I thought were appropriate murmurs of appreciation."

Susan wished she had seen that, but she didn't speak.

"Mr. Harvey then explained that he had already visited everyone else in town who might be sponsoring a project that could benefit from his generosity. And, by the way, he did refer to this as his own generosity. Very uncouth, I thought."

"Did he explain why he was visiting you last?" Susan asked.

"No. I assumed it was because I had this surgery right before he arrived in Hancock. Or maybe he was just going about his visiting in alphabetical order."

"I suppose anything is possible. But you said he was promising everyone his money. Does that mean he promised it to you, too?"

"Yes. But I don't think even he thought that I believed him. He said that I was the last person he would visit before making the public announcement at the Inn, and that he wanted me to know that he thought I had presented the most deserving project."

"And you didn't believe him," Ethan asked.

"Not at all. In the first place, I know something about what H.E.C. wants to do in the parks, and I certainly appreciate what P.A.P. and F.O.P.P. are doing for quality of life in town—my little dig is really only of interest to scholars, historians, and a few local history buffs."

"And in the second place?" Susan prompted.

"I think he lost interest in me and in my site when he realized that there was no way I was going to be in the room for his official presentation."

Susan was sitting in the hospital coffee shop considering what Martha Trumbull had told her when Ethan Trumbull appeared at her booth, a brimming tray in his hands.

"Do you have a few minutes to talk with me?" he asked politely.

"Of course. Sit down," she offered, moving her own meal closer to her seat. "You know, I was just wondering about something that you might be able to help me with."

"Anything," he answered happily, squeezing lemon into a tall glass of iced tea.

"Did your aunt say that Horace Harvey said he was going to write his will or rewrite his will?"

Ethan thought for a few minutes before answering. "I think she said write, but we could check. My aunt is very precise—about everything. Even with all her mind and body have been through in the last week, she will remember what he said. Do you think it makes a big difference?"

"A big difference, no. Probably not. But it may make a difference. A man worth all that money wouldn't go around without a will, would he?"

"Well, I doubt it, but maybe he was eccentric or something. Or maybe the money just came into his possession recently."

"And he dashed right back to Hancock, Connecticut, to find someone to will it to in case he died?"

"No, I guess that doesn't seem very likely, does it?" Ethan frowned as he spoke.

Susan peeked inside the tuna salad sandwich she'd selected at the counter before biting into it. She had finished half her meal before he spoke again.

"It's a little strange that he would be killed at the end of a week when he promised his estate to a lot of people, isn't it?"

Susan didn't argue.

"You and my aunt both think this Tillie woman isn't the murderer," he began.

"That's true."

"But the murderer is probably one of the people who expected to benefit from his death."

"It looks like that right now, but that doesn't mean it's true," Susan disagreed. "For all we know, the man has an ex-wife who killed him out of revenge. There are a lot of possibilities, in fact," she added, not believing her own words. It would be too much coincidence if all this talk about wills hadn't led to Horace Harvey's death.

"My aunt says you've had some experience investigating murders," the young man said after thinking about her words for a few minutes.

Susan nodded.

"And you're investigating this one, aren't you?"

"I don't believe Tillie Greenleaf is the murderer, and I'm a little concerned about how competent James Malarkey actually is. I'm just asking questions, trying to find out as much as possible."

"Investigating, in fact."

Susan laughed. "Yes, I guess so. Nothing official, of course, but I couldn't just sit back and do nothing under the circumstances. . . ."

"Then you understand how I feel!" Ethan exclaimed. "I can't just sit around and do nothing. My aunt is very upset about all this, and she doesn't need the extra strain in her life right now. I can't just sit around and do nothing," he repeated, looking up from his food and directly at Susan. "You understand what I'm leading up to, don't you?"

"You want to help investigate this crime, don't you?" she asked, a puzzled expression on her face.

"Yes. I don't know much about crime and nothing about murder, but maybe I could . . . you know, assist you."

Susan didn't know. "I'm not the police. I don't have any official standing here." Especially since Brett is out of town, she added to herself. "And you're needed at your aunt's house, aren't you?"

The young man chuckled. "Not really. I let the cats out at night and let them back inside in the morning—being sure they leave any trophies of their evening expeditions outside the door—and I feed them and make sure there's enough fresh water around. . . ." He looked up at Susan. "It doesn't fill many hours in the day."

"But you visit your aunt. . . ."

"True. But that's only for four or five hours a day at the most. And she'll be coming home soon to twenty-four-hour professional nursing. I'll do the grocery shopping, but not much else. She has a daily cleaning woman, a yard service . . . There's not much to keep me occupied. If you're worried that my aunt will suffer without my constant attention, you shouldn't be. I'll make sure everything is all right. And I can help you, too."

"What about your studies? I thought this was just a semester break. Don't you have work to do?"

"Well, that's another story." He paused and glanced around the room.

Susan sat quietly and waited for him to continue.

"I've left Yale," he announced, and Susan had the feeling that she was the first person he had told. "I asked to take a leave of absence and it was granted—happily, in fact. I haven't been doing very good work recently. Everyone is hoping a break will do me good." He grimaced. "I'm hoping so, too. I'm in American studies—the Puritans are my specialty. I've been waiting years and years to concentrate on them, to do some serious scholarship. But now it seems . . . I don't know . . ."

"Irrelevant?" Susan suggested, realizing immediately that she had offended him.

"Absolutely not. The Puritan principles of the sixteen hundreds are still alive in this century, and if people understood more about their past, they might be able to make much more constructive decisions about their future. . . . I won't lecture you. I promise. It's just that I feel so isolated. I've been waiting for years for the opportunity to live in libraries, and now I can't stand it! I don't know what's wrong with me!"

If he hadn't seemed so anguished, Susan might have thought he was suffering from a bad case of spring fever.

"So you see why I need something to occupy my mind. Why I'm asking you if I can help with your investigation."

Susan, in fact, didn't understand at all.

SEVEN

Susan had a couple of errands to do in Hancock's small downtown area. Although the most basic needs of its citizens were handled by the shops in the mall outside of town, a few dozen specialty stores served the community. Here you could buy *les petit pain* but not Wonder bread, Godiva but not Hershey's, couture but not Claiborne, behind the two-story Tudor facades that lined Main Street. At the end of one string of storefronts was something called "Bow Wow and Meow." Until today, Susan had never had the opportunity (or desire) to enter this particular establishment. But little what's-her-name needed dinner, and this was closer than the nearest grocery—and there couldn't possibly be a long checkout line.

A black Lab was sprawled across a large tartan pillow directly inside the doorway, raising its square head as Susan entered. "Don't worry about Skye—he's very friendly," a voice called from behind the counter at the rear of the store.

"So I see," Susan said, bending down to pet him. "I like the dog bed. Do you sell them?"

"Over your head," the voice instructed, and Susan looked up at a shelf running along the ceiling. On it were puffs in dozens of colors, plaids to delight the most loyal clan member, and prints with hearts, dog bones, and black cats.

"Wow."

"There's also a choice of filling. Polyester or cedar. Cedar smells better. Polyester, you can wash. What's your breed?"

"Pardon?"

"What type of dog do you have?"

"A golden retriever. A puppy."

"And you're looking for a dog bed?"

"Actually, I'm looking for puppy chow. She ran out at breakfast."

"To your left in the back."

There was almost as much selection here as above her head—no, more, Susan decided, looking around the area indicated.

"Need some help?"

Susan gladly accepted the young woman's offer, and twenty minutes later she was filling her trunk with bags of dog food scientifically formulated to keep her puppy healthy, a large box of beef hide and hooves (and she was not going to think about that), plastic toys, fuzzy soft Frisbees, and the filling of her puppy's very own dog bed. The cover (blue and green plaid) remained behind to be monogrammed with whatever name was chosen for the dog. To help with that task, Susan carried in her purse a large paperback entitled *Lovely Names for the Puppy You Love*. She planned on hiding most of this stuff around the house before her husband saw it; he would have a hard time resisting making a sarcastic comment or two.

And then, she decided, maybe she should make a few calls and figure out how quickly she could see Bob Arnold. She was more than a little curious about his thoughts on Horace Harvey's murder. Certainly he was as likely a suspect as anyone else who ran an organization in town. And she couldn't quite figure out why Ralph Spinoza had made such an effort not to mention Bob. Under normal circumstances, he trashed his fellow citizen and competitor every chance he got.

There were other people she should see, too, she thought, scrounging around in her purse for the notebook that was never there when she needed it. But she found the book she had just purchased, and she pulled that out. There were lined pages in the back, and she used one of them to write down the names of suspects she should visit. She was just wondering if Alissa had one or two *s*'s when she spied something on the side of the road that inspired her to slam on her brakes.

Alissa was standing in the center of the lawn of an old deserted stone building. She was yanking a FOR SALE sign from the ground. That is, she was trying to. It would have been easier to accomplish if another woman, whose back was to Susan, would stop working just as hard to push it back in. Susan parked on the side of the road, leapt from her car, and jogged up the lawn to . . .

To what? she asked herself, slowing down. What had looked like a mugging from the street seemed to be an almost friendly contest of strengths now that she was closer. Alissa was even laughing—perhaps just a little nervously. "Is there anything I can do?" Susan asked hesitantly.

"Susan, Susan. I'm so glad to see you. Could you please tell this woman that I have every intention of buying this building?"

Susan recognized Alissa's opponent as a well-known real estate agent in town.

"It is our agency's policy to keep the sign in the ground until a contract has been signed. Otherwise everyone doesn't get an equal opportunity to make each sale. And you haven't even made a deposit, Alissa."

"I explained all that to you. There's probate. . . ."

"There are grand juries, too. You're ignoring the fact that Horace Harvey was murdered. It could be months, even years, before you see any of that man's money, Alissa Anthony—if you ever see it."

"What?" Alissa reacted to the other woman's statement with a shriek. "Are you accusing me of lying? Do you think you're the only real estate agent in this town?"

"No, but I know the market, and I know I'm listing the only building in Hancock that's suitable for conversion into a theater."

Alissa stepped back, apparently deciding to try another tactic. "I thought you supported the idea of theater in Hancock. I thought you understood the importance of culture. I thought—"

"There's been a recession recently, if you haven't heard.

I'm fighting to save my agency. I've worked over twenty-five years to build it up, and I'm not going to miss a sale like this one. Everyone in town knows that Horace Harvey was promising his estate to more than one group. Why should I believe that he thought your group more important than the others?"

"Because he told me so. That's why."

The agent yanked the sign from the ground and stepped back a few feet. "I'll wait one week. Unless I have the money then, this sign is going back up. If he really left his money to you, you should be able to get a bank to set up some sort of bridging loan by then."

"Fine—bitch," Alissa added as the other woman strode off, presumably to her car. "Do you think she's right?"

"About what?" Susan asked, startled.

"About a bank giving me money—not that the money is going to me," Alissa added quickly. "This is all for the theater. But do you think I could get a loan right away? This is the only building suitable in Hancock—or anyplace else around here. I know. I've looked for years. Do you want to see it?"

"Sure. Can we get inside?"

Alissa looked over her shoulder. "Just wait till she's gone. I have the key here."

"How did you get—"

"Don't ask. Just look as if you're admiring these crocus with me."

Susan did as requested, wondering what Alissa wanted to see her about. There had to be some reason other than her desire to show off the building she hoped to purchase. Susan feigned interest in the tiny flowers emerging in clumps from the yard and waited for an explanation, knowing that Alissa's idea of a long silence was usually described as a pregnant pause—a very short pregnant pause.

And she was right. "Do you believe that woman?" Alissa asked in a loud whisper as the real estate agent got into her sedan. "And to think I accepted an old Victorian couch from her for our production of *Empress Jones*." She sniffed indignantly while Susan decided not to ask the obvious question. "Wait until you see the inside of this place. It's beautiful—and perfect for us. Just follow me."

Susan did, trailing Alissa to the side door of what Susan had always thought was a Quaker-type meetinghouse. "You know," Alissa began, jamming the key in the old lock, "this place is supposed to be one of the last standing granges in southeastern Connecticut. And it's going to be perfect. Not only does it have a stage, but there's room downstairs for dressing rooms, costume storage—there's even a tiny place right next to my office that will serve as a green room!" She pushed Susan through the door ahead of her. "What do you think of that?" she asked, flipping a switch near the door and illuminating the large area.

Susan was stunned. "It's going to take a lot of work, isn't it?"

Alissa frowned. "I'd expected more vision from you. Look!"

"Well, I . . ." Susan could hardly believe that this grubby, beaten-up interior was hidden behind the old but elegant facade.

"We'll need new curtains, a proscenium, chairs, lighting—oh, everything. I know that. After all, that private school outside of town used this as their gym for years," (a fact Susan had already guessed from the lines painted on the scuffed floors and the basketball hoops jury-rigged from the ceiling at either end of the long room) "but Horace Harvey's estate is going to transform this. It will be a showplace. We may even get some off-Broadway professionals to join our little troop for a performance once in a while. An excellent facility can make all the difference."

"If—"

"I know what you're going to say. You don't think he left the theater his money, but you're wrong. I spoke to him just yesterday morning, and he assured me that I . . . that our theater was very important to him."

"Is that exactly what he said? That the theater group was important to him? He didn't actually promise you the money?" Susan had been wondering about this point for the past twelve hours and was glad to finally be receiving an answer.

"Well . . ." Alissa began.

Susan was sure she knew what was coming.

"I suppose it doesn't matter. Now that he's dead and all. I mean, he can't change his will now. . . ."

"So he didn't promise you the money."

Alissa opened her eyes wide. "Of course he did! Why would I lie about it? It's just that . . . well, this sounds a little strange. . . ."

"What?"

"He said that I was the only person to know. That if anyone else found out—either in the theater group or outside of it—he would change his will and leave the money to a different group."

"You're kidding." Susan couldn't imagine why.

"No. He called me early yesterday morning and told me that it was important that we get together before the meeting last night. Naturally I agreed. He sounded very cheerful, and I guess I knew then that the money was going to my group. . . ."

"Did you ask him about that?"

"No." Alissa paused. "Well, maybe I did say something like 'do you have any good news for me?'—something like that. I'm so impetuous."

"And what did he answer?"

"Well, he was very rude. He said that I shouldn't make such casual comments about something so important and that if I didn't take his inheritance seriously, then maybe he shouldn't even consider leaving me the money to buy and refurbish this building. He scared me to death. To think I'd come so close and missed . . . Well, naturally, I assured him that I took the whole affair very, very seriously. I explained again how much theater meant to Hancock, and how much good his money would do for us. I'm certain he understood and agreed with me."

"Why do you say that?"

"Because when I met him later, he told me that he had

chosen the Horace Harvey Theater Company to be the honored recipient of his estate."

"When was this?"

"After he died, of course."

"That's not what I mean. When did you see him yesterday?"

"Sometime right after lunch—I think it was around one o'clock. He was late for our meeting, in fact. I thought we were going to meet at noon, but then he didn't show up. I wasn't wearing a watch—I think all this attention paid to time is very pedestrian, don't you?—and the clock in the hospital cafeteria wasn't working, so—"

"Why were you in the hospital?"

"That's where we met. He asked me to meet him for lunch in the cafeteria there. I thought it was an odd place to meet—certainly the food is nothing to write home about—but, well . . ."

"You weren't going to disagree with him about anything at that point." Susan finished her sentence for her.

"Theater is the one thing that Hancock lacks—and I'm the person who can do something about it. I consider it a mission."

Susan wasn't going to argue—not when she was getting such interesting information. "Alissa, what did you have to do to qualify for the money? What I mean is," she added, seeing the look on Alissa's face and being afraid of another soliloquy in the making, "did he need financial records? Plans to redo this space? Information about plays put on in the past? Or maybe the number of people involved in each production—or who attend each performance?"

"You think he didn't trust me!"

"I think he must have had some way of choosing which organization he was going to give his money to—some sort of standard—and I was wondering exactly what it was."

"Well, let me think. He came to see all this." She waved her arms at the large room. "And he looked around very thoroughly. I took him downstairs as well as all over the property. And I explained a little of what we had done in the past—what plays had been performed and where—

things like that. And then I told him the sort of things we would like to do with his money."

"Like the names of the plays your group wants to perform?" Susan asked, wondering what else there was.

"No. He didn't ask for information like that. I just gave him an overview of my goals."

"So he didn't ask for anything as specific as the number of people involved or the money you needed to get a mortgage on this building?"

"I told you. No."

"And was he specific?"

"About what?" Alissa asked, waving away a spider that was sliding down from the ceiling on its thread.

"Did he tell you when the money would be available? If he was going to be advancing any of it before his death? Or even how much money he actually had to give away?"

"No." Alissa frowned. "I wondered about that, in fact, but I didn't want to . . . to be rude."

Or offend him, Susan added silently.

"And everyone was talking about the millions that he'd made. Besides, he assured me that I would have the money to do what was necessary—those were his exact words. And this place is going to take a lot of money to fix up."

Susan nodded. That part, at least, was definitely true. She headed back to her car.

Susan glanced at her watch as she left Alissa behind on the lawn of the building she was planning to convert. She didn't think wearing a watch was pedestrian—she thought it was necessary. The puppy had been alone for a few hours. She just hoped she'd remembered to turn the ends of the tablecloth up—the dog loved chewing on them. She ought to start another list, too, she thought. Something about the times that Horace Harvey had talked with people on the day of his death. Had he spoken with Alissa before or after he saw Martha? And was he at the hospital for any reason other than to visit Martha? Was it possible that Horace Harvey was ill? Was that the reason for this urgency over writing his will? What was in that will, anyway? Susan knew that, with Brett out of town, she'd have a difficult time getting any information like that from the police department—if they even knew by now. If Horace Harvey was like everyone she knew, he wasn't carrying his will around with him.

She continued to head home, thinking about all of this. Where had Horace Harvey come from? Where had his money come from? Why was he so anxious to leave his money to a group in Hancock? Why Hancock? What had happened to him here that he felt so grateful?

She looked at her watch again. The puppy had probably already passed the time to go out; a quick detour to the library wouldn't make much difference now.

Susan had never spent any time in the Hancock Public Library's historical collection—and it was fascinating. Records, maps, pamphlets, books . . . all the documents since the town's incorporation in the eighteenth century were stored here. And, unlike H.E.C.'s records, everything was in perfect order. School records, records of churches, Boy Scouts, clubs . . . Susan forgot her dog and became involved in the search. After two hours, she had found only six mentions of Horace Harvey—all of them in his high school yearbooks. He was pictured with the rest of his class for his first three years of attendance at Hancock High School. He was also included in the photos of the biology club his sophomore year and the junior varsity basketball team. (He was team manager his junior year.) The only other information was included under the individual picture of him his senior year. Next to the list of activities that Susan had already noted, there was a quote. "The secret of success is constancy of purpose—Disraeli."

Susan stared at the shiny black-and-white photo of Horace Harvey at eighteen. Apparently neither a student leader, an outstanding scholar, nor as good-looking as the average person in his class, Horace Harvey was an unlikely man most likely to succeed. She frowned and flipped to the back of the book. The listing of students was complete with their addresses, and Susan wrote down where Horace Harvey had lived while attending Hancock High in the back of the

puppy-naming book. Then she thanked the librarian who
had assisted her in her search and left. Whatever had happened to Horace Harvey that made him so grateful to his
hometown, there was no written record of it here. She decided to go home to the puppy, grab a snack, and check out
the address now tucked safely in her purse. Maybe she
would get some sort of idea of Horace Harvey's youth from
the place where he had lived. Hancock was a suburb, and
as such, the population tended to turn over a good bit, but
there were still people around who had lived all their lives
in this town. If she was lucky, she'd find someone like that
living next to the house in which Horace Harvey grew up.

If she ever made it there, she thought, entering her
kitchen to the enthusiastic response of the puppy. As she let
her pet out the back door, she noticed that a red number
was flashing on her answering machine. Six calls. She
turned the animal in to the large pen built especially for it
and returned to the house, but not before noticing that the
puppy, instead of exercising, was lying next to the gate with
a forlorn expression on its face.

The machine was a new one, and she had pressed almost
every button on its ebony surface before she convinced it to
release the recorded messages.

"Mrs. Henshaw, this is James Malarkey. I need to speak
with you. I'm at the police station now, and when I leave,
someone here will know how to reach me. Thank you."

"Susan. It's Kathleen. You won't believe what that idiot
at the police station has done now. I have to go out, but I
need to speak with you. Don't talk to him until you've spoken with me. I'll call again."

"Susan. It's Kathleen again. I was thinking. You have to
leave home, because he can reach you there. Go out someplace and call me. And don't return home until I talk to
you—don't worry. If I miss you, I'll be at the Inn this
afternoon—you can find me there."

"Mrs. Henshaw? This is Detective Malarkey. It's very
important that I speak with you as soon as you arrive home.
Thank you."

"Mom. It's me. I'm going to be home late tonight. We're

going to a party in the city. Oh, I talked to my guidance counselor today, and she said that we're scheduled for Monday morning in Boston. Could you drop my black raincoat off at the cleaners? And ask them to hurry. I'll need it in Boston. 'Bye."

Susan ground her teeth.

"Sue. It's Jed. I'm on my way back to the city. I forgot the folder that I need to finish this report tomorrow. I won't make dinner."

Susan stood still for a moment, thinking. The urge to track down her daughter and scream at her was almost immediately replaced by the decision to leave her house, and do it quickly. The dog could go with her, she decided, locking the door behind her. Chrissy would just have to live without a clean raincoat.

But two minutes later she was back in the kitchen, grabbing a yogurt, the raincoat in her hand.

"Well, she's going to be interviewed by people at these colleges," she informed the dog as she started the car. "Otherwise, I'd never do this for her. Really," she insisted, amazed to discover an expression of disbelief on that sweet fuzzy face. "Oh, no," she added, accelerating to speed down the street, after spying a police car near the corner of the block.

But either the person driving the official car didn't see her or else wasn't looking for her, because she made it to the cleaners without incident. After dropping off the coat, she asked to use the phone, but Kathleen's answering machine was on and she had the dubious pleasure of hearing that Bananas had learned his ABCs. Susan, in turn, said hi into the machine, omitting any mention of James Malarkey's desire to see her or the fact that there was no *K* in the youngest Gordon's alphabet, then she returned to her car.

The neighborhood where Horace Harvey had grown up was on the far side of town from the Henshaw home, and Susan shared a peach yogurt with the puppy as they traveled. The trip took longer than usual as she had decided to stay away from the main thoroughfares. It wasn't, she told herself, as though there were anything illegal about avoiding the police. . . .

The street named in the yearbook had sounded familiar, and once Susan found it, she realized why. Her son had taken trumpet lessons from a man who lived around the block about six years ago. The teacher habitually ran late, and she had spent more time than she cared to remember waiting in her car for Chad to appear. This particular neighborhood was possibly one of the least expensive in a very expensive town, and looking around, Susan wondered if it hadn't been definitely working-class fifty years ago when Horace Harvey was a boy. The two-story homes had a uniformity about them that was rare in town, and she suspected that more than one had been built as a duplex.

Glancing down at the back of the book she had written on, Susan noted the address she sought. And, she thought, smiling at her yogurt-covered puppy, she had a wonderful excuse to check out the neighborhood.

Dog walking had some interesting side benefits, she decided, wandering slowly down the street. When you're with a dog, you belong. And people stopped to talk, Susan remembered, slowing down at an elderly man's approach.

"Hi," Susan said with a smile.

"Good afternoon. Golden retriever?"

Susan correctly interpreted the words and smiled as the man slowly bent down to pet the puppy.

"What's her name?"

Susan admitted the animal's lack, and the man chuckled. "I know how that is. My father brought a puppy home one evening, and the entire family got into the act to name the little guy. And I have six brothers and a sister, so it didn't look likely that we'd ever agree."

"What name did you finally decide upon?"

"Boomer. And I have no idea why or how. He was a great dog, though. This one is going to be big, isn't she?"

"She's not growing, she's blowing up," Susan admitted, starting to stroll along with the man. "Have you lived in Hancock long?"

"About two decades. My wife and I moved here when

she inherited the house she'd grown up in from her father. I was retiring that year, and we were glad to get out of the city to such a charming town. . . ."

He continued and Susan listened, waiting for a moment when she could figure out a way to meet his wife. But that was not to be.

". . . So when she died, I just stayed. I enjoy the house and I have my garden. And there's a lot to do at the Senior Center. It's a nice life."

"I'm sure it is," Susan assured him. "You know, I was wondering . . . is there anyone still living on the block that grew up here—like your wife?" she added.

"Hmmm. Nope, I don't think so. No one's ever mentioned it to me here, and my wife never spoke of it. Why do you ask? Does it have something to do with the murder last night?" He chuckled. "Don't look so surprised. Retired people have a lot of time and are interested in what's going on. I read about Horace Harvey's murder in the paper over breakfast this morning. And I've read about you solving other murders before this. But I'm not real good at names . . . ?"

Susan held out her hand for him to shake. "Susan Henshaw. And it does have to do with the murder—that is, indirectly it does. Horace Harvey grew up on this block. In that house there," she added, pointing at a white two-story Victorian with dark green trim. "Number 319. He lived there while he was in high school."

"He did? Well, the couple that live there will find that interesting. They've been in the house almost as long as I've lived here. We could ask them if they know anything, though. But you know what?" He stopped walking. "I could ask around down at the Senior Center. If that would be any help. There are people there who've lived in Hancock their entire lives. They may not have lived on this block, but they could have known Horace Harvey. Back then, Hancock wasn't as large a town as it is now. It wouldn't hurt."

"No, it would be wonderful."

"Well, I'm due there for my t'ai chi ch'uan class in about half an hour. Maybe you'd like to go along with me?"

"I'd love to . . . but maybe I shouldn't."

"Oh, of course, you're probably too busy helping the police and all. . . ."

"No, it's not that! Actually, I'm trying to avoid the police right now."

"You certainly lead an exciting life, Mrs. Henshaw."

"I can try to explain, but you're not going to understand it. I know that," she added, seeing the puzzled expression on his face, "because I don't understand it. All I know is that James Malarkey—"

"The acting police chief."

"Exactly. Well, I know that he's looking for me and that there's some reason that it's important that I don't talk to him until I talk to someone else."

"That is confusing. Very. But it doesn't have to be a big problem. I assume that you're expecting to speak with this other person soon?"

"As soon as possible. I left a message on her machine, and she's left more than one on mine. But it's been a while. I could try again."

"Good idea. Maybe you could use the phone in my kitchen. I have to change my clothing before class. You can bring her in," he added, seeing the look on her face. "I have an old tabby, but she's too smart to mess with an energetic animal like yours. As you get older, you learn to accept your limits."

Susan could see his point. This case was too confusing, there were too many people and organizations involved. Maybe she had reached her limit, too.

EIGHT

So IF YOU CAN'T DO IT YOURSELF, WHY ARE YOU SO RELUCTANT to let me help out? I'm old, Mrs. Henshaw. I'm old, but I'm not senile. I'm perfectly able to ask questions and remember the answers.

The last sentence had convinced Susan. She didn't want to hurt this charming man's feelings by refusing his offer. Besides, she really needed his help, she reminded herself, following her cheerful puppy through the park. Up ahead was the reproduction Victorian gazebo where she had promised to meet her elderly helper. Susan cut across the lawn, tripping on a granite block that seemed to have sprouted up from the roots of a massive beech tree.

Naturally, there was an audience for her clumsiness. Two women, vaguely familiar, were jogging on a nearby path. "Are you all right?" the one closest to her called out.

When Susan assured them of her safety, they continued their exercise plan, the other calling back over her shoulder, "You have to be careful in our parks, you know. Tillie Greenleaf and her group have filled them with dozens of memorials, plaques, and tablets. H.E.C. is turning our parks into cemeteries."

"Well, you know how she's always lecturing about the benefits of natural fertilizers!" They both shrieked with glee over the presumed cleverness of the comment.

Susan ignored them. "Come on, dog," she urged, bending down to help the puppy up the steps into the gazebo. The animal immediately began to lick the brass dedication plaque set in the center of the structure's floor, and Susan plopped down on a bench, pulling the scribbled-upon paperback and a pen from her purse. "How does Truffles sound to you?" she asked the animal, flipping through the pages. "Or maybe Chesapeake? Chessie? Cheesecake? Crumbcake? Clancey? No, that's for a male, isn't it? What about Buddy? Or Babette?" The animal showed complete disinterest in the whole question of nomenclature, and Susan decided she had more pressing things to worry about. "Like where did Horace Harvey live after leaving Hancock? . . . Oh, damn!"

Two police cars had just stopped in the lot where she'd left her car, and James Malarkey was getting out and starting to walk in her direction. The gazebo was in the middle of a large, tree-studded lawn. There was absolutely no way to slip off unnoticed. And she saw no value in publicly fleeing from the police. So she sat and waited.

James Malarkey was a good-looking man, and he seemed to prefer the type of clothing more common in Ralph Lauren ads than in a police station. Today he wore a fine herringbone suit under his Burberry. His silk tie sported a print that was discreet but interesting. A long fringed silk scarf hung over his shoulders, and well-polished tan shoes completed the image. He looked affluent, but he didn't look happy.

Susan tried to remember the lecture her dentist had given her about the dangers of grinding her teeth. Pet the dog! Petting animals was known to calm people down, to actually lower their blood pressure. She bent down to scratch the puppy and wait.

She wasn't going to be the first to speak! She wasn't going to admit to listening to the messages he had left on her answering machine! She was going to shut up and pet her dog.

Unless he didn't say anything. James Malarkey slowly mounted the steps and joined her in the gazebo, choosing to sit down on the bench directly across from her. He allowed a faint smile to crinkle his lips; he didn't speak. Susan tried to emulate his example.

And she did until she couldn't stand it anymore. "Hi."

Well, that wasn't giving anything away. It was merely being polite.

He nodded.

Susan glanced over at the twin cars in the lot. Would anyone there notice if she ripped one of the ornate pillars off its base and beaned this guy? "Did you want to see me?" she asked in as innocent a tone as she could manage. Was it only her ears that heard the underlying lie?

He nodded again. Susan slipped down to the wooden floor, determined to sit silently by her pet until he started the conversation.

"We could, of course, keep this up forever," the policeman said after a few minutes had passed.

"We could." Susan tried to keep all expression out of her voice. Not a completely successful effort, and she was aware of it. "I have to go to Boston Monday, though, so maybe we could—"

"Why Boston? What do you plan to do there?"

Susan opened her mouth and then closed it. Think before you speak, even if you grind your teeth while you do it, she lectured mutely. There was something significant here. Why was he so interested in her travel plans? "Are you telling me not to leave town?" She tried to make the question sound casual.

"I want to know why you need to go to Boston." He didn't bother to act like his question was unimportant. In fact, Susan got the impression that her answer had a significance that she didn't understand—yet.

"I'm taking my daughter to visit some colleges that she's interested in attending the year after next. The trip was arranged by the college counselor at her school. Chrissy is interested in a fine arts program. She's quite a talented artist, although she hasn't narrowed down the field she wants to work in. . . ."

"When?"

"Monday."

"I mean, when was the trip planned?"

Susan paused. "Well, Chrissy has been talking about

Boston College and Boston University for years, and then she found out more about Emerson College and—"

"When did you plan on going to Boston?"

"Well, actually, I was thinking about sometime next week, but Chrissy's guidance counselor arranged all this. I just found out . . . a few hours ago." At least she had explained without admitting to answering her phone machine.

"Oh."

It was obvious to Susan that her companion had completely lost interest in her travels. "Why were you looking for me?" Susan asked, bored by this entire discussion.

"Why do you think I was looking for you?"

Susan waved her arm about the field. "Why else would you come here?"

"Late lunch." That grin again. He reached into his coat pocket and pulled out a neat brown packet. Susan recognized a croissant sandwich that one of the specialty shops in town sold. "There isn't quite enough to share, I'm afraid."

"That's fine." She wasn't going to admit how hungry she was feeling. The dog had eaten most of the yogurt. "I'm planning to eat later at the Inn, as a matter of fact," she added, remembering Kathleen.

"Really? Why?"

This was becoming ridiculous. "Because the food is good. Because it's convenient. Because I like it there. What business is it of yours where I eat anyway?" she ended belligerently. "If you're only here to have a picnic, I guess I'll leave you alone." She started to get up.

"Actually, Mrs. Henshaw, I think I'll join you at the Inn for lunch. The bakery made a mistake," he added, seeing her eyebrows rise. "I asked for Brie on the croissant. They gave me cheddar." He tossed the package, half-opened, into the garbage container provided at the bottom of the stairs. "Shall we go?"

What could she say? "Of course. I'll meet you there, I guess," she added as they started walking to their cars.

"Why don't I ride with you? Then my men can go about

their business. . . . Mrs. Henshaw? Is that all right with you?" he asked when she didn't answer right away.

"Yes. Yes. Of course." She had been thinking of other things. Like why did James Malarkey want to eat with her? Especially since she had seen the telltale rind of creamy Brie spilling from the package he'd thrown away.

The Inn certainly didn't look like the scene of a crime, Susan thought, directing her car into a familiar parking spot. Huge magnolia trees were budding on the lawn. Forsythia were spilling their buttery petals onto the flagstone walks. Tiny yellow daffodils were blooming in copper boxes beneath the wide windows flanking the door. Certainly peace and happiness were here. That was the general atmosphere until one got a look at Charles. The host walked out the door, and sunshine fell on his pale, distressed face.

Susan was shocked. "Charles, are you okay?" she asked, leading James Malarkey up the path. She was holding the puppy, hoping they could find someone to care for the animal while they ate.

Charles rearranged his face into its usual professional facade. It occurred to Susan that she knew very little about this man whom she had been seeing regularly for many years. "Mrs. Henshaw. What a nice surprise. And Detective Malarkey. Are you joining Mrs. Gordon for dinner?"

Susan opened her mouth, but the policeman managed to answer.

"We would rather be alone. Maybe you have a booth in a private corner for us?"

"Of course. Just follow me."

"Maybe you could find someone to take care of my puppy during our meal?" Susan asked, preceding the men inside. "She's just a few weeks old, and I hate to leave her in the car."

Charles glanced around quickly, spied a waitress walking toward the kitchen, and motioned her over. "Ellen, would you help Mrs. Henshaw? She needs to leave her pet with someone while she eats.... Maybe someone is in the office?"

"Julie's up there working on the orders for next month. I'll take the sweetie." She reached out for the dog.

"I'll just go make sure everything is okay," Susan suggested, pulling her dog away from a dangling tablecloth.

"We'll be at the large booth in the back of the main dining room," Charles said. "You know where it is: the one under the brass sun, Mrs. Henshaw."

"Of course. Of course. I'll be there in just a few seconds," Susan called over her shoulder as she followed the young woman up the main stairs of the Inn.

"If you'll just follow me," Charles said to the detective, who had little choice but to do as asked. "Perhaps there's some news about the burglary here last week...."

When they were out of hearing range, Susan whispered to the waitress, "Do you know who Kathleen Gordon is?"

"Yes, of course. She's been coming here for years."

"She's here now. And I want to see her, but privately. Could you possibly find her and tell her I'm here? And ask if she would meet me in the ladies' room at—" she looked at her watch "—at six o'clock."

"Yes, ma'am, of course."

Susan realized that the girl thought she was a little eccentric—at the very least. "But it's very important that you don't let on that I've asked you this. That the man I'm with doesn't know about it," she said, not wanting to admit that she was keeping secrets from the acting chief of police.

It was an unnecessary precaution. "You mean that Malarkey man," the girl said with disgust. "Don't worry, I won't tell him anything. I was the first person to come on duty the morning after the burglary," she continued to explain, "and he acted like I had robbed the place myself. He refused to believe the answers that Charles had given him, so he asked me the same things—question after question. All about the layout of the Inn, its alarm system, the schedules of the employees, and things that I don't know anything about. And then he didn't act like he believed my answers.

Don't worry, I won't tell him anything. And I'll take care of this little puppy," she added. "Does he like liver?"

"He's a she, and she likes anything—maybe you shouldn't leave those shoes under the desk."

"Gotcha! Come on, sweetie."

Susan hurried back down the stairs, confident that her puppy was going to be spoiled to death and that she was soon going to find out what Kathleen wanted to tell her.

Charles wasn't looking any better, Susan thought, hurrying to the large banquette in the rear of the room. She had expected to find the Inn fairly empty. There were three dining rooms besides the large bar on the first floor of the building. There was a medium-sized dining room next to the bar. The large dining room extended half of the building, from front to back. The third room was a small, private room that sat fifty people at most; it had been created by enclosing a porch. Usually only one room was needed for the lunch crowd.

Today all the rooms were open and full of customers. Maybe Charles had been wrong last night: It seemed that people loved eating in a place where a murder had occurred. Who would have thought ...

"Here's Mrs. Henshaw now." Susan thought she heard relief in the maître d's voice. "I'll send someone over to take your order immediately."

"We'd like to see the wine list," James Malarkey announced.

"I ..." She stopped. Why not? She didn't need to drink any, and the detective needed to relax. She leaned back and looked out the window. "It's been a pretty day."

"A pretty day in a pretty town," he replied, taking the long wine list from the woman who had appeared almost instantly. He scanned the pages as though looking for something, and when he found it, he ordered, not bothering to ask Susan if she had any preferences. The waitress hurried off, leaving behind menus. Susan picked hers up, although she knew what she wanted. She was determined to stay in control.

So, apparently, was James Malarkey. After breezing through the wine list, he was taking his time with the menu.

Susan looked around the room. She recognized a few customers and she was considering an acquaintance's new hair color when she realized that she was being stared at by Tillie Greenleaf. Susan gasped and looked away, but not before realizing that Kathleen was Tillie's dinner companion.

"Are you all right?"

"I just realized they have lobster salad on the menu—it's one of my favorites." It was the only excuse she could think of. "We ... we have a house in Maine. Lobster is one of my favorite foods. Ah ... it really is," she ended, remembering her vow of silence. Good thing she'd never wanted to be a monk.

"How interesting." Obviously it wasn't.

Maybe those monks chanted silently. Shut up. Shut up. Shut up. Susan, shut up. What was Tillie doing here? Out of jail. Did James Malarkey know she was here? She glanced at the man. He stared back at her.

"Are you okay?"

"Yes."

"You don't look very well."

"I'm fine," she insisted.

"Here comes the wine; maybe that will help."

"Well ..." Susan paused.

"This is a celebration," he insisted, filling her glass with tawny liquid. "Your friend, Mrs. Greenleaf, was released from jail a few hours ago."

"I'm glad to hear that, but she's not really a friend. I mean, I don't know her very well."

"That's probably for the best. I think she did it, you know."

"I assumed you thought that—after all, you arrested her." Susan was becoming irritated.

"Arrests are based on facts, not opinions."

Susan took a sip from her glass. And then another. This man might not know much about murder, but he knew how to pick out wine.

"They have an excellent wine list. Not many restaurants carry this vineyard."

"This is very good. I don't think I've had it before," Susan said, reading the label as he refilled her glass.

"It's one of my favorites. I guess you could say I feel about this the way you feel about lobster."

Susan took another sip of wine. "Why did you release Mrs. Greenleaf?"

His shrugged shoulders that could only be called elegant. "We weren't prepared to go before a grand jury at this time.

"Ah ... here's our charming waitress. Mrs. Henshaw will have the lobster salad, and I'll have the soft-shell crabs."

Susan only smiled at the waitress, who winked at her and then glanced at her watch.

Susan looked down too. "I need to visit the ladies' room. I'll be back in a few minutes."

He stood as she left. Susan walked by the table where Kathleen and Tillie had been. It was empty. She continued on to her destination.

Kathleen was waiting, leaning against a white pedestal sink, examining the ivy stenciled on the walls of the room.

"Where's Tillie?" Susan asked.

"On the phone. She had to call her husband and let him know that she's going to be home later than she had told him."

"I could hardly believe my eyes when I saw her. I assumed that she was still being held by the police. She's not out on bond, is she?"

"No, they just let her go this afternoon without any explanation."

"Malarkey says that they didn't have enough evidence to present to a grand jury."

"Her lawyer thinks that he has enough evidence to sue for false arrest—but I don't think you need to tell James Malarkey that.

"Meeting in here was good thinking," she added. "But I

guess we can't spend too much time. What has he been saying?"

"Nothing."

"You're kidding."

"No. We met over at the park about fifteen minutes ago, we drove here, we sat down. About all he's told me was what I just said to you about evidence and that he likes Italian wines."

"And what have you told him?"

Susan was more than a little offended by the question. "Nothing. Not a thing. Although he knows how much I love lobster."

Kathleen resisted asking the obvious question. "He hasn't explained why he wanted to see you?"

"He doesn't know that I know that he wanted to see me," Susan answered, and then explained about the messages on her answering machine. "But I still don't know why you wanted to talk to me. You sounded pretty desperate."

"Oh, that doesn't matter now. I was trying to get Tillie out of jail, and I thought you could help."

"Wait a second," Susan said, squinting into the mirror. "Why did you want to see me before James Malarkey?"

"I didn't want you to tell him about H.E.C. and Chrissy."

Susan stopped fiddling with her earring and turned to stare at her friend. "I haven't the foggiest idea what you're talking about. How are my daughter and H.E.C. connected?"

"She didn't tell you? I thought she'd be so thrilled!"

"About what?"

"You know how a lot of the organizations give awards to graduating seniors?"

"Yes," Susan said a bit impatiently.

"Well, Chrissy is going to receive the H.E.C. award as a junior—it's practically unheard-of, and it almost guarantees that she'll receive the student service award in her senior year. I thought she'd be thrilled to death!"

"Why would they give her the award? She's not a gardener."

"Because of the work she did designing for the landscape-of-the-future contest." Kathleen looked closely at her friend. "Don't tell me you know nothing about this?"

"Nothing at all," Susan said sadly. "Well, it will give us something to talk about on the way to Boston."

"Boston . . . You're going to Boston? Susan, that's terrific! Then we'll really have something to work with!"

"What does my trip have to do with anything? I'm taking Chrissy to visit a few colleges and art schools in Boston. Of course, I'm not sure what my part is in all of this. She has interviews to go to. . . ."

"And you can use your free time to do some research into Horace Harvey's background. Find out more about his business interests, where he lived, maybe even talk to some of his old friends and colleagues. . . ."

"Horace Harvey is from Boston?"

"If it's where he made his money. I know it's where he's been living for the past twenty years or so—maybe ever since he left Hancock."

"If he's been living so close by, why didn't he ever come back to visit? Or did he?" Susan asked, momentarily diverted.

"I have no idea. All I know is that he lived in Boston. . . . Here's Tillie. She can explain."

Tillie Greenleaf entered the room and headed straight for one of the booths that lined one wall. "I've got to go," she explained.

"Could you explain what you overheard about Horace Harvey's past while you're in there?" Kathleen asked.

"Sure. Did you explain what happened?"

"Tillie was talking with her lawyer this morning—"

"In an office belonging to one of the policemen. The juvenile officer, I think," she called out. "It was right next to the room that Detective Malarkey is using while he's in town."

"And the doors were open to the hall," Kathleen added, "so she could hear what was being said next door."

"While I was waiting for my lawyer. He was on the

phone in another room," Tillie elaborated. "The doors were both open at the same time for only a few minutes."

"What did you hear?" Susan asked.

"Someone was reporting on a background check on the dead man."

"That's how you know that he lived in Boston!" Susan exclaimed.

"Exactly." Kathleen took over the story as the toilet flushed. "We don't know how long he lived there, but he lived there before coming here, and he had a business there."

"The business that made him the money!" Susan exclaimed. "What did he do? Deal in the stock market?" It was the only field she knew where friends and neighbors had made millions in just one decade.

"No," Kathleen said bluntly.

"He's a venture capitalist," Tillie said.

"How could he have made so much money doing that?" Susan asked, astounded.

"Good question," Tillie said.

"You'll have lots of free time in Boston. Maybe you can find out something."

"Maybe I will," Susan agreed.

NINE

"YOU'RE BACK. I WAS CONSIDERING ASKING CHARLES TO send a waitress on a rescue mission."

"It was nice of you to worry about me," Susan said, sitting down across from him. Her meal was waiting, and the lobster did look awfully good.

"I wasn't worried. I just prefer not to eat food that is no longer warm."

"You should have started without me." Susan was still trying to be polite.

"I did."

Susan glanced down and saw that he was halfway through his meal. She picked up her fork without another word.

But James Malarkey wasn't content to eat in silence. "I assume you ran into Mrs. Greenleaf in the ladies' room."

"I . . ."

"You don't have to bother to deny it. She's still our primary suspect. I have a man watching her."

"Then you can stop asking me questions that you already know answers to and let me eat my dinner."

After Susan had finished her lobster and was buttering an onion roll, her companion spoke again.

"It's just possible that I could have you arrested for obstructing justice—or aiding a criminal after a crime has taken place."

"I doubt that," Susan said with more confidence than she felt. She took what she hoped was a jaunty swig from her wineglass. And, naturally, choked.

As her coughing grew worse and, horror of horrors, she could feel her nose beginning to run, fellow diners and waitresses hurried from all points of the room to offer handkerchiefs and fresh napkins. "I'm okay. I'm fine," she croaked, trying to avoid anyone determined to display knowledge of the Heimlich maneuver. "I just need some air."

Charles had appeared by her side. "Mrs. Henshaw needs air. If everyone will step back please."

"Here. Take this." Susan couldn't determine the identity of the person who slipped the large fresh damask napkin into her hand. But she could feel the crispness of the note tucked inside. She dabbed her eyes and tucked the fabric firmly around the paper and under her seat cushion. Life was so interesting during a murder investigation, she thought, scanning the faces around her.

"I believe Mrs. Henshaw is going to be fine. Thank you all so much for your help." The policeman stood up and graciously dismissed the crowd.

Susan smiled weakly and reached for the goblet of water that had appeared by her side. "Thank you." She waited until they were alone again, after Charles had been reassured of her health and comfort and had returned to the front desk. "Why did you want to see me?" she asked frankly. "You found me in the park, you asked me to dinner. Why?"

"I guess there's no reason to pretend that it's merely for the pleasure of your company."

"None."

"And what if I told you that I need your help?"

I wouldn't believe you, Susan said to herself. "To do what?" she asked aloud.

"I seem to have rubbed some of the people involved in this case the wrong way."

Doesn't surprise me. It was such a strong thought that, for a moment, she was afraid she'd spoken out loud.

"Not everybody, of course," the policeman continued, putting down his fork. "I've found Mrs. Bradshaw very reasonable. In fact, she had me over to her house for breakfast this morning."

Trust Honey to think that morning was an appropriate time for entertaining. "She has a very good cook," Susan answered inconsequentially.

"Hmm. Fresh melon, German pancakes with brown sugar and strawberries, Canadian bacon. She even offered maple syrup from their own trees—they have a cabin in the Adirondacks, she told me. But . . ." Susan thought he was rather reluctant to return to the point. "Some of you seem more interested in protecting each other than in helping the police. My conversation with Mr. Arnold was less than revealing. He seemed intent upon blaming one of your councilmen. . . ."

"Ralph Spinoza." Susan filled in the name he obviously had forgotten.

"Exactly. Mr. Spinoza, however, was concerned that we might suspect Mr. Arnold—in fact, he was most emphatic about the other man's innocence. I find that very suspicious." He nodded at his own perceptions and, picking up his fork, started to finish his meal.

Susan was convinced that Ralph Spinoza had intended just that, but she kept the thought to herself. "You're talking with everyone on your own?" she asked, trying to force herself to forgo another roll.

"Of course. I've done some preliminary interviewing of everyone Horace Harvey promised his money to."

"Then . . ."

"Despite my belief that Tillie Greenleaf is the person we're looking for, I felt an obligation to talk with everyone else."

"How do you know that the murderer is someone who runs one of these organizations? Why don't you consider other people? After all, these people aren't going to benefit personally from the inheritance."

"You are kidding me." He placed his fork in the middle of his empty plate and drained his wineglass. "These people aren't normal. They don't just belong to these organizations, they're obsessed with them. They probably care more about their organizations than their children. That lady who runs the theater group—Alissa Anthony—I was at her house last night, and she was making some sort of Italian soup that takes three days to cook—three days! I couldn't believe it! It was for her friends who are trying out for the next production. Her family was trying to move around her in the kitchen to heat up Lean Cuisines in the microwave. Does this make sense to you?"

"Well ..." Susan knew that the demands on volunteer workers sometimes did interfere with their family lives— even if their families had been the original reason they'd gotten involved in the first place. It didn't make sense, but not everything did. "What about other members of these organizations? Aren't some of them equally fanatic? Maybe past presidents?" She felt that the larger the field, the less likely he could possibly be of Tillie's guilt.

"I thought of that. It doesn't hold water. Q.U.I.E.T., S.O.D., P.A.P., and H.O.P.E. are all brand-new—they don't have past presidents. They don't actually have elected presidents; they have founders. H.E.C., F.O.P.P., and the theater group have been around for a longer time, but they are run a lot like benevolent dictatorships. It wasn't hard to make the list. Do you eat dessert?"

"Excuse me?" Susan was surprised by the change of topic.

"I thought I'd order chocolate mousse and cappuccino. How about you?"

"I ... I still don't know why you wanted to talk with me," Susan blurted out.

"I'll order mousse for you and explain."

"No. Yes. Well, then, make mine almond praline," she succumbed.

"Do you have a notebook or something to write in?" he surprised her by beginning.

"No, but I've been writing things in the back of this." Susan pulled the puppy name book from her purse. She scrounged around for a pen in the bottom of her bag and, when she'd found one, opened to a fresh page (entitled "names I like best"), waiting for him to tell her what he wanted.

"When are you leaving for Boston?" he surprised her by beginning.

"Monday. Early in the morning. We're due at Boston University at nine A.M."

"Then you're going to be busy between now and then—if you agree to help me."

Susan tried to keep a neutral, noncommitted look on her face.

"You see, I have questions about all these people. You're a respected part of this community. People listen to you."

This is where all this began two days ago, Susan thought, smiling at the waitress who set a discreetly small custard cup before her, a cloud of whipped cream topped with a dusting of crumbs shrouding the contents. "You want me to ask questions of the suspects?" Susan asked. "Things you don't want to ask?"

"Questions that I need honest answers to—right away. Do you think you can help me? I know you've assisted the Hancock Police Department before."

"I've helped Brett," Susan muttered. "Unofficially, of course."

"Of course. Can you do it? You understand that I don't want to give you a list of questions before I can depend on your assistance." He had finished his dessert in three large spoonfuls, and Susan got the feeling that he would have encouraged her to hurry up if he could have done so without being rude.

She looked around the room as if searching for an answer. And found one. Standing in the corner, between a portable serving cart and a flourishing ficus tree, stood Kathleen Gordon, waving her hands and nodding her head.

"Yes," Susan interpreted her friend's gestures. "I'd be glad to help you. What do you need?" she asked, finishing her food and sitting with her pen poised. He had opened a leather-bound notebook, holding it at an angle so she couldn't see inside.

"Let's start with Mrs. Bradshaw. She's the easiest. I need you to find out, first, where she was when Horace Harvey was found, and next, where did she go to high school?"

"High school?"

"Exactly. I can't tell you why I need to know these things—not right now," he added solemnly.

"Fine." She tried to make her voice match his tone. She finished writing and looked up. He was picking fur from his sleeve.

"Damn poodles," he commented.

Susan raised her eyebrows. If Honey Bradshaw had let him believe her dogs were ordinary poodles, maybe she did have something to hide. "Anything else?"

"No, that's all for Mrs. Bradshaw. Now, about Alissa Anthony ..."

Twenty-five minutes later, Susan was sitting alone, her puppy book open on the table.

"What have you been writing? I thought I'd die of curiosity waiting 'til that man left!" Kathleen slid into the chair James Malarkey had recently vacated.

Susan pushed the book over for Kathleen to read. "This doesn't make any sense," she said long before she could possibly have finished.

"What doesn't?"

"Look at this." Kathleen pointed. "It says Alissa. Dot. Dot. Dot. Bob Arnold's wife's affair." She looked up. "Did Shirley Arnold have an affair?"

Susan looked around to see that they couldn't be overheard before answering. "According to James Malarkey, there's a rumor around that she was involved with Ralph Spinoza."

"What?"

"Quiet! Everyone in the room is going to be staring at us."

"They already are. You know how interested people get in your life whenever there's a murder around here."

"Okay. Then let's just keep it down and I'll explain—and read my notes to you."

"Go ahead."

"James Malarkey wants me to help him with his investigation," she started, ignoring Kathleen's raised eyebrows.

"He gave me a list of questions that he believes very important to answer—as soon as possible."

"Which, in your case, is before you leave town."

"Exactly. Well, the weekend is beginning. At least most people will be home. Do you want me to read this to you?"

"Please."

"Okay. There are three things he wants to know about Bob Arnold: if his wife had an affair with Ralph Spinoza and if he knew about it; also, how well does he get along with Olive Spinoza?"

"Implying that he was having a relationship with her? What sort of wife-swapping lifestyle does James Malarkey think we're all living here?"

"Wait 'til I get to the end of this. He is looking for information about who the Spinozas made the guardian of their children in case they die. Let me just list the questions. Then we'll get done before one of the waitresses or Charles comes over and interrupts."

Kathleen nodded her agreement.

"Alissa Anthony. Has she ever needed to have a paying job? Has she ever had anything published? Has she ever been sued?

"Tillie Greenleaf. Where did she meet her husband? How long did they know each other before they were married? Where does their money come from? I gather he thinks that they couldn't maintain the lifestyle that they do on the salary of a college professor." Susan looked up, a serious expression on her face. "Which might be true. I've heard other people comment about that from time to time.

"Martha Trumbull. Well, this one is easy. He wants to know if she knows that Ethan . . . her nephew," she added, before Kathleen could ask. "He's living with her right now. Well, evidently Ethan has dropped out of college, and he wants to know if his aunt knows that, if she supports him, if he is her heir.

"And last, but not least, he wants to know why Patty Taylor refused to speak with him at all."

"You're kidding."

"No, apparently he said he wanted to ask her some questions, and she said she would not speak with him unless her lawyer was present."

"And . . . ?"

"And he decided he had other things to do and put it off." Susan shrugged. "I think he'd already chosen Tillie as the most likely suspect and just didn't bother."

"Why you?"

"Why does he want me to find out these things?"

"Exactly."

"He says that he thinks everyone will tell me the truth, that I don't threaten them in any way."

"And what do you think?" Kathleen asked seriously.

"I think he's jerking me around, that he wants to keep me busy asking questions until I leave town." Susan frowned. "These questions sound like something out of a soap opera. He's fishing—and wasting my time."

"So what are you going to do?"

"I'm going to investigate. I'd be crazy not to," Susan laughed, "especially since I now have official police blessing."

Kathleen nodded. "So where do we start?"

"I think we'd better go upstairs. I left the dog in the office; it's probably time I collected her and headed home. I really should spend some quality time with my family tonight—especially since I'm going to be running all over town asking questions this weekend."

TEN

THEY WERE IN SUSAN'S CAR, ON THE WAY TO THE BRAD-shaws' house.

"Why Honey first?" Kathleen asked.

"Because the questions he wanted answered about her are so innocuous."

"You're going to ask the questions that man listed?"

"Those and more," Susan admitted. "It's a starting point, after all. Besides, Honey had James Malarkey over for breakfast yesterday morning."

"Good thought. There might be leftovers. I don't like the woman, but she sure serves wonderful food."

"You just ate breakfast," Susan protested, once again envying her friend's ability to eat almost constantly and retain her fabulous figure.

"It's the most important meal of the day," Kathleen muttered, looking at the messy list Susan had made. "Why in heaven's name would he want to know where Honey went to high school? And I know where Honey was when Harvey was found. She was sitting in front of the fireplace in the bar at the Inn. I was on the other side of the room and I was watching her."

"Why?"

"I don't know. I was thinking about F.O.P.P. and H.E.C. ..."

"What about F.O.P.P. and H.E.C.?" Susan asked, glancing at her companion. Kathleen had a very serious expression on her face.

"Oh, nothing that's significant now. It just strikes me as

strange that they were both being considered as equals. You know, there's no comparison between the two groups—except for the fact that they both deal with plants. H.E.C. has acres and acres of parklands that they maintain and support. F.O.P.P. probably has a quarter of an acre at the most, if you add together all their pots and window boxes. They're not real gardeners even. They buy plants and stick them in planters and tend them. Mostly, though, F.O.P.P. is a group of social fund-raisers."

"H.E.C. does fund-raising. I always go to their Mother's Day plant sale—and we bought our Christmas tree from them last year."

"Oh, we do. We probably raise a couple of thousand dollars a year—sometimes more. And we have a large number of endowments."

"Endowments?"

"People who leave H.E.C. money to plant and maintain part of a garden." Susan remembered the comments she'd heard yesterday about tripping over plaques in the park. "Do you know that the gazebo and both small greenhouses over in Riverview Park were built with funds from the family of the old superintendent of schools? I think we've benefited from over fifty estates."

"You're kidding." Susan glanced out the window as they passed the Fiske Home.

"No. We have a completely volunteer staff except for our treasurer—she's a professional. It's too much money and too much responsibility. There are I don't know how many thousands of dollars involved."

Susan was driving up the long, curving brick driveway to the Bradshaw home. "How much money do you think F.O.P.P. needs to carry out their work?"

"Good question. They buy hundreds of flats of plants every year, fertilizers, insecticides. . . . That's about it after the initial amount of money to buy the containers and soil mixtures. Maybe a few thousand a year."

"How do they raise it?" Soil mixtures? She had always called it dirt.

"Balls, parties, garden tours. You know Honey. She'll tell

us all about it." Kathleen waved through the window to the elegant woman walking out her equally elegant front door.

"How does she do it?" Susan muttered. The sun had just moved from behind a cloud, and bright light illuminated Honey's hair (the color of the purest of all the bee's products) that fell over her eggshell blue sweater set (cashmere, naturally); her stone house (massive yet homey) was trimmed with shining white paint, bracketed by gleaming black shutters; the lawn and trees were prematurely green, the gardens rioting with every type of bulb (flown directly from Holland, of course) Susan had ever heard of and some she hadn't. "I always get the feeling that Martha Stewart just dashed out the back door."

"It is photo-perfect, isn't it? Hi!" Kathleen called out.

Honey returned her wave. "Come on in. I have to get back to the kitchen," she replied, and reentered her home.

"That sounds more like you than Honey," Kathleen commented. "And where are those dogs?" she added, glancing around nervously.

Susan followed her friend into the house and across the gleaming chestnut floors of the center hallway, slowing down to admire the hand-painted walls. Honey had agonized for months over these walls, examining design after design, choosing, discarding, and rechoosing colors. She claimed not to have slept for the entire six weeks that it took to complete the job. As her husband said, you would have thought she was actually doing the work. Instead, she had hired an artist from California who, after finishing the house, turned down numerous offers from neighbors and friends who admired and envied the result of his efforts. He said he couldn't be trusted to enter Connecticut ever again; he was afraid he might accidentally run into Honey Bradshaw, and he just knew he couldn't resist killing her. But the walls were beautiful, museum quality; everyone agreed on it.

Honey looked up from the work island in the center of her kitchen. She appeared to be decorating lemons. *"Citrons givres,"* she announced, using her wrist to push her hair off her forehead. "They're for a small dinner party we're giving tonight. Some of William's colleagues. I would have canceled after the murder, but they're from the city and they're not involved, so . . ." She left her explanation unfinished.

"It's not as though Horace Harvey was a personal friend," Kathleen agreed.

Susan said nothing, busily examining Honey's creations. "There's some sort of gratiné inside the frosted lemon peel, isn't there? And you piped green marzipan on for leaves?"

"Yes. They were a favorite at my cooking school in Paris. I like to do dessert myself."

Susan crinkled the corners of her lips into something resembling a smile—if you didn't look too closely. Why couldn't Honey cut recipes from magazines like everyone else? "What else are you serving?" she asked.

But Kathleen wasn't going to let menus interfere with the reason for their visit. "We came to talk with Honey about the murder," she reminded her friend.

"Oh, I had that nice James Malarkey over for breakfast yesterday. He really isn't at all what I would expect from a policeman. Almost our class . . ." Honey barged on, apparently forgetting that Kathleen's father had been in the Philadelphia Police Department long before she had been a policewoman herself.

"Why?" Susan interrupted bluntly.

Honey opened her perfectly made-up eyes wide, as though astounded that such rudeness was being directed at her. "Excuse me?"

"Why did you have him over for breakfast?"

"Susan means that you probably wouldn't entertain the acting chief of police under normal circumstances," Kathleen suggested.

Susan glanced at her friend. Was this some version of the good cop–bad cop routine? Good friend–bad friend, so to speak? "That's exactly what I mean," she agreed.

Honey put down her pastry brush and removed the pan of lemon confections to the top shelf of her freezer. "Let's sit down and talk." She glanced at her watch. "I have about half an hour before I have to go pick up my babies. They're out at Poochie Parlor being groomed. I think you should be absolutely clear about what my position here is. This is not just a murder case, it could also damage F.O.P.P.—as well as H.E.C. and all the other organizations like us."

"Why?" Susan persisted.

"We exist because of the town's enthusiasm for us. We're a volunteer organization, Susan. You know what that means."

She did. If an organization fell out of favor, if there were no longer people who thought it worth their time and money, it would die. "So what does that have to do with entertaining Malarkey at breakfast?"

"I am F.O.P.P.," Honey declared. "I saw a need. I created an organization. I keep it going. I wanted him to understand that F.O.P.P. is essential to gracious living in Hancock."

"And what did you want him to do?" Kathleen asked for some specifics.

"Tread gently."

Fine. The one time she was hoping for a dose of Honey's famous garrulousness, the woman became a minimalist. "What exactly do you mean?" she asked quietly.

Honey leaned across the antique English pine kitchen table, hands clasped before her, an intense expression on her face. "I want him to talk to me, not my members. I am so fortunate. I have wonderful, wonderful people involved in F.O.P.P." (And Susan had always thought her name came from the color of her hair, not the cloying sweetness of her voice.) "I must protect them from all of this."

"So they don't leave F.O.P.P.," Kathleen suggested, returning to the point.

"So they will defend F.O.P.P.," Honey answered, anger flushing her face. "Don't tell me that H.E.C. doesn't have things they would rather keep to themselves, Kathleen Gordon. We're just asking for some privacy. We deserve it."

"You mean things like the marijuana growing in the urns near the police station," Susan said.

Honey seemed startled by Susan's statement. "That had very little to do with F.O.P.P. . . ."

"They're your urns. Your volunteers had been tending

them all summer, hadn't they?" Susan asked, wondering why Kathleen wasn't joining in.

"Listen, that was such a minor thing. But I take full responsibility. I always have. No one from F.O.P.P. planted those seeds. Even the police said that it was probably some teenagers who thought they were being clever. My mistake was assigning some of our newest members to maintain those planters. Of course, I never thought—"

"Why the newest members? I mean, was there any particular reason that you chose them instead of someone else?"

"Of course. I work very hard deciding who is going to work where every spring. I make charts and exact schedules. Nothing is left to chance. But first I decide what is going to be planted. Let me show you." She stood up and walked over to the massive painted primitive wardrobe that filled most of one kitchen wall. Opening a door that displayed improbably stylized flowers drooping artistically in a vase, she removed two marbleized portfolios. Untying the grosgrain ribbons that bound them, she spread sheets of paper across the table in front of her guests.

Kathleen picked up long lists of names, phone numbers, and dates. Susan focused on the marvelous diagrams of the town. Almost baroque in their detail, blocks where F.O.P.P. gardened were blown up, labeled, and, amazingly enough, beautifully watercolored. She would have loved to take the time to examine them, but Honey had a purpose. "Let me explain. These are the plans for the entire town. Each planter is lettered and numbered on the diagram. The numbers indicate the plants that are to be planted. They're on these sheets here." She pulled long lists over the pictures.

"There's more written there than plant names," Susan protested.

"Of course. Growing conditions, soil and fertilizer requirements, blooming times . . . What did you expect? And the letters are my volunteers. That way it's easy to know exactly what is supposed to be planted, the care it requires, and who is going to take care of it—as well as vacation substitutes."

"And the planters around the municipal center are different?"

"The planters around the municipal center are easy."

"Easy?"

"Easily grown varieties," Kathleen elaborated, going through the charts.

Honey smiled approvingly. "Exactly. They have to be. They're abused constantly. People feel free to pick the flowers. They drop garbage around them. We even find cigarette butts in them. Disgusting. You wouldn't think things like that would happen in a place like Hancock. Anyway, they're planted with pansies in the spring, geraniums, white marguerites, and ivy in the summer, mums in the fall—the type of plant it's impossible to kill. That's why I always give those planters to the least experienced members of F.O.P.P. It's not surprising that they didn't recognize the hemp plants. Although I would have thought the workers in the building would have paid more attention. . . ."

Susan nodded. Kathleen was still examining the plans, so she decided to get on with her questions. "Where did you go to high school?"

"Why, Susan, you know that I'm an alumna of Hancock High. Valedictorian. Art editor of the yearbook. Head cheerleader. Prom queen. Why, those were some of the favorite years of my life. We weren't in the new building, of course, but what we lacked in facilities, we made up for in enthusiasm. When I got to Bryn Mawr, I met many girls who had been to private school, but I sometimes think they didn't get the education that I did and—"

"You know, I was wondering where you were when Horace Harvey was discovered," Susan interrupted, not interested in Honey's curriculum vitae.

Her answer caused Kathleen to stop examining the plans. "The ladies' room."

Kathleen had been so startled that she had forgotten her hunger. She and Susan had said good-bye, returned to the car, and were almost out of the driveway before Susan asked the question they were both wondering about.

"Why would she lie?"

"Why would she spend so much time and effort on those diagrams and lists?" Kathleen ignored Susan's question and asked one of her own. "Surely there's an easier way to do it. Computers, maybe."

"That's just the way Honey is. Everything has to be perfect from the inside out."

"I guess she won't have to worry about her underwear if she's in an auto accident," Kathleen laughed.

"She once explained to me how she ordered lingerie by the dozen from a specialty shop in Geneva."

"Switzerland?"

"Naturally. Where else do they produce such marvelous cottons?" Susan's imitation of Honey Bradshaw left them both giggling as they traveled down the road.

"So why did she lie and where are we going?" Kathleen asked.

"She lied because she had something to hide. No one could have forgotten where they were when Horace Harvey was found. Not in less than forty-eight hours. You saw her in the bar—and you don't have any reason to lie. We'll just have to get your statement confirmed by someone else. And I think we should go see Patty Taylor—to answer your second question."

"Because she wouldn't speak with the police?"

"She is the only person who refused."

"I don't know her," Kathleen said.

"Neither do I, but I know where to find her."

"Where?"

"The high school—she's Chrissy's college counselor."

"On Saturday morning?"

"Chrissy has had meetings with her on Saturday." Susan shrugged. "But I have a friend who works at the high school; maybe we should call her first," she added, spying a phone booth on the corner they were passing.

"Good idea."

Susan was out of the car before Kathleen had gotten the two words out of her mouth. She spent only a few minutes at the phone booth, the expression on her face changing from a smile to a frown during the short conversation. Kathleen didn't have to wait long to find out what had happened. Susan was ready to explode when she got back into the driver's seat.

"That girl! I can't believe she's been lying to me all this time!" she exploded, jerking on the steering wheel.

"It's not a good idea to drive when you're mad."

"I'm fine. Chrissy's not going to be, though. I may kill her."

"It's one way to avoid paying college tuition. Not necessarily the best way, of course. You're going to tell me what's wrong, aren't you?"

"Chrissy has been lying about seeing her counselor on weekends. According to my friend, the new teacher's contract demands that all teachers work only during regular school hours. No late meetings with students. No Saturday hours. Clubs and school-sponsored events are paid for separately. Patty Taylor isn't a club or activity sponsor."

"You think she's been with that boy."

"Where else?"

"About three thousand other places," Kathleen insisted. "At the mall. With her other friends or—"

"No way. Why would she lie to me about being with someone else? No, she was with him."

"Susan—" Kathleen didn't know what to say, so she was relieved when Susan interrupted.

"No, this is no time to worry about Chrissy. I'm going to be spending a lot of time with her the day after tomorrow. We can discuss it then. I got Pat Taylor's address. Shall we go see her?"

"Sure. Jerry is playing househusband with Bananas today. I have all the time in the world—or at least a few more hours."

Susan laughed. "Okay. She lives in one of the new condos down on the water. We're not far. And if she's out, Alissa's house is nearby."

"Good planning. And I've wondered about those condos. My mother talks about leaving Philadelphia and moving closer to her favorite grandson sometimes. Those are probably the only apartment vacancies in town."

"Would you like that?"

"I hope the condos are dreadful," Kathleen admitted.

"We'll hate them even if we love them," Susan said. "They are in a very convenient location, though, aren't they?" she added, driving through the wooden pilings that introduced the nautical theme favored by the condominium's developers. "It's apartment 26—easy to remember because Jed's birthday is the twenty-sixth."

"You can park over there by that brass sea gull," Kathleen said, pointing to an empty parking slot.

"Everything seems very well marked," Susan commented.

"Hmm . . . Why do you think this woman will talk with you? After all, she refused the police."

"I don't know. But we may as well try." Susan wondered if Kathleen guessed that she was also interested in meeting Chrissy's college counselor.

Kathleen was noticeably silent as they wound their way through the condo complex. Number 26 was on the second floor, and presently they arrived at a blue door with the appropriate number prominently displayed.

"Here goes," Susan said, and pressed the bell.

The door was opened almost immediately by a young blond woman who reminded Susan of the camp counselor she'd idolized the year she became a teenager. Could this woman possibly be old enough to teach in a high school? She looked more like a student. "Hi. Come on in. Would you like a Coke, or beer, or something?"

Susan was surprised by such cordiality from someone she hadn't even introduced herself to, but willing to take advantage of it. "Thank you, we'd love something to drink." She accepted the offer as she followed Kathleen in the door.

They entered a living room scantily furnished with mismatched furniture, brick-and-board shelves full of college texts, books, an expensive stereo system, and an elegant burnished leather couch. Posters and art prints hung on the walls. Susan knew immediately that this was Pat Taylor's first apartment. She sat down on the couch next to Kathleen.

"I'll be right back with our drinks."

As their hostess left the room, the two women exchanged looks. But there wasn't enough time for more than that. Patty Taylor reappeared in the room, a tray in her hands. She laid it down on the straw basket that served as a coffee table. Three green Mexican goblets bubbled soda beside a basket of blue corn chips and a clay bowl of salsa. Everything must have been waiting in the kitchen.

Susan noticed an unremoved price tag on the tray as she chose a glass. She sank back into the soft leather.

"Wonderful couch," Kathleen commented, doing the same.

"Thanks. It's new," Pat Taylor admitted. She was perched on a disintegrating brown tweed Barcalounger, nervously sipping her Coke.

"Have you lived here long?" Susan asked politely, although the answer was pretty obvious.

"Since last September. I moved in right before school started." She forced a smile onto her face. "Have some salsa."

Kathleen, who was always, Susan thought, interested in seeing just how many calories she could consume before one or two of them showed up as fat, accepted the offer and began to eat.

"You probably want to ask me questions," Pat Taylor said.

"Yes. If you don't mind."

"No, of course not. Go ahead."

"Well . . ." Susan paused, not knowing exactly where to begin.

"Maybe I should tell you something about my background."

"Excellent idea," Kathleen enthused. "Good salsa; is it homemade?"

"Yes. I spent a year in New Mexico—well, you may know about that. . . ."

"Why don't you go ahead as though we don't know anything," Susan suggested.

"Okay." Pat frowned and then, taking a deep breath, began. "I went to the University of Maine at Orono, graduating two years ago with a bachelor's degree in education. Then I worked for Outward Bound. First at Hurricane Island and then in Utah—mainly in the Canyonlands and Zion National Park. I did mostly hiking and backpacking. I assisted on some raft trips, but it's not my specialty. You're not really interested in that, though, are you?"

She continued quickly, like someone too nervous to leave any normal spaces in the conversation. Susan was thinking how natural it was that Pat had reminded her of a camp counselor when Kathleen started asking questions.

"This is the first year you've actually worked in a school?" she asked.

"Yes. I don't think it's for me, which is why I'm thinking about a change right now."

Susan jumped in. "You don't like your job?"

"Being a college counselor is miserable. The kids are nervous—to put it mildly. They start getting nervous in the fall of their junior year, and by spring of their senior year, they're miserable wrecks. And that's nothing compared to their parents. They call constantly. Every single one of them believes that there is either an SAT course that only twenty people know about that will get their little darling into an Ivy League school or that there is something the kid can do at the last minute that will impress the college of their choice so much that they'll be welcomed with open arms—and a full scholarship. In a word, I hate it."

Kathleen suspected that Susan was dying to ask a question about Chrissy, and she decided to forge on regardless. "How did you get involved in P.A.P.?"

The young woman smiled. "It's my first love right now. I actually started it." She leaned forward as she forgot her nervousness in her building enthusiasm. "Hancock is a wonderful town. Lots of money. Lots of resources. And the park system is not to be believed. And it's hardly used at all. Just by a bunch of gardeners and families walking in the afternoon and picnicking on weekends."

"And P.A.P. wants to change all that?" Susan asked.

"P.A.P. stands for Parks Are People. I want the parks used by everyone for everything. Poetry readings and concerts in the evenings. Classes during the day. Things that are appropriate in the parks like wreath making or herb growing. Early morning T'ai Chi Ch'uan classes with the whole community participating. Stuff like that."

"Sounds wonderful," Susan commented.

"Have you talked with Tillie Greenleaf about this?" Kathleen asked.

"The woman who runs the Hancock Environmental Committee?"

Kathleen nodded.

"No. I got a call from a Mrs. Bradshaw when I announced the formation of P.A.P., and she said that H.E.C. was not at all happy about my plans and that Mrs. Greenleaf would try to stop me. And Horace Harvey said that, too."

"He did!" Susan was surprised.

"I can't imagine Tillie not thinking that your ideas are wonderful," Kathleen said.

"I—"

"When did you talk to Horace Harvey about P.A.P.?" Susan insisted on getting back to the point.

"He came here the first night he was in town. Sunday night. I had the entire group here for a wine tasting."

"How many members do you have?"

"Fifteen. Mostly young teachers like myself. But it's not just the high school. We have broad support. Two librarians from the public library and the Methodist minister are involved, too. There's a lot of enthusiasm."

"You sound like you've really gotten something important started," Kathleen commented.

The young woman blushed, and Susan smiled. "Did you get the impression that Mr. Harvey was going to leave his inheritance to P.A.P.?"

A puzzled expression appeared on Pat Taylor's face. "I

thought so at the time, but now it sounds like he promised his money to everyone. I was at the Inn when he was killed, and it was incredible. A lot of people actually seemed happy. Everyone thought their project was going to benefit from his death." She shook her head. "It was really strange."

"Did you see him after he died?" Kathleen asked.

"No. I thought all the rush to view the man was more than a little ghoulish, to be honest." She sighed. "I do wonder which organization is going to get all his money now."

No one said anything for a moment.

"Did you like him?" Susan broke the silence to ask.

"Who? Horace Harvey?"

"Yes. Did you think he was a nice person?"

Pat Taylor looked puzzled. "Why are you asking that? What does Horace Harvey have to do with me being hired by Woman's World?"

"Woman's World?" Susan repeated, puzzled by the girl's reaction. "Isn't that a magazine?"

"A magazine? I don't understand. Is this some sort of test?"

Susan shook her head. "I think we need to clear some things up here. What is Woman's World?"

"A travel adventure company for women only," the young woman replied, sitting up very straight and beginning to look very angry. "You're not the people who were sent to interview me for a position with them, are you?"

"No."

"Then who the hell are you? Why are you here?"

"I'm Susan Henshaw and this is Kathleen Gordon. We're investigating the murder of Horace Harvey."

"You're policewomen?"

"We're sort of unofficial," Susan admitted.

"Unofficial?"

Susan heard the anger in Pat Taylor's voice, and she couldn't say she blamed her. She also couldn't figure out how she was going to pacify the young woman.

Pat Taylor stood up. "You should leave now," she stated.

"I wish you'd let us explain," Kathleen said, not moving.

"Yes, please," Susan joined in, thinking hard. "You know, I've heard a lot about you from my daughter. She ... she says that you're always fair with the kids. You know, giving them equal time, even the ones that don't have a prayer of getting into the Ivys ... Won't you give us a chance to explain?"

It was lame, but it seemed to work. The angry young woman sat back down. "Who's your daughter?"

"Chrissy Henshaw," Susan said eagerly.

"Chrissy ... Oh, Chris. The artist, of course."

Susan had no idea that her daughter had ever been called anything other than Chrissy, but she knew this wasn't the time to go into it. "Yes, you made arrangements for us to look at colleges in Boston the day after tomorrow," she agreed.

"Oh, I didn't know you were going, too. Well, that's okay. One parent more or less on the walk around campus probably doesn't matter at all."

"But we came here to talk about the murder," Kathleen reminded them both. She knew how likely Susan was to go off on any tangent that led to her children.

"I refused to talk with the police about it," Pat Taylor said.

"Why? You must know that refusing to answer questions makes it look like you have something to hide," Kathleen said.

To the astonishment of both women, tears appeared in the other woman's eyes. Susan leaned across the improvised coffee table. "Is there anything we can do for you? We don't think you killed Horace Harvey, if that makes you feel any better. In fact, we came to you first because we thought you were the least likely of all the suspects," she admitted, hoping to cheer the woman.

"That's because you don't really know me, do you?"

Well, neither woman could argue with that. "But you didn't do it, did you?" Susan asked gently.

"Of course not. Why would I? He wasn't going to leave P.A.P. his money—and I'm hoping to see the last of this area of the country soon. P.A.P. will be taken over by its members as soon as school is out. And I had no connection to Mr. Harvey other than that."

"Then why would anyone suspect you?" Kathleen asked.

"Because I was involved in a murder investigation before," she answered quietly. "It was just last year. My best friend, my roommate, in fact, was murdered by her boyfriend's mother. It happened in the apartment that we shared, and I found the body. . . . Oh, it's okay," she reassured the two women, both of whom instinctively leaned forward to offer sympathy. "The woman was insane—totally. But I was suspected for a while, and it was a nightmare—one I could feel myself slipping back into when I heard that Horace Harvey had been killed."

"And that's why you refused to answer any questions?"

Patty looked at Kathleen. "I was afraid that someone would find out about the other death. I've been trying to keep it quiet. I had nothing to do with the murder, except for being friends with the victim, but when they find out about it, people treat me differently. That's why I came to Hancock. I thought a career change would help bury the past."

"But . . . ?" Susan asked gently.

"But there's been another murder, and, in fact, I hate my job—" There was a knock on the door, and she gasped. "That must be the woman who really is coming to interview me." She leapt up and grabbed the now-depleted tray. "What am I going to do? She's not going to be impressed with me now."

"Why not?" Susan asked, taking the tray and handing it to Kathleen. "Take this to the kitchen, refill it, and leave it there. Answer the door, Pat; everything is going to be fine."

They were back in Susan's car, leaving behind the brass sea gulls. "You were wonderful." Kathleen admired her friend. "Although that woman probably thinks it was a setup—the parent of a student just happening to be on hand to rave about the teacher who is being interviewed for a new job."

"Did I overdo it?"

"Maybe just slightly, but when we left, I got the impression that she had gotten the job."

Susan smiled contentedly. "Me, too. I'm glad we didn't hurt her chances. Sounds like she's been through enough."

"Hmm. So we've talked with Honey and Patty. Who's next?"

"You still have time?"

"Sure. What about you?"

"I left homemade chowder for the family's lunch. I think they can manage without me for a few more hours. You know," Susan continued, "I haven't talked to Bob Arnold about this."

"I've heard he's always in over his head. Always trying to succeed at something that he's almost bound to fail in."

"You're kidding. I don't know him well, but he's always struck me as a slightly tense, but very nice man. Doesn't sound much like a murderer, does he?"

"Sounds exactly like a murderer," Kathleen disagreed. "Where are you going?"

"To his house. He lives a few blocks from here. His son was on Chad's Little League team about three years ago—we carpooled."

"You seem to have carpooled with everyone in town."

"There have been days when it felt like that," Susan agreed. "But it's only a feeling. I've never even met Bob's wife. He had custody of his kids on weekends."

"I think I have. Her name's Shirley, right?"

"I think so. How do you know her?"

"We met at a dinner party back in January. She was there with a date. I gather they're divorced?"

"I guess so. The Arnolds were one of these couples that split apart, got back together, and then split again. It's not that unusual around here. A lot of people try again—especially when there are children involved."

"James Malarkey seemed to think that Shirley and Ralph Spinoza had an affair."

"Apparently so," Susan agreed, remembering the questions he had given her.

"And did they?"

"I have no idea. In this particular case, I'm definitely not in the loop. They're not in our circle of friends, and I haven't heard anything."

"So you're just going to walk up to these people and ask about their sex lives?"

Susan chuckled. "I guess so."

"They might get just a tad offended."

"Well, we'll know soon. Here's his house." Susan drove into the driveway of a large, rambling fifties ranch.

"He remarried?"

"Not that I know of. I think Shirley moved out with the kids, and he stayed in the house. Must be interesting for him. There aren't a lot of single men living alone in three-bedroom homes in the suburbs."

"Interesting?" Kathleen wondered aloud about Susan's choice of words as they walked up the brick path to the front door. "I don't even know what Bob Arnold does for a living."

"You're about to find out."

Susan knew the door would be opened immediately. Bob Arnold was nothing if not prompt. She glanced at Kathleen; she was always interested in the first impression Bob Arnold made on those who didn't know him.

He looked the way he always did: Handsome in a turn-around-and-look-twice type of way, he could have fallen from the pages of a chic advertisement—into an accountant's nightmare. She knew his looks were natural; Susan once had seen Bob Arnold when he wasn't surrounded by sheaves of papers, but then he'd had a laptop computer with him—at a PTA meeting. He was busy computing the future profits of a multinational corporation while other parents argued about the financing of a new, safer jungle gym. His wife left him a few weeks later.

A neighbor had once told Susan about the reason her cousin had quit his job on the New York Stock Exchange floor. He claimed that a trader had had a heart attack in the pit—and the sick man's colleagues had moved him aside and continued their work. After meeting Bob Arnold, Susan believed the story. It wasn't that he was cruel or excessively greedy; the correct term was, she thought, *single-minded.*

So she had been surprised to hear that Bob had created and was running an organization dedicated to keeping Hancock free of increasing corporate expansion and development. She didn't need to have overheard Ralph Spinoza berating Bob Arnold to think that maybe the organization was just another example of the intense competition between the two men.

All this went through her head as she followed Kathleen into the Arnold home.

"I guess we were lucky to find you here," Kathleen said. Susan could tell that her friend was trying hard to act as though the home's interior were nothing to stare at.

"I'm here all the time. I work at home."

"Oh."

There was, of course, no other explanation for the fact that the conventional living room furniture (two brocade couches, a Lawson chair with matching footstool, marble coffee tables, end tables, and three or four lamps tangled into one mass) was pushed together in one corner while elegant examples of modern abstract oils hung on walls above long Formica tables, file cabinets, and more piles of paper than Susan had seen in one place before. There were stacks of magazines, newspapers, and brochures. Three computer printers had contributed mounds of printed sheets that spilled off tables and were stacked on the floor. Susan had counted five personal computers, two copy machines, one fax machine, four telephones, three answering machines, and five pieces of office equipment with functions she didn't know, before she realized Bob Arnold was speaking to her.

". . . but I guess that wouldn't work for Jed, would it? Advertising agencies expect people to work at the office."

"Yes, I guess so." Susan hoped she was right; she wasn't too sure what she had just agreed to. "Kathleen's husband works with Jed," she added, feeling herself to be on safer ground.

"Of course, Jerry Gordon. I should have known." He

took Kathleen's hand in a weak handshake. "I've heard about you for years. I'm not quite sure why we haven't met before."

"It's nice to meet you now," Kathleen said. She looked nervous, and Susan wondered if she was concerned about questioning a man who was claiming a long relationship with her husband. Well, there was nothing to do but get on with it.

"I saw you at the Inn Thursday night," Susan introduced the subject.

"The night Horace Harvey was murdered," Bob Arnold agreed, nodding.

"Kathleen and I are helping the police with their investigation," Susan continued, exaggerating only slightly.

"Then you must want to ask me some questions about that night. . . . Excuse me a second, will you?" He interrupted himself as the fax machine began to spew papers onto the floor. He checked out the messages coming in while Susan noticed that the once elegant Berber carpeting was imprinted with his route between the various machines. How long, she wondered, had it been since Shirley Arnold had left home? Kathleen was standing awkwardly in the middle of the room, a position that was highly unlike her, Susan thought. She was starting to move toward her friend when the front door opened and Olive Spinoza blew in.

The quintessential clubwoman, Olive was frequently dressed in this year's version of Chanel's famous suit, and Susan had thought more than once that she must own every low-heeled style of Ferragamos ever made. Today she looked dreadful. Her stockings had runs in each leg, mud covered the bottom of her nubby pink wool skirt, her blouse wasn't tucked in, one of her necklaces was dripping fake pearls, and she was missing the ever-present headband that held back her lacquered blond pageboy.

She slung her tiny chain-strap purse over one shoulder and stood, visibly quivering, on the flagstones that were laid right inside the door.

"Bob Arnold," she cried, then realized that he was not alone. "I . . ." She bit her lips and spun around, breaking the heel off her left pump, and departed, slamming the door behind her.

Bob Arnold looked up from his faxes, a vague smile on his face.

ELEVEN

"But why would he admit to having an affair with Olive Spinoza if it isn't true?"

"Now, hon, you know how those two men have been competing for years. Isn't it possible that Shirley and Ralph had an affair—which would be a major point for Ralph in this stupid game of one-upmanship that the two of them play—and claiming to have seduced Olive is the only way Bob can achieve match point?"

Susan and Jed were sipping decaf cappuccino in his study. Chad had vanished to a friend's house immediately after dinner. Chrissy was still out, and Susan suspected that her husband's willingness to risk the inferno their imported cappuccino maker spewed forth was more an attempt to distract her than a real desire for the brew. Susan was determined to ignore her daughter's absence. They would have time to discuss her behavior on the way to Boston. She reached for a needlepoint pillow to tuck into the small of her back.

"Damn! I don't believe this!" She shook the pillow under her husband's nose.

"What's wrong?" Jed protected his cup from flying kapok.

"The dog chewed a hole in this. I spent an entire summer working this pattern. She's not supposed to be alone in this room."

The puppy, lying contentedly at Jed's feet, seemed to recognize her part in Susan's distress and ducked her head under the chair.

"She's just a puppy, hon. She doesn't know any better."

"I know." Susan frowned. "I'm just a little stressed out these days."

"Maybe you should stop worrying about this murder. . . ."

"No, the murder investigation is keeping me sane. At least I can do something. Everything else I'm worrying about is out of my hands." She sighed. "'Where did I put my purse?'"

"I think I saw it next to the telephone in the kitchen. Would you like me to get it for you?"

"No. I'll do it. I'm hungry. I really wish I could learn not to eat when I'm worried. . . ." she muttered, leaving the room.

Jed absentmindedly reached down to pet the puppy; the animal was happily teething on the sleeve of his Brooks Brothers oxford cloth when Susan returned. "Do you want her to do that?" she asked, pointing at the dog.

"Oh, shit. Stop that!" There was a ripping sound as he jerked his arm away.

"Give her this," Susan suggested, offering a homemade gingersnap. "It probably tastes better than your shirt."

"Isn't that rewarding her for chewing on clothing?"

"I don't think she connects things that well," Susan answered as the puppy fell at her feet, apparently too delighted with the unexpected treat to remain standing. "I want to read you something," she continued, displaying a paperback.

"Anything; it's about time we agreed on a name."

"Oh." Susan opened the dog-naming book. "I wasn't thinking of dog names. I've been writing notes on the blank pages at the back of the book. Do you mind if I go over the things that are bugging me about all this?"

"Go ahead," Jed agreed, rightly interpreting "all this" to mean the murder investigation.

But she read for a few minutes before speaking. Then she tossed him the book. "Maybe it would be easier if you just looked at this yourself."

"Okay."

Susan played with the puppy while her husband read through the questions. It took him longer than necessary, and she noticed that he was glancing at her periodically as he read. "Something wrong?"

"These questions don't seem very significant," he said slowly. "Of course, I may be missing something. . . ."

"Oh, I agree with you. That's just what I thought when James Malarkey gave them to me."

"He what?"

Susan explained how the list of questions had come into being.

"And you've changed your opinion of their importance now?"

"I wonder if they're red herrings. I thought that he wanted me to ask them so I would be kept busy until I left town, but now I'm wondering if he wanted me to ask these questions hoping that I wouldn't ask the things that I'm curious about. Or maybe he hopes to lead me in the exact opposite direction."

"So you think you can find a key to the investigation in the opposite direction he's led you?"

"Exactly!"

Jed spent more time looking at the list before responding. "I don't think so," he said slowly.

"Why not?" Susan loved her husband as much as she hated him contradicting her. She pulled the book from his hand. "Look at this. What if he wants us to look at the personal relationships between the Spinozas and the Arnolds because he doesn't want us to look at the professional relationships? Or what if he wants to direct our attention toward Ethan Trumbull rather than . . . than . . ."

"Yes. What is the opposite of Ethan Trumbull quitting school?"

Susan thought she heard sarcasm in the question. She told herself that Jed was feeling the same stress over Chrissy as she was, but she still had to bite her lip to keep from snapping at him. "That's not quite the point, Jed. Or maybe . . ." She stopped and thought for a moment. "Maybe it is."

"Huh?"

"Well, think of it. Maybe James Malarkey is concerned about Ethan going away. Maybe he's afraid for some reason or another that Ethan will leave and take something with him."

"Frankly, I think you're stretching it."

"But maybe I'm not. Maybe I'll just go find Ethan and talk to him about going back to school and what it might mean if he stays here. You," she added, becoming a little angry, "you can walk the dog."

Jed looked down. "She seems to be sleeping. And you know what they say to do with sleeping dogs."

Susan slammed the door on the way from the house. And then she smiled as she heard the puppy wake up barking.

Susan knew that being angry with the world wouldn't accomplish anything. And it might cause an automobile accident, she reminded herself, skidding to a stop as the traffic light changed from yellow to red. She had driven to the Trumbull house and discovered it empty. It was getting late, but she decided to go to the hospital regardless. There was a chance she'd see Ethan there, and she really didn't have any idea where else to look.

She arrived at the modern facility and parked in the lot provided for visitors. Most of the traffic, both pedestrian and vehicular, seemed to be going rather than coming, but she continued on regardless. She entered the lobby of the immense main building and was heading for the correct elevator when she heard someone calling her name. Susan had to look carefully before she saw someone she thought she recognized, the pretty young girl who had taken over her aunt's job as police dispatcher. Today she had exchanged her purple glasses for green, and her hair was tied back with paisley chiffon. Ethan Trumbull was standing at her side.

"Mrs. Henshaw, what are you doing here?" he asked. "Visiting hours ended fifteen minutes ago."

"I was coming to see you," she admitted. "Although I did expect to check in with your aunt. And you're here visiting your aunt, too, aren't you?" she added to his female companion.

"Yes. She likes to keep up on what is going on down at the station. It distracts her. She's pretty miserable here," she added.

"We were just going to get some coffee. Would you like to join us?" Ethan asked.

Susan suspected that the two of them wanted to be alone together. Well, they were young; there would be time enough later. She followed them to a round Formica table in the corner of the coffee shop. "How did you two meet?" she asked the girl when Ethan had gone off to fetch coffee.

"We kept running into each other in the hallway and we smiled. . . ." She looked a little embarrassed. "You know how it is."

"Sure do, but I don't think I remember your name. . . ."

"You don't have to worry that you forgot it. You probably never heard it. I doubt if Detective Malarkey introduced us. I'm Betsy Sawyer." She offered her hand.

"How's your aunt?"

"Better. She had some surgery on her elbow, and the recovery is pretty painful, but she'll be okay. She loves her job and she misses it, so I come over every evening and tell her what happened during the day—or at least I tell her as much as I can without worrying her."

"You don't talk about the murder, then?"

"Oh, I do; she finds it interesting. I don't tell her about Malarkey. That would upset her."

"Why?"

"The man is an idiot."

"Really?"

"Well, not really an idiot." Betsy began to back off.

"But not Brett Fortesque," Susan suggested, hoping Betsy would continue.

"Not if you go by what my aunt says. She says Brett is wonderful, that he doesn't act important all the time, that he takes care of everybody who works with him."

"I've had a hard time figuring out Detective Malarkey," Susan said.

"It's not that he's mean or anything." Betsy frowned and nervously fidgeted with the sugar canister on the table. "But he's inconsistent. I'm majoring in child psychology, and one of the biggest mistakes people make raising children is inconsistency. I keep thinking that it's a good thing James Malarkey isn't a father."

"Then he isn't married?" Susan knew it was probably irrelevant, but she did want to understand the man.

"No. He keeps talking about how free he is to move around—that a woman would just tie him down. The general feeling down at the station is that no woman would have him."

"He's good-looking. . . ."

"He's conceited, inconsiderate, and inconsistent. I've never met the real police chief here. What's his name again?"

"Brett Fortesque," Susan supplied.

"That's right. Everyone talks about him. The men respect him, and it seems to me that half of the women who work down there have a crush on him. Even my aunt starts to simper when she mentions him. I actually think she wanted me to take over for her this week because she was hoping I'd marry him!"

"Who are you talking about? Am I supposed to be jealous?" Ethan appeared at their table, a tray of food in his hands.

Susan thought he was trying to sound like he was kidding, but that his feelings were more serious. She glanced over at Betsy and smiled with relief. She was staring up at Ethan with an unmistakable look. Obviously good things could happen in hospital coffee shops. "How is your aunt feeling?" Susan asked, accepting a Styrofoam cup from Ethan. "I was hoping to get in to see her today, but I've been busy."

"Mrs. Henshaw is investigating the murder," he explained. "She knows a lot about murders."

"I've been involved in a few investigations—unofficially," she admitted.

"Is that why you were down at the police station the night of the murder?"

"I was there to help Mrs. Greenleaf."

"You don't think she did it, do you?"

"No."

"Then why did she lie about knowing Horace Harvey before he came to Hancock?"

"What?" Susan was astounded by this information. "How do you know that?"

"Oh . . ." Betsy paused and looked across the table at the young man. He nodded and she continued, but quietly. "I probably shouldn't be talking about this. . . ."

"Actually, James Malarkey asked me to help him with his investigation," Susan said, hoping Betsy wouldn't wonder why she hadn't heard this before.

"Then I guess it's okay. You may even already know about it."

"You said that Tillie Greenleaf knew Horace Harvey before he came to Hancock. Do you know when or where?"

"No. I know that she was very upset that James Malarkey found out about it, though."

"Why don't you start from the beginning and tell Mrs. Henshaw all about it," Ethan suggested, passing plastic-wrapped cheese Danish to his guests.

"Well, it really started before Mrs. Greenleaf was arrested," Betsy began. "I think it was on the list that Horace Harvey had in his pocket when he died."

Susan put down her coffee so hard that it sloshed on the table. "What list?"

"You know about the lilac and the pipe bowl, don't you?"

"Start a little further back," Susan suggested. "I know that there was white French lilac found in Horace Harvey's hand. That's the only lilac I know about."

"That's what I'm talking about. And you know about the marijuana that was found in his other hand?"

"Really?"

"Well, it was. And there was the white bowl of a pipe found in his jacket pocket."

"For the pot?" Susan suggested.

"No," Ethan answered. "It came . . . well, we think it came from my aunt's dump site. Apparently it was a colonial pipe."

"There was also a program from one of the theater group's productions of *Lysistrata* in the same pocket."

"Anything else? Some sort of representative article from Q.U.I.E.T., P.A.P., or H.O.P.E.?"

"I don't think so. I just heard about this from one of the police officers." She hesitated and looked at Ethan.

"One of the guys was trying to impress her with his knowledge and pick her up," he explained.

"But there was a list found?"

Betsy nodded.

"Did you see it?"

"Well, it was waved in front of my face, but I didn't get a chance to actually read it. But I do know some of what it said. Detective Malarkey was in one of his friendly moods. . . ."

"He was probably trying to pick you up, too."

Susan glared at Ethan. "Please let her tell the story. Go on."

"Well, the list was long. A computer printout that was pretty much completely filled—single-space. And he didn't tell me all that much."

"But he did tell you about a previous connection between Tillie Greenleaf and Horace Harvey."

"Yes. But not what it was. All he said was that Tillie Greenleaf had known Mr. Harvey before he came to town and that she had a good reason to kill him—other than to inherit his money. I thought that was strange."

"Why?"

"Because he wouldn't leave his money to someone who hated him, would he?"

"That's true!" Ethan exclaimed.

"But he wasn't leaving his money to the people, he was leaving it to the organizations they ran," Susan protested. "What else was written on the paper?"

"Something about a teacher being involved in a murder

before. I don't know who it was, but he had copies of police reports from out of town."

Susan remembered Patty Taylor's fears that her past would catch up with her. It seemed that they had—in the worst way. And how would that influence what James Malarkey made of her refusal to speak with him?

"Is something wrong?" Ethan asked.

"No, just thinking," Susan answered. "What else?" she asked the girl.

"That's all he mentioned to me, but I did just happen to glance at the paper. . . ."

"Go on."

"I couldn't read the writing, at least not without looking obvious, but I did see something strange in the margins."

"What?"

"A bunch of hearts with arrows going through them— like valentines, you know?"

Susan nodded.

"And they had names in them—the same names in different order. I don't really remember exactly, but one was Oliver and Bob, and one was Oliver and Ralph. And there were two or three others; I know at least Ralph was mentioned again. That isn't very helpful, is it?"

"If you think that Oliver could be Olive, it might be very helpful, in fact," Susan argued.

"It could be. In fact, it probably was, wasn't it?"

"Probably," Susan agreed, absently biting into the stale Danish.

"People do just scribble things that have no significance on the edges of paper," Ethan said.

"True." Susan looked up at the young man. "Are you really planning to return to Yale?" she asked suddenly.

"Who told you that I wasn't?"

"I didn't say anything," Betsy spoke up.

Susan decided there was nothing to be gained by hiding the truth from him. "Detective Malarkey," she answered quietly. "He said you had dropped out of college, and he implied that the reason you were in Hancock was that you were after your aunt's money."

She expected a protest, maybe even anger, but she didn't expect Ethan to stand up so quickly that his chair crashed on the floor as he charged from the room. Susan reached out and grabbed Betsy's arm before she could follow him. "Don't leave," she urged. "It won't help him."

Betsy bit her lip anxiously, but she remained in her seat. "He's probably already left," she muttered, turning to look out the window as car lights moved from the parking lot. Then she returned to Susan. "You shouldn't have said that to him. He's feeling dreadful."

"About leaving school?" Susan asked gently.

"About wanting his aunt's money."

"Would it be betraying a trust if you told me about it?"

"I don't think so." She paused and picked the cheese from the middle of her pastry. "I think it might even be better if you understood."

Susan finished her Danish while she waited for Betsy to begin.

"It's so sad. Ethan has a real problem, Mrs. Henshaw."

Susan was mentally running through such possibilities as drug addiction or a fatal disease when Betsy continued. "He wants to be a minister."

Susan opened her mouth and, finding that her brain had failed her completely, closed it again without saying a word.

"Of course, it will never be accepted in his family."

"Why?"

"They are what Ethan calls serious agnostics. They believe that organized religion has caused more evil than politics. They even give examples like Northern Ireland and the Crusades!" She opened her young eyes wide with disbelief. Susan, who didn't completely disagree with the Trumbull family stance, waited for the rest of the story. "He says that his aunt is one of the most dedicated of the family. She keeps talking about how the Puritans almost destroyed this country and things like that. She'll never forgive him for converting."

"To what?"

"He's become a Presbyterian."

Susan had a hard time reconciling that answer with her vision of fanatic cults.

"And he wants to be a youth minister. He's really wonderful with children."

"But he's an adult. Why does he need his family's approval?" She was a little jealous. Why didn't Chrissy feel such a commitment to her family's values?

"His aunt controls his money."

"But—"

"It's in a trust fund and she's the executor. He's allowed a small amount to live on as long as he's in school studying something that the family approved of. He says it's not like they were worried about seminary. The trust was set up when he was thirteen or fourteen years old, and his parents didn't want their money spent on something like correspondence courses in motorcycle repair. There isn't all that much money, though. He has a fellowship to Yale."

"Well . . ."

"He truly loves his aunt and he certainly doesn't want to disappoint her. And it's true that he's her only heir. He says he has to be realistic about his future. He would like to go to seminary, get his degree, and work with inner-city kids. Money is needed in places like that. It's not himself that he's thinking about. . . ."

"He's a lovely person. You don't have to convince me. And his aunt is a fine person, too. All this will work out in the long run. But there is something I don't understand."

"What?"

"I don't understand what this has to do with the murder of Horace Harvey."

"What does any of it have to do with the murder of Horace Harvey?" Betsy answered, finally licking the cheese filling off her fingertips. "It sounds to me as though Detective Malarkey is what my father would call a nosey parker. Except for that teacher, everything he's investigating seems awfully irrelevant."

Susan didn't argue, but she wasn't so sure. Murder investigations frequently look into some of the most intimate aspects of life—and find something significant. But Ethan wasn't involved in the quest for Horace Harvey's money, and he wasn't, as far as she knew, involved in S.O.D. Or was he? She asked Betsy the question.

"Not that I know of. We haven't talked about it much, but he did say that he was glad the dump had been discovered, that it gave his aunt something to think about and plan for while she was in the hospital and after she goes home. There will be a long recovery period for her, of course. He thinks that the excavation and all the surrounding excitement will give her an interest."

Susan couldn't think of anything else to ask. "I guess I'd better be going."

"I don't suppose you're going to pass the police station, are you?"

"I can. Do you need a ride?"

"Yes. Ethan drove me here, and I have to be back at work soon."

"No problem. My car's in the lot," she said, leading the way.

Both women were silent until the municipal center was in sight, then Betsy spoke up. "Are you going to talk with Ethan?"

"I was thinking about it," Susan admitted. "Do you think he went back to his aunt's house?"

"Probably. He doesn't know many people in town. Although he might have gone to a bar, or maybe just for a drive." The car had stopped, but she didn't get out. "You'll tell him that I thought I had to explain. I mean, you won't make it sound like I was just gossiping."

"Of course not. Don't worry. I'll be very discreet."

"Thanks. I'd better get going. Detective Malarkey might be in one of his moods."

"I'll be seeing you!" Susan called out as she turned her car in the direction of the Trumbull home. It was only a short drive, and she was pleased to notice a large black Mercedes in the driveway as she pulled up to the curb in front of the house. As was appropriate for a historian, the facade of the building was colonial. A curving slate path wound between tall blue spruce on its way to the door.

Brass lamps were lit on either side of the walk and over the curved fanlight above the door. Susan knocked and then waited patiently for an answer. In moments, Ethan Trumbull opened the door, a sheepish look on his face.

"Hi. I was expecting you. Would you like to come in for some tea? Is it too late? Or are you allergic to cats?"

Susan spied three chocolate Burmese cats peeking down from the top of the stairway and walked in the door. "I love cats, and I could use a drink if you'll offer me one," she answered.

"That's a fine idea. Follow me." He led the way through a chestnut-paneled hallway past a beautifully furnished living room and an elegant dining room to a door disguised by the woodwork. He opened the door for her, and Susan walked into a magnificent small library. The room was fabulous. She decided then and there that if she had to spend the rest of her life between four walls, these were the four walls she would choose.

There were two windows opposite the door and a fireplace set into an inglenook on the same wall. Everything else was shelves, and the shelves were stuffed full of books. Books standing on spine end, books piled on books, books across the top of the mantel, books seemingly cantilevered out into space. The woodwork was white. The fitted rug was sisal, and the twin sofas and comfy chairs were the soft blue of faded chambray and piled with an interesting and varied collection of pillows. Plants grew up from terra-cotta pots and draped down from hanging baskets. A brass tray with a generous selection of bottles and glasses stood in the middle of the antique child's sled that served as a coffee table.

"Wow. Can I move in?" Susan asked, flopping down on one of the couches.

"That's exactly how I feel. The rest of the house is so formal. Even the bathrooms have brass and wood fittings; I'm afraid to splash in the shower for fear I'll damage something. This place strikes me as perfect. What would you like to drink?"

Susan glanced at the possibilities. "Some of that Laiphroing would be perfect."

"The thistle glasses?"

Susan nodded. She almost held out her hand but resisted appearing anxious. "Thank you." She accepted the drink.

"Betsy called," he said, choosing the same drink and sitting down across from her. "Thank you for taking her back to work. I just wasn't thinking when I left."

"You're going to have to stop making mistakes like that if you're going to be a minister, aren't you?"

"She told you." He took a too large gulp of the Scotch. "I thought she had. She was just a little too anxious to get off the phone."

"She's very sympathetic and kind."

He beamed. "I know. I think she's wonderful. Was she mad at me for leaving her at the hospital?"

"No. She's worried about you—and about your relationship with your aunt. But to tell you the truth, I don't understand what's going on here."

"Like what?"

"Like why you ran from the hospital."

"Oh." He looked down at the empty fireplace. "I keep thinking that I will have a fire, but I spend so much time at the hospital and I'm always afraid of going to bed with embers left glowing."

TWELVE

Another middle-of-the-night meditation: Was Ethan hiding something? Was he going to end up marrying Betsy? Were the Arnolds and the Spinozas involved in some sort of wife swapping? Where had Chrissy gone tonight? What was going to happen to her relationship with this young man? Were she and her daughter going to grow closer in Boston? Should she wear boots or trust the weather to stay nice? This was getting her nowhere. But if she got up, she'd have to walk the dog, and worse than that, she'd probably find herself eating every fattening food in the kitchen.

She swung her feet to the ground, deciding to accept the inevitable.

So what else was there to do at two-fifteen in the morning? she wondered. The puppy, happily walked, was at her feet in the kitchen. They were sharing a bowl of jelly beans. Two for Susan, one for the dog. After all, everyone knows sweets are bad for babies.

"Hey, there, jelly bean, try orange," Susan asked, throwing the candy in the air. "Nice catch!"

"Jelly Bean's a pretty good name."

Chrissy was standing in the doorway, a pink chenille robe over the large U.C.L.A. T-shirt she wore to bed. Her long blond hair sprouted from a fluffy elastic on the top of her head, and she wore one chartreuse and one purple sock. Susan thought she looked adorable.

"Hi. Want some?" She offered the bowl of tiny eggs.

"No. I'm on a diet. I told you yesterday."

"Maybe some sugar-free hot chocolate?"

"Just some Perrier. I can get it myself." There was a pause. "Thank you, though."

The puppy's head flew back and forth; she was unable to decide who was more worthy of attention, the woman with a bowl of jelly beans in her hands or the girl opening the refrigerator. Her tail beat in time to her head. Chrissy's choice of snack disappointed the puppy and she moved an inch or two closer to Susan, dripping drool on her slipper.

"She sure does love to eat. Maybe we should think of food names. Like Butterscotch or Brandy or Caramel Custard," Chrissy suggested, drinking straight from the bottle.

Susan ground her teeth. Why should she waste her time trying to correct behavior that was almost universal? "Where were you tonight?"

It was obvious from the expression on her daughter's face that she would have been better off commenting on her manners. "We went to a gallery opening in the city."

Susan mistakenly tossed her favorite flavor jelly bean (licorice) to the pup. "I took your coat to the cleaners," she offered as an apology for the intrusion.

"Are they going to be able to finish it before we leave Monday morning?" Chrissy asked, placing the empty bottle in the sink.

"That goes in the recycle bin in the garage."

"Mother, it's the middle of the night. I'll put it away in the morning."

Everyone in the room, except for the dog, knew that Susan would be the one to put the bottle in the correct place. She started to say something when her daughter interrupted.

"Brian says that you get involved in these murder things because you're suffering from empty-nest syndrome."

"Really?" If Susan hadn't been so irritated, she would have been amused: Children were always positive that their parents' lives would end when they were no longer around.

"I get involved to help people," Susan said, knowing that was only part of the story. She did, in fact, enjoy the puzzle and the chase.

"Couldn't you just serve stew at a homeless shelter?" Chrissy asked, not waiting around for an answer.

"You know, Chrissy ..." Susan began before realizing her only companionship was canine. "Damn." She tossed the last orange candy to the dog and, turning off the light, left the room. Tomorrow was going to be a busy day.

But at least it was going to begin with Sunday brunch at the Inn.

Susan was feeling pretty good, despite not sleeping well. She was wearing a new dress that she was convinced made her look at least five pounds lighter. Even Jed had noticed when they were leaving the house. Her children were still snug in their beds, the puppy was asleep under the kitchen table, the day was warm, and she was hungry.

Kathleen and Jerry were waiting for them at a round, tulip-adorned table. Bananas was nearby in a high chair, trying to break his previous record of stacking nine sugar cubes. They all exchanged greetings (Bananas offering a sugar cube, which Jed accepted, popping it into his mouth) and then settled down to enjoy their mimosas. As usual, they divided into two groups.

"Are you going to be able to investigate with me today?" Susan immediately asked what was on her mind. "I need to talk with Tillie Greenleaf."

Kathleen accepted the menu that a waitress held out. "I would like to be there when you do," she agreed slowly.

"And I was thinking about starting here," Susan continued, noticing that the men were talking about a recent crisis at the ad agency where they both worked.

"Here at the Inn?"

"Yes. I should have done it sooner. I've been getting distracted by these interviews. We don't know things like who last saw Harvey alive—and when. I thought I'd try to talk with Charles before we left."

"Is he here?"

"Isn't he always?" Susan asked. "You know, I can't remember ever being here when he wasn't."

Kathleen finished the important business of ordering her

meal before answering. "It must be a good job," she commented. "How old is this place?"

"Well, it's been around since colonial times," Susan began. "Someone told me that the offices and rest rooms upstairs were once bedrooms for guests. I don't think there have been any overnight guests in this century. But it certainly wasn't always like this," she added, looking around the luxurious room. "In fact, it was pretty stodgy when we moved in."

"Stodgy?"

"Not bad, just the way these places used to be. You know, dark beams on the ceiling, dark wallpaper, brass sconces, mahogany tables and captain's chairs. Nice, but not chic. And the food tended to be the turkey-with-stuffing or pork-chops-and-fruited-rice type of meal."

"When was it redone?"

"I think about ten or eleven years ago. It was closed for at least a year. The interior was completely remodeled. I think the fireplaces and the woodwork around the bar are the only originals in the place. The porch was enclosed to make that small dining room at the back of the building. . . ."

"The one with the exit to the outside?"

"Yes." Susan stopped to sample the potted shrimp that had just been placed in the middle of the table. "And it was landscaped at the same time. Some of the trees out back that look like they've been there forever were brought in full grown and replanted. Jed's always been jealous. He'd love to replace those sugar maples that came down in the hurricane the year we moved in."

"When we were down in the wine cellar, it looked like it had been renovated, too," Kathleen mused, but getting her share of the appetizer at the same time.

"True. And it's not just those cherry shelves that are impressive. There have been articles in *The New York Times* about how extensive the wine list is here."

"Must be a gold mine for someone," Kathleen commented. "Do you think there's crab in this as well as shrimp?"

"I don't know."

"Susan?" Kathleen was surprised by her friend's sudden silence.

"I was just thinking ... I don't know who owns this place."

"So?"

"It's just that it's odd," Susan insisted. "I've been coming here for years. I've read articles about it in the *Hancock Gazette*, in the throwaway shoppers, in *The New York Times*, in *Connecticut Magazine* ... but none of them have mentioned ownership. Doesn't that strike you as unusual?"

"A little," Kathleen conceded, "but not necessarily ominous—or significant to this situation."

"No, but still ... It's worth asking a question or two, don't you think?"

"I think. What else are you going to do today?"

"I want to go to the hospital and talk with Martha Trumbull about Ethan. And Alissa Anthony."

"You don't sound like you're looking forward to Alissa."

"It's so difficult to get a straight answer from her. She's always quoting and emoting."

"I know what you mean."

"And it's so hard to find her," Susan added.

"At least you know where you're going to find Martha," Kathleen said.

"Captive suspect," Susan agreed. She was frowning.

"You're thinking about Martha Trumbull." Kathleen said.

"Actually, I was thinking about Ethan Trumbull. ... Ah, here's our meal."

"Great," Kathleen said, pulling a bib from her purse and tying it around her son's neck. "I was starving."

Susan decided not to mention that her friend had eaten most of the group's appetizer; she was planning her day. Maybe the hospital first. ...

"Hi, how's your sweet puppy?"

Susan looked up to discover that their waitress had been her dog's sitter the day before. "Fine, thank you. I hope Charles told you how much I appreciated your help yesterday."

"Don't mention it. I enjoyed it."

"Is Charles in the office upstairs?" Kathleen asked.

"He's not here today," their waitress said.

"We were just saying that we couldn't remember him ever being away from the Inn," Kathleen said.

"You were right. I've been here for three years, and I can only remember him missing a few days right before Christmas with the flu."

"You work full-time?" Jed asked, hungrily eyeing his eggs Benedict.

"Just weekends and four nights a week. I'm finishing up at the community college. I'll be done in May."

"Well, congratulations."

"Thank you." She noticed someone waving at her from a nearby table. "I'd better be going."

"Could I talk with you for a moment after we eat?" Susan asked quickly.

"No problem. I'm going to go on break in forty-five minutes. If I'm not on the floor, come on up to the office where you found me Friday."

"Great," Susan agreed, and they all got down to some serious eating.

"Anyone want to see the dessert cart?" Jed asked, being the last person at the table to put down his knife and fork.

Susan told herself that she was an adult, she could resist. She could resist the best chocolate fudge cake in the world, orange flan, strawberry shortcake, lemon mousse, coconut almond pound cake. . . . "Why don't you three go on without me. I'll just see if I can find out a few things from our waitress." She spied the desserts arriving and practically fled from the table.

Their waitress had taken her break, and Susan found the girl sipping coffee from a fragile cup in the office where she'd been yesterday. "Can I take up some of your time?" she asked hesitantly.

"Sure. What can I do for you?"

Susan started right off with the question she had been considering silently for the last hour. "Who owns the Hancock Inn?"

"Well, the person who owns it really doesn't want anyone to know." She stopped. "That's sort of a hint. If you think about it, you'll probably know the answer."

Susan thought about it, but no one came to mind. "Do a lot of people know?" she asked, wondering if she might find a more friendly witness.

"Not many. I only know because I help out with the bookkeeping here."

Susan asked another question when the young woman didn't continue. "Do you have time to answer some questions about the Inn for me?"

"Of course. Charles insists that we be cooperative with customers at all times."

"This first question sounds a little like something from an old English mystery novel, but is the wine cellar locked up?"

"Only overnight. There are a lot of people coming and going in there from lunch until around midnight. The Inn is known for its cellar, and customers come here just to taste some of our stock. It's very important to the Inn—the profit margin there is enormous."

"So any waiter or waitress can go down and bring up a few bottles?" Susan had been hoping otherwise.

"Of course." There was a silence before she continued. "Everyone who works here is very reliable. It's an awfully good place to work, and there is very little staff turnover. At least that's the way it's been since I've been here."

"So the night of the murder, anyone could have gone down into the wine cellar. . . ."

"Any of the staff, but it's unusual for a customer to make their way down there."

"Why?"

"The wine cellar is the only thing in the basement. Well, that's not quite true. There is a completely separate basement under the kitchen that is used for food storage, but there's no passageway between the two cellars. The wine cellar is the only thing that's down the back stairway. And there's really no reason for the customers to go that way.

Everything—the rest rooms, the cloakroom—is up on the second floor, and the way is very well marked."

"There are two entrances to the Inn. . . ."

"There are three," the young woman corrected her. "There's the front door, the door to the porch—which is kept closed and locked unless that room is rented out for a private party—and there's the door to the basement. I mean the basement under the kitchen. That's where all the food, supplies, and things like laundry are delivered. The night of the murder, only the front door and the basement door would have been open."

"Emergency exits . . . ?"

"Yes, I was forgetting. There are four emergency exits. One from the bar and each of the dining rooms. But they're alarmed. Anytime one is opened an alarm goes off."

"Were you here the night of the murder?"

"Yes. I always work on Thursday night."

"What time did you get here?"

"My shift runs from five to one. That's usual for waitresses. The chefs and kitchen helpers start at three and work until eleven. Although we're all on call to come in earlier or stay later if necessary for a special occasion."

"And was the night of the murder what you call a special occasion?"

"I'll say!"

"Because so many people were invited to what was a private party?"

"No. It wasn't really a private party like we're used to. . . . I'd better explain."

"Please."

"We frequently have parties where one or more of the dining rooms is closed to the public, but the party guests do mingle with our regular customers at the bar before and sometimes after the event."

Susan nodded. "I've been to wedding receptions here that were like that."

"Then you know what I'm talking about. I'm glad. I'm not sure that I'm explaining very well."

"You're doing fine; go on." Susan was puzzled by how

nervous the other woman was. "The party where Horace Harvey was murdered wasn't like that?"

"Not at all. It's the only time I can remember when the Inn has been completely turned over to a group on a Thursday night. It's been done on Monday nights when we're normally closed, and I was talking with one of the chefs, and he said that years ago it was closed early on a Sunday night for the wedding reception of one of the daughters of the governor. . . ."

"I remember hearing about that. It was evidently some fancy occasion. But it hadn't happened before on any other day."

"No. Thursday is a big night—almost as big as Friday. It used to be Saturday, but now that so many women work, a lot of couples go out to dinner every Friday. And that's not all that was different. When there are special occasions here, they're always planned out months—sometimes years—in advance. Horace Harvey's party wasn't even planned until Thursday morning. So the Inn couldn't be closed, and the people who had reservations for dinner just walked into all these suburban women. I mean . . ."

"I know. Don't worry about insulting me. I'm too old not to have come to terms with what I am. Did anyone explain why this unusual thing was happening?"

"No, and some people were pretty upset. I overheard one of the waiters complaining that the people with reservations were being treated like second-class customers, but Charles said that many of the women coming to the meeting were not only community leaders, but they were some of the best customers that the Inn had. And he's right about that. Alissa Anthony eats dinner here at least once a week. And Mr. Spinoza eats lunch here regularly. I could go on and on."

"So you can understand why Charles agreed that the party could take place?"

"I suppose so. It's just that it was really very unusual."

"Do you think that the reasons Charles gave were enough reason for the party to be held?"

"I guess so. What else could there be?"

"I wish I knew," Susan said. "Do you know why Charles isn't here today?"

"Personal reasons."

"That's what you heard?"

"That's what was written on the day sheet. Have you seen the day sheet?" she asked, reaching under some copies of *Gourmet* that were on the desk.

"I haven't even heard about it."

"Here it is." She handed a computer printout across the table.

Susan read for a few minutes before making any comments. The page began with a note that Charles was going to be gone for the day for, as she already knew, personal reasons, and named the two people, a waitress for the dinner crowd and a waiter at lunch, who would greet the guests and take care of any problems that might develop. It continued to explain that the most unusual thing to take place that day was that a church group from a neighboring town was scheduled to have brunch in the porch room. A final paragraph was dedicated to the specials that the chef had prepared and his explanation of any special ingredients. "This is amazing. Who writes it?"

"Charles."

"And it's the same format every day?"

"Yes."

"Are they saved?"

"Sure. It helps to avoid repetition. Do you want to see the one for Thursday?" she asked, her hand on the desk drawer anticipating the answer.

"Yes." Susan reached out, and a similar sheet was placed in her hand. It took her less time to go through this one. "The party that night isn't mentioned here."

"I don't think it was even planned until around lunchtime. I know that I came in at the regular time, around one, and the place was in an uproar trying to get ready for the evening. Tables were being rearranged, extra appetizers and desserts were being ordered. . . . There's a lot of extra work when an event like this takes place."

"And you're sure that it wasn't planned when this was written?"

"Positive. I think Charles writes them the night before, but he frequently does an update in the morning. Chefs discover that there's something new and fresh on the market and frequently want to change their specials. Sometimes large parties make reservations early in the morning—not parties as large as this, though. And Charles turns down parties of a dozen or more if they don't give enough notice. But lunchtime is not the time that this type of thing happens."

"And when did this party get put on the schedule?"

"I'm not completely sure, but I think just before I got here, just before one."

"And the plans were made by Horace Harvey?"

"Yes. Do you have any more questions?"

"No, you've been a big help," Susan said, standing up. The other woman had been doodling on the desk's blotter, and Susan was astounded to see that her scribbles displayed the same distinctive capital letters as the note that had been slipped to her during her meal with James Malarkey.

THIRTEEN

"I HAD FORGOTTEN ALL ABOUT IT," SUSAN SAID, RUMMAGing in her copious purse. "Ah . . . here it is."

"Maybe you should read it to me so I don't crash the car," Kathleen suggested.

"It doesn't make any sense. That's probably why I forgot. It doesn't really go anywhere as far as I can tell."

"We're almost at Tillie's house. Are you going to tell me what it says?"

" 'Please help him. He's innocent and he can't prove it.' "

"And does that mean anything at all to you?"

"Nothing. I guess the writer means that one of the men involved in this case didn't kill Horace Harvey, but I don't see how that idea gets us anywhere."

"Unless you're sure that waitress wrote it—why didn't you ask her about it when you were there?"

"I'm not positive that she wrote it, but I'm sure I'll be talking with her again. While I was there, it occurred to me that the Inn itself is more significant than I first thought."

"Maybe," Kathleen begrudgingly agreed. "But we're here. We can talk about it after we talk with Tillie."

They had arrived at a charming small Tudor home on a quiet cul-de-sac.

"Wow."

"That's what everyone says." Kathleen agreed with Susan's assessment. "You know, I took my mother to Holland the spring after my father died, but I don't think the bulb displays there had much on Tillie's yard."

"It's beautiful. Do you think she's here?"

"It's a gorgeous Sunday afternoon. I don't know Tillie well, but I have a hard time imagining her anywhere else but her garden on a day like this."

"And you're so right about that."

Susan and Kathleen turned toward the speaker. The man coming around the corner of the house was wearing chinos, a light blue turtleneck, and a well-worn Harris tweed jacket with leather patches on the elbows. The pipe poking up from his breast pocket spoke the word *professor* before Kathleen said, "Professor Greenleaf, it's nice to see you. I don't know if you remember me. . . ."

"I do. Kathleen Gordon. One of the most beautiful gardeners to join H.E.C. as well as the woman who has been such a kind friend to Tillie for the last few days. I'm glad to see you. I've wanted to thank you for everything you did for us."

"I think your lawyer did a lot more than I could. We're here to see Tillie. Is she free?"

"She's out back, in her garden as you guessed. Just follow the path. And please, let me thank you again. You were a good friend when Tillie needed one desperately."

Susan and Kathleen followed the brick walkway around the house. Either side was lined with mounds of tiny blue and white grape hyacinths. Next to the house, multicolored primroses fought with narcissus for space in the dark loam. Baskets hung from eaves, full of ferns and red species tulips. Susan stopped exclaiming and just enjoyed the view.

Tillie Greenleaf was sitting on a wooden lounge, a trug of garden tools at her feet and stains on the knees of her chinos, betraying the work she had been doing since dawn. She got up to greet her guests, putting a smile on her face. "Kathleen. Susan. How nice to see you."

Susan waited until Kathleen and Tillie had exchanged greetings before she asked any questions. She would have liked to wait all day. How was she going to ask this nice woman the questions that James Malarkey had given her? Everything was so personal: How long had she known her husband before they got married? Where did they meet?

Where did the money supporting their lifestyle come from? Susan looked around the yard that ended down with a tiny elegant glass gazebo by a pond. Maybe being a professor paid better than she imagined.

Or maybe she shouldn't ask about those things. What possible difference could they make to the murder investigation? Except, she reminded herself, it was possible that Tillie still was the main suspect, and as such, anything about her life that James Malarkey was interested in was worth more than a second look. She leaned back in the chair and looked at the budding trees against the blue sky. She must have dozed off, because it took Kathleen more than a few minutes to get her attention.

"Susan? Are you asleep?"

"Oh, I'm sorry. I didn't sleep well last night."

"Kathleen says you have some questions to ask," Tillie reminded her gently. "You don't have to worry about offending me. The most important thing now is to find out who killed Horace Harvey."

"Detective Malarkey wanted to know some things about your past," Kathleen started.

"About your past with your husband," Susan added.

Tillie Greenleaf smiled slightly and picked up a piece of trailing ivy. "Some things just never go away, do they?"

"Maybe you should talk directly to Detective Malarkey?" Susan suggested.

"I'd rather talk with you and Kathleen. God help me, I hate that man."

"Would anyone like some lemonade? And maybe, Mrs. Henshaw, it would be easier for me to answer questions about my life with Tillie than for her to do so." Professor Greenleaf appeared with a large tray in his hands.

"Dear . . ."

"Let me," he insisted, sitting down next to his wife. "I think what the police are interested in is my war record—so to speak. You see, I was a draft resister, and I was imprisoned for more than three years in the beginning of the Vietnam War. I met Tillie there. She was a visitor to the prison. Tillie is a Friend . . . Quaker, if you will . . . and she was very involved in her prison work. She's a lot younger than I am, of course. She was a senior in high school when I met her. We were married the afternoon of her graduation from Swarthmore. It had been a long five years. The courts then were not entirely sympathetic with the plight of prisoners of conscience. I was not incarcerated in what people now call country club prisons. I was in a maximum security prison with murderers, rapists, and the like. Possibly a better man than I am would have studied these people and searched for a way to understand and possibly change their miserable lives. I chose to continue my studies of English literature. I wrote my doctoral dissertation on Donne in prison."

"And that was not an easy task under the circumstances," his wife insisted.

"The experience changed both our lives. Tillie was happy at Swarthmore, but she chose to go there to be close to me. And I guess I naively thought that was going to be the only permanent change in our lives stemming from my original decision, but I was wrong."

"What happened?" Susan asked.

"I couldn't get a job. The most liberal colleges and universities didn't require my services. I'd always wanted to be a college professor. I'd always expected to be a college professor. I had, over the years, received a lot of support—verbally—from my colleagues and mentors. But they all forgot about me when I was finally released from prison. Politically correct is sometimes difficult to distinguish from the middle of the road."

"But I thought you were a university professor," Kathleen said.

"I was, but never in the ivy-covered walls that I had envisioned. A relative of mine got me a job as an assistant at a small offshore medical school—there was a feeling that there should be a humanities course or two thrown into the science curriculum. I shouldn't complain. I was lucky to get it. And in time and with a lot of publishing credits, I did manage to move to a fine little school in Texas, and from there to a university in the Midwest. I had a nice life there and my share of professional respect. But the only ivy I've ever come to know intimately is that which my good wife has planted."

Susan wondered how she was going to ask about anything as crass as money when he had just been so honest with them.

"My mother had been a widow for years, a fairly wealthy widow, to be honest, and when she died, we moved to Hancock. I was going to continue my writing, but it's not always easy to do what we intend to do."

"We have a lovely life here," Tillie said in a firm voice. "A lovely life. I, for one, wouldn't change it for the world." She turned to the others. "My husband made a decision of conscience, and it changed his life. But he had the courage to make the decision and the courage to live with the result. I am very proud of him. Very proud. And, as he said, I am a member of the Society of Friends. I would not take the life of another for any reason. I don't expect a man like Detective Malarkey to understand that, but I know you both do."

"Thank you," Kathleen said, understanding the compliment.

"Do you have other questions for us?" Professor Greenleaf added.

"I don't think so, at least nothing that Detective Malarkey asked us."

"I have a few questions of my own, if you don't mind us intruding more," Susan said somewhat reluctantly.

"We will answer anything. You and Kathleen know that Tillie isn't guilty. I have found that it doesn't do to depend on receiving justice from our judicial system. I appreciate the time and effort you're willing to put in to prove my wife's innocence."

"Were you at the Inn with your wife Thursday night?"

"No. I do not have a green thumb and I'm not active in H.E.C.—although my wife occasionally co-ops my aged back for digging and spreading compost. I was, if I may anticipate your next question, at an ale-tasting party at a tavern in Norwalk. I consider myself something of a beer connoisseur, and I was happy for the opportunity to taste the products of the new smaller breweries. I came home rather late, and Tillie was picked up by the police almost immediately."

Susan took a deep breath and asked the question she had been dreading. She looked straight into Tillie Greenleaf's eyes. "Why did you say you were glad that Horace Harvey was dead?"

Tillie glanced at her husband. "Did I say that? I was so surprised by his death that I probably didn't know what I was saying."

Susan decided to skip it for the moment. "Apparently everyone in town knows that white lilacs are your favorite flower," she began. "And you said that there was some blooming in your greenhouse right now, didn't you?" She glanced down at the glass house at the end of the yard as she spoke.

Tillie got up. "Do you want to see it?"

"I'd love to," Susan answered quickly.

"You two go ahead. I'll entertain Kathleen while you show off your pride and joy," her husband suggested.

"He's bragging, in a sense," Tillie explained, starting off. "The greenhouse was a birthday present from him—and he designed it as well."

"It's really wonderful. It looks like one of those little glass houses that people have in England."

"That's what it's supposed to resemble. But it's very practical. Triple-glazed, solar as well as gas-heated . . . et cetera, et cetera. I know that I bore people when I start talking about gardening."

"Do you take care of all this by yourself?"

"We hire people for the heavy work, but gardening is my second love—right after my husband—and I'm inclined to become jealous when someone else is doing what I can do."

They had reached the greenhouse, and Tillie opened the many-paned door into the interior. "Wow. Aroma therapy," Susan said, taking a deep breath.

"That's the lilac." Tillie nodded at the large flowering

bushes on either side of the doorway. "And probably some of the citrus trees ..."

"Citrus trees ... ?" Susan was so impressed that she was about to forget what she had come here for. She gathered her thoughts while Tillie explained the nature of the plants in her orangery.

"You didn't come here just because you're interested in the plants, did you?"

"No," Susan admitted. "I was mainly interested in whether or not someone could break in here and steal some flowers without anyone detecting the break-in."

"You mean the lilacs found in Horace Harvey's pocket, don't you? Well, the answer is, as you can see, that it is more than possible. There are no locks on the doors; anyone could walk in and take whatever they wanted. We didn't think security would be a big problem when we had this built."

"Of course not," Susan agreed. "It really is beautiful."

"Anything else?"

"Did Horace Harvey ask any questions about you or your husband as well as H.E.C.?"

"Nothing. Absolutely nothing. His approach to picking the group to receive his inheritance was unusual, but the process of looking at the organization was completely professional. He checked out our bank statements, looked at the parks, asked what I would have thought were the right questions."

"Tillie ..." Susan hesitated.

"Go ahead," Tillie insisted with a smile.

"Did you know Horace Harvey before?"

"No, of course not."

Susan stared at the garden wonderland around her. She believed Tillie Greenleaf, but ... things just weren't making sense.

Susan had been to Alissa Anthony's house many times, but she had never been left alone in the room that Alissa referred to as her own private green room.

"This is the most extraordinary place," Kathleen was

saying, leaning over the leather tuxedo couch to read one of the dozens of framed clippings that hung on the deep green silk-covered walls. " 'A sensation! —the *Hancock Gazette*. Alissa Anthony was a theatrical success last weekend in an original version of *Empress Jones*.' They're kidding!"

"What?" Susan turned away from some rather garish watercolors of turn-of-the-century costumes.

"Listen to this! 'Ms. Anthony's sensitive depiction of *Empress Jones* as a white feminist—' "

"Alissa, I'm so glad you could take the time to talk with us," Susan interrupted Kathleen, hoping her enthusiasm would cover anything sarcastic that was about to be said.

"I'm very busy today." Alissa used both arms to lift her abundant hair off her shoulders, thus decreasing at least one burden on them. She flung herself on the chaise lounge that, together with a large ornate Victorian papier-mâché table, seemed to serve as her desk and chair, and continued. "Of course, I'm always busy. I thrive on work. Simply thrive on it. Like a small orchid struggling up toward the sun, like a moth to the flame, like Icarus flying to the—"

"We have some questions to ask you," Susan continued.

"You're investigating the murder, aren't you?" Alissa's tone conveyed an unspoken "how quaint."

"Detective Malarkey asked for our help." Susan put as much authority as she could muster behind her words.

Alissa opened her eyes wide and spread her arms to the room. "So investigate."

"You rewrite so many of the plays that your group performs. . . ." Susan began.

Alissa gathered herself into an attentive position. "Yes?"

Wow, talk about a mood swing. "Well, I was wondering," Susan continued, "if you've ever done any other writing. You know, short stories, maybe even a book?"

"What exactly have you heard, Susan?"

"Well, Det—" Susan would have explained that these questions had been given to her by the policeman if Kathleen hadn't interrupted.

"Then you are a writer."

Alissa paused. "I must admit that I found my destiny

rather late in life. I did have early hopes of being a writer, and I must confess that I received some encouragement for my early, and admittedly immature, work."

"Books?" Kathleen insisted on a more specific answer.

"I did have one novel published. Yes."

"And what happened?" It was certainly a vague enough question to elicit some sort of response.

"My art was betrayed by the philistines."

"Could you be just a little more specific?"

"All art is derivative. None of us work in a vacuum. There is always an awareness of the hard work and genius that has gone before. Do you understand?"

"Of course," Susan assured her.

Kathleen merely nodded.

"And, naturally, the dedicated artist strives to be aware of the previous as well as the current work being done in his or her genre."

She paused.

This time they both nodded.

"And the artist creates out of a large body of work as well as one's own mind, both the conscious mind and the subconscious."

They waited.

"And sometimes, as they say, mistakes will happen."

"What sort of mistakes?" Kathleen was bold enough to ask.

"I wrote my roman à clef, I poured my heart, my soul, my life's blood, into it. Only to discover that I had accidentally copied someone else's work."

"Someone else's heart, soul, and blood were there, too?" Susan asked.

Kathleen was more direct. "Plagiarism? You plagiarized someone else's novel?"

"You make it sound so pedestrian, so legal," Alissa protested.

"Illegal rather," Susan muttered.

"You were accused of plagiarism? Did the case ever go to trial?" Kathleen asked.

"It did not. And I did not commit plagiarism. It was

merely a manifestation of my unconscious admiration for a novel that I had read a year or two before that caused me to emulate it perhaps just slightly more than the law allowed." She took a long, deep breath and settled back into the seat. "We settled out of court."

"And you gave up writing," Kathleen suggested.

"No. Rather, after a period of intense crisis, I found myself and, I am happy to report, my true calling."

"When did you do this writing?" Susan asked.

"Right after I graduated from college. I moved to Greenwich Village, to what could only be known as a garret, convinced that I was going to write the Great American Novel." She shrugged. "Alas. That was not to be."

"Did you work?" Susan asked.

"Do you think writing is play?"

"Did you get paid? How did you support yourself?" Kathleen asked more succinctly.

"My parents had given me a very generous graduation present. Like the very best presents, it allowed me to pursue my dream.

"And what, may I ask, do these questions have to do with the murder of Horace Harvey? Or have you just become curious about my life?"

"We didn't mean to pry," Susan said. "These are actually questions that Detective Malarkey asked me to ask you."

"Why didn't he ask them himself? Is he so busy? Can I assume that I'm only a minor suspect? That if I held the position of, say, Tillie Greenleaf, he would interview me himself?"

"We just left Tillie Greenleaf," Kathleen answered coldly, rising to her feet.

Susan wondered if there was anything else they should ask. "Did you find out about a bridging loan?" she asked quickly, that being all she could come up with on the spur of the moment.

"My husband spoke with a friend of ours who is very highly connected in the Bank of America, and he said that the Hancock Community Players were screwed by Horace Harvey. The man never intended to leave us his money."

The phone rang before anything else could be said. Alissa picked up the receiver and spoke briefly before hanging up. "That was Jed. He said that a man from the Senior Citizens Center dropped a letter off at your house for you a few minutes ago."

Susan was startled. She had forgotten the lovely man she had met the day before. And she wondered what it was that he had found out talking with his friends.

Susan reached across Kathleen and pulled a Mint Milano from the bag Jed had found in the top of a cupboard and started to read, waving the cookie around to emphasize points.

" 'Two people at the center this afternoon remembered knowing Horace Harvey when he (and they) were growing up. A few other members of the afternoon film study group (we're doing urban film images from *Backstreet* to *Midnight Cowboy* this spring) thought that they might remember him sitting in the back of one class or another in high school, but that's about all they remembered if it even was Horace Harvey.

" 'Back to the two people who actually remember Mr. Harvey: Their main impression is that he was distinctly forgettable. Many of the classes at Hancock High School in those days seated the students in alphabetical order. Denise Harwin (her maiden name) remembers sitting behind Horace Harvey in a lot of classes.' " She stopped and took a bite of the cookie.

"Keep reading," Kathleen insisted, shaking the bag to see how many cookies were left.

"Fine. 'She actually remembers very little about Horace Harvey except that he started wearing too much after-shave during his senior year and that he asked her to the senior prom. She refused, and went instead with the man she was married to for forty-one years until he died. She says that Harvey was an average student except in math. She is sure he wasn't in her math classes, which means he was probably advanced in that subject. She's sure because her husband's last name was Gilbert, and he sat by her in math for all four years. She says that she can't imagine how he became so wealthy since he wasn't a particularly promising student and he was what her grandson would call a dork.

" 'However, there is one more person who remembers Horace Harvey, and she remembers him very well. She was in many of his classes and went to all the basketball games for two years to watch him sitting on the bench "managing" the team. She had a terrible crush on him. She thinks, though, that it was inspired by the fact that she felt sorry for him. She says that although he wasn't ugly, he certainly wasn't attractive, that he was a mediocre student except for math (she's sure he took calculus his junior year), and that he was one of those lonely, unpopular students that each school has. She remembers how cruel the other students were—teasing him and making fun of him even to his face. She remembers that she found him sitting on the bleachers after some sort of event in their senior year—she thinks maybe it was a pep rally—and that he was crying. She's a very perceptive woman and she says that you could have knocked her over with a feather when she heard he was coming back to town to give away his money. She says that just goes to prove that people are bigger than you think and that he had been underestimated throughout high school.' " Susan stopped reading and laughed.

"What?" Kathleen asked.

"He says he thought this last woman was so sweet that he asked her to Sunday dinner at the Inn and that he would be happy to help me out any time at all. Also that he'll let me know if he hears anything else."

FOURTEEN

SUNDAY AFTERNOON WAS APPARENTLY A BIG DAY FOR VISIT-
ing at the hospital, and Susan and Kathleen had a long hike
from the farthest parking lot. They had spent the drive trying to organize the information they had collected.

"Why are we still writing in the back of this dumb
book?" Kathleen asked, dotting the last *i* and dropping her
pen into her purse. "If you're going to be carrying it
around, the least you could do is find a name for that poor
puppy. Maybe you should try doing it like people used to
do with the Bible: open it at a random page, stick a pin in,
and just call her that name."

"It is ridiculous, isn't it?" Susan muttered, not paying
much attention to her friend.

"What are you thinking about?"

"I was thinking about Martha Trumbull's house."

"From what you told me, it sounds wonderful."

"It is," Susan agreed. "And it's very large. Ethan said
there are four bedrooms, one with a dressing room attached,
and two bathrooms on the second floor, and two attic rooms
and a half bath above that."

"So?"

"So why does one elderly lady living alone in a house
that size decide she needs to build an addition?"

Kathleen thought for a moment before answering.
"That's an excellent question."

"One I think we should ask immediately," Susan continued, walking in the automatic door to the hospital. "Oh,
look, Ethan's in the coffee shop with Betsy."

"That's the niece of the dispatcher down at the station?"

"Uh-huh. Just let me go say hello. If he knows I'm visiting his aunt, he may stay away longer. And I'd really rather speak with her alone."

"Fine. I'll go to the gift shop and pick out something to take up. I suppose her room is already filled with flowers." And Kathleen went off, intent on her task.

Susan was carrying a vanilla malt, and Kathleen a small wrapped package, when they met at the elevator a few minutes later.

"You found something."

"Some English violet body lotion. If she has six bottles already sitting by her bed, Ethan can exchange it for her."

"What a good idea," Susan said as they arrived at the right floor. "It's room 418. Down that corridor."

Susan knocked on the correct door, then led the way in at Martha's command. "Martha, you look much better," she said immediately.

"I must, because everyone is saying the same thing in that same surprised tone of voice. It makes me wonder how terrible I've been looking for the past week."

"Ethan asked me to bring you this," Susan said, handing over the drink, "and I don't think you know Kathleen Gordon."

"No, but I did know Jerry Gordon's first wife—she was very active in the historical society—and I have always heard that you're just as fine a person as she was. And you're beautiful, too," she added, holding out her hand. "I hope you don't mind me mentioning her."

"Not at all. I know how happy she made Jerry and what a tragedy her death was," Kathleen said, meaning every word of it. Marrying a widower had not been a problem for her. "And I'm very glad to meet you, too. I brought you a present," she added, handing it to the woman.

"How lovely. I must admit that the best thing about being in the hospital is receiving gifts. I feel a little like a child at Christmas." She pulled the paper off the boxed cream. "Oh, how lovely, and what a good idea. This place is so hot and dry, I've been needing this." She promptly used the cream on her hands and arms. "Lovely, absolutely lovely. Thank you so much.

"Now, let's get down to business. How's your investigation going, and what else do you need to ask me?"

"The investigation is going very slowly," Susan admitted, "and I have to go to Boston tomorrow. . . ."

"Boston. Now, where did I read something about Boston and the murder?" Martha Trumbull reached out to the large pile of newspapers on a chair by her bed.

"I'm not really going to find out anything about the murder. This trip is to take Chrissy to see some colleges."

"But you did say that you would check into Horace Harvey's background up there if you have the time," Kathleen reminded her. "Mr. Harvey lived in Boston and made his fortune up there," she explained to the other woman.

"Oh, that must be what I read about in the paper." She sounded doubtful.

"We would like to ask you a question or two," Susan said gently.

"I'm glad I'm still a suspect. I know it sounds strange, but you have no idea how insignificant you begin to feel lying in a hospital bed."

"I was at your house last night," Susan began, "talking with Ethan. It's a beautiful house, but large, and I was wondering why you decided that you needed an addition. I mean, you live alone and all."

Martha put down the milk shake she had been sipping, a serious expression on her face. "You haven't added my nephew to your list of suspects, have you? Because he couldn't have done it. He was here with me that entire evening."

She didn't pause long enough for Susan to explain that Ethan had already admitted to being away from the hospital for a while on Thursday night—or that she had not come up with a motive for the young man.

"That is not to say that I'm not worried about Ethan. Did he tell you that he's dropped out of Yale?"

"I didn't know that you knew!" Susan exclaimed. "And he—"

"He certainly thinks it is his secret," Martha agreed. "But I happen to be old friends with one of his professors, and the gentleman told me about it all a few months ago. That's why I'm adding to the house."

"I don't think I follow that," Kathleen admitted.

"Are you expecting him to move in with you?" Susan asked.

"No. I was hoping that it would renew his interest in colonial history—not that it worked. Old women should know better than to try to manipulate the young. All I have now is a hole in the middle of the old rose garden and a nephew who's a suspect in a murder case. No fool like an old fool, to coin a phrase that I've always hated. I suppose I'd better explain. Why don't you both sit down and get comfortable?

"I really don't spy on Ethan. I was thrilled when he got into the graduate program at Yale and I do have some friends in the American Studies program there, but I did not have anything to do with his admission and I did not check up on him there. I even resisted inviting him to my home except for Christmas and Thanksgiving. But it has been obvious for a while that his interests have changed, that his studies are no longer the most important thing in his life. I thought maybe the dump would change all that."

"You knew it was there before you began to excavate," Kathleen said slowly.

"I've known about it for years. It was discovered right after we moved in. My husband had multiple sclerosis, and we were thinking of having a pool put in the backyard for him to use to get exercise. There were some preliminary excavations made, and the top of the dump site was uncovered then."

"But you decided not to excavate."

"No. My husband wasn't terribly interested in the whole project, and I thought I could always do it at a later date. We were busier back in those days. Despite my husband's disabilities—or maybe because we wanted to do as much as we could before they increased considerably—we were doing a lot of traveling and visiting with friends we had made over the years. But my husband died about ten years ago, and so, when I realized that Ethan was losing interest in his studies, I thought that maybe an archaeological site of his very own would reinspire him, so to speak. The addition was just an excuse to dig. I had no intention of increasing the size of my home, as you correctly guessed."

"So you didn't actually care about receiving an inheritance from Horace Harvey?" Kathleen asked.

"I didn't expect it and would have had very little idea what to do with it," she admitted.

"Then how did you get on Horace Harvey's list of possible organizations?" Susan asked.

"I have no idea. I told you that he arrived here Friday morning offering the possibility of great wealth—and I was lucky enough to be in the position of being amused rather than envious."

"But people did know about S.O.D.," Kathleen said.

"Yes. I formed the organization and gave it a name. Then I called in the local press, who very obligingly put some stories in some of the papers, and I invited some of my friends from the Hancock Historical Society in for tea and told them about it."

"All to keep your nephew from becoming a Presbyterian minister?" Susan sounded as astounded as she felt.

"It sounds worse than it is," Martha Trumbull said. "You see, my brother left a rather unusual will. To be blunt, he said that his money could only be left to an atheist, an agnostic, or a heathen. My brother was a very colorful person, but he did not believe in freedom of expression. I have frequently thought that it's a good thing that he didn't believe in religion. Otherwise, he probably would have created and led some kind of fanatic cult. But I've been thinking about all this while I lie here, and I have a solution to the problem. A solution so obvious that there's no excuse for not having thought of it much earlier."

"What?"

"I'm going to give Ethan the money that he would receive from his father. I'm the only other person in the family that the money could go to if Ethan doesn't get it, and I'm certainly enough of a heathen for anyone."

Susan smiled at the admission. "Then you don't care whether or not he's a minister?"

"I was very happy to discover that the only other living member of my family loved history as much as I do, but I know that everyone has to live their own life. Ethan's decisions might not be mine, but they shouldn't be. And come to think of it, a young man wanting to dedicate his life to God isn't a very good suspect in a murder case, now is he?"

"Maybe not," Kathleen agreed. "But it doesn't depend on us; Detective Malarkey makes that decision."

"I can't say I've heard anything positive about him. That young woman that Ethan likes so much . . ."

"Betsy?" Susan offered the name. She thought it was time to leave; Martha Trumbull suddenly looked very tired.

"Yes. Well, she's been stopping in from time to time after visiting her aunt, and she says that everyone down at the police station is very unhappy about working for him."

"Any reason other than that he's just generally one of the more obnoxious people on the face of the planet?" Susan asked.

"I don't know specifically. Why don't you ask her aunt? She's right next door." Martha pointed to the wall over her head. "Or maybe over there," she said, pointing in the other direction with a frown on her face.

"Don't worry, we'll find it." Susan stood up as a nurse entered the room.

"Who are you looking for?" the nurse asked, popping a thermometer in Martha's mouth without ceremony.

"A patient who's the dispatcher for the town's police," Kathleen explained.

"Right next door." The nurse pointed.

Susan and Kathleen said quick farewells to Martha Trumbull and hurried from the room.

"Do you want to take the time to talk with her?" Kathleen asked when they were together in the hall.

"Why not? The only other person I want to talk with is Ralph, and that couldn't possibly take the rest of the afternoon."

"Then let's give it a try," Kathleen agreed, knocking on the door.

"Come on in!" called out a cheerful voice, and Susan and Kathleen did as they were told.

The woman sitting up in the hospital bed looked very much like a branch of the tree from which her niece had dropped. For one thing, they shared a taste in hairstyles. A shocking white poofy ponytail stuck straight up from the patient's head. She was also as cheerful as her niece. "Kathleen! How wonderful to see you."

"Oh, my goodness, I didn't know who you were," Kathleen cried out, entering the room more quickly. "I should have, though; your niece looks a lot like you."

"Kathleen and I flunked out of the same quilting class last year."

"Do you remember me telling you about it?" Kathleen asked Susan.

Susan had heard so many stories of Kathleen's attempts to find a domestic outlet that they all ran together. She just nodded and smiled.

"Are you two looking for someone else?" asked the woman in the bed.

"No, we were looking for you," Susan admitted. "Is your name Sawyer, too?"

"Elizabeth Sawyer. My niece was named after me. What can I do for you? We'd better talk before a nurse comes in to wheel me off to physical therapy. There's not a lot of freedom in this place."

"We're looking into the murder," Kathleen began.

"And we have some questions that we'd like you to answer," Susan added.

"I sure will, but I don't know how I can help you. I've been lying here in this bed reading about it in the papers. Except for what my niece and a few people who are nice enough to take the time to visit me have said, I really don't know very much at all. Mostly, what everyone at the police department does is complain about Detective Malarkey. It sure is too bad that this murder had to take place when Brett is out of town."

"Is there a second-in-command under Detective Malarkey?" Kathleen asked.

"Sure is. Brett is very big on the line of command. But as I understand it, Detective Malarkey doesn't work like that. He likes to work alone. He tells people what he expects them to do, and then they report back to him. But he doesn't treat them as a team that's working together toward a common goal. At least that's what I hear. Everyone is complaining about it."

"About the same thing?"

"It's just a difference in working style, isn't it?" Susan asked.

"Not really," Kathleen started.

"Not at all, according to my friends down at the department," Elizabeth Sawyer disagreed. "After all, the whole point is to find the person who killed Horace Harvey and make an arrest that will hold up in court. That isn't a one-person job, and if everyone is accomplishing their own task rather than working on pieces and trying to put everything together into a whole, things go more slowly. And, of course, it isn't as satisfying. Betsy says that everyone is unhappy."

"And are they getting closer to an answer?" Susan wondered.

"I don't know. From what everyone says, Malarkey is sure that Tillie Greenleaf is guilty, and he's just trying to amass enough evidence to make it stick."

"Damn." Kathleen frowned.

"Well, that's stupid," Susan said bluntly. "He might as well have just picked any one of the suspects and spent all the police department's time and effort trying to convict them."

"And I guess we'd better get going and figure out exactly who did it," Kathleen said, standing up to leave.

"I'm stuck in this place for another week or so, but if there's anything I can do . . ."

"We'll give you a call," Susan promised.

* * *

"Do you think we're going to be able to figure this out?" Kathleen sounded doubtful.

"I sure hope so. I'd love to pin it on Ralph Spinoza. Well, why not? If James Malarkey can have his favorite suspect, so can I."

"Why? And how are you going to prove it?" Kathleen asked, removing the dog book from the dashboard of Susan's car.

"Because I don't like him, and I have no idea at all how I'm going to prove it—probably because he didn't do it."

"Why are you so sure?"

"He's such a careful, organized man. He doesn't strike me as someone who would kill anyone—it's such a messy way to accomplish something. And no one gives out certificates of appreciation for murder," Susan added, and explained about the bathroom decorations.

"Wow. A little egocentric, don't you think?"

"He claims that his wife did it, if you ask about them. As though anyone who knows the two of them would believe that she makes any decisions on her own."

"Not even to have an affair with Bob Arnold?"

"I would assume that, if she's involved with Bob Arnold, it was an autonomous decision," Susan agreed. "But we don't know that she is, do we?"

"No. We just know that James Malarkey wants us to look into it. I wonder how many people who work for him down at the station are looking into the same things, don't you?" Kathleen asked.

"I sure do. Sounds like he has the entire police department running around doing his bidding," Susan answered. "I do hope we're not going to end up feeling like the world's greatest suckers when all this is over."

"I just hope it ends without Tillie spending any more time in jail."

"Why do you think he's picking on Tillie? To me, it doesn't look like she's a more likely suspect than anyone else."

"Maybe he's some sort of fanatic military supporter and he wants to punish her for marrying a draft resister."

"That doesn't make any sense. . . . Though maybe it does when you think about it. When James Malarkey was asking us to investigate Tillie, he didn't say something like 'find out if Horace Harvey threatened to foreclose on her mortgage or expose her past and ruin her life,' he just asked about her husband's past—in ways that would make it impossible for us to discover anything but his military record. And I don't think most people in this town would be at all bothered if they found out about Professor Greenleaf's prison record. Even people who aren't liberal accept that other people made other decisions. It probably wouldn't make a difference to Tillie or H.E.C. And it has absolutely nothing to do with Horace Harvey."

"That we know of," Kathleen said quietly. "And we really don't know very much about Horace Harvey."

Susan thought for a few moments. "You're right. Maybe he was in prison with Professor Greenleaf and does know something that would change their lives. Or maybe he was on the draft board that . . . No, maybe he was a member of the jury that sent him to prison. Or . . ."

"I think you're getting a little crazy. We don't know about any connection between Horace Harvey and the Greenleafs except through H.E.C. There's no reason to assume anything else."

"So why Tillie?" Susan repeated. "The white lilac theory doesn't hold water since there were other clues left with the body."

"You did walk outside with her, and the bottle that Horace Harvey was hit with was found there," Kathleen reminded her gently.

"She was not carrying a large bottle in her hand when we left the Inn. The policeman at the door should be able to tell him that."

"Well, that's the only thing I can think of that distinguishes her from the other suspects that night," Kathleen said. "Can you think of anything?"

Susan thought. The murder had taken place three days ago, but it was getting difficult to distinguish between what happened Thursday night and what she had heard since then.

Kathleen was flipping through the dog-naming book again. "I have a list of suspects here. Do you want me to read it?"

"Sure."

"Honey Bradshaw. Bob Arnold. Ralph Spinoza. Martha Trumbull. Of course, that's impossible because she was in the hospital in a body cast."

"Cross out Martha and put in Ethan. I don't think he did it, and he claims that he wasn't at the Inn that night, but there's over an hour of his evening unaccounted for. I don't know why he'd do it, but Malarkey is looking at him, so we may as well, too."

"Okay." Kathleen wrote for a few minutes and then continued. "Ethan Trumbull. Alissa Anthony. Patty Taylor, but I'm including her just because she runs P.A.P.; I don't think she's a real suspect."

"I agree with you."

"And that's it except for Tillie Greenleaf."

"That's it as far as people whose groups were hoping to benefit from Horace Harvey's death. It could be someone else, couldn't it?"

"You're trying to drive us crazy, aren't you?"

"Not me. James Malarkey is trying to drive us crazy. If Brett were here, he'd be helping us out with information rather than trying to get us to ask questions for him."

Kathleen looked at the list she had in her hands. "You know, it would be a big help if you'd spend some time doing research in Boston. We need to know more about Horace Harvey and his business."

"I'll try. I don't suppose you'd like to come along?"

"With you and Chrissy? I don't think I can stand so much sweetness and light. Besides, I have to take care of Bananas. His play group is meeting at my house Monday morning."

"Enjoy him while he's young," Susan advised.

"Parents of teenagers keep telling me that. One thing

about being a teenager, it's something that we all grow out of."

"And how many parents die of anxiety before then? Oh, well, we're almost at the Spinozas'—a couple with four perfect children."

"Really?"

"You sound like you don't believe it. You should see that family perform at the high school family talent show each year. One year they all performed on their violins—first they played a sonata by Beethoven, then a short concerto composed by the oldest boy. The next year was a scene from Shakespeare, costumes designed by Olive and sewn by the girls. Then there was the gymnastics display."

"Only three years?"

"You don't happen to know that one of the four children is a mass murderer, do you?" Susan asked.

"Nope. I did hear that the oldest boy just received a full scholarship to Stanford, but you probably don't want to hear about that," Kathleen said.

"The youngest is probably on the short list for the Nobel Prize. You know, though . . ." Susan stopped without finishing.

"What?"

"I'll tell you after we talk to them," Susan promised.

FIFTEEN

SUSAN AND KATHLEEN WERE SITTING UNCOMFORTABLY ON very comfortable overstuffed furniture in the Spinozas' elegant living room. They had knocked on the front door and been admitted to the fringes of a family fight.

The tall young man who greeted them at the door had let them in and shown them to the living room as cries from the second floor gathered momentum and threatened to spill down the wide, spiraling stairway. "Television," he lied abruptly. "I'll tell them you're here," he added, then took the stairs two at a time. As he disappeared down the hallway, the shouting diminished considerably.

"So much for the perfect family," Kathleen said.

"Everyone fights."

"True. You should hear Jerry and me exchanging views on whether Bananas is going to go to public school or start on the upper-class, pressure-filled private school track."

Susan laughed. "It's not hard to guess which side you're on."

"Yeah, well. I got a good education at public schools. . . . We'll talk about that some other time. And he's only three, for heaven's sake."

"Hmm. Wait till he starts talking about skipping college and bumming around Europe for a year or two."

"Please. I can only think of one thing at a time. First toilet training, then nursery school. After that, he can drop out of college."

There was a loud crash from the room over their heads.

"Something must have fallen," Susan said.

"Or been thrown."

Susan didn't respond. She leaned back and glanced around the room. "I wonder where all the pictures are."

Kathleen looked around and noted the large dark rectangles in the deep pink walls scattered around the room in three different areas. "Seven of them are missing, aren't they?" she asked, after a quick count.

"Yes. Ralph and Olive collect modern European Impressionists. They're a little too pastel and perky for me, but they adore them. I suppose they're out being cleaned or something."

There was another crash and then footsteps on the stairs.

Ralph Spinoza appeared in the room, brushed his hair off his forehead, and headed straight for the large teak bar set up along one wall. He had poured himself a large portion of generic-brand bourbon before he noticed that he had guests. Susan didn't know what surprised her more: the fact that his hands were shaking or that he was pouring cheap, unbonded liquor.

"Ralph?" She spoke as quietly as possible, but still surprised him enough to spill bourbon on the carpet. She didn't think it was the first time. "I'm sorry if we scared you."

Like most men, Ralph zoomed in on Kathleen and her good looks, changing his scowl into a smile. "You're Jerry Gordon's wife, aren't you? We met at the club a few times last summer. Are you still taking paddle lessons? And," he added, looking down at the glass in his hands, "would you lovely ladies like a Sunday afternoon drink? Olive often joins me for a glass of sherry or . . . something."

"I'm fine."

"Me, too," Susan agreed, wondering if she heard someone else coming down the stairs. She turned in her seat, hoping to see Olive. Instead, the large Rottweiler she had met the other day appeared in the doorway and looked at his master.

Ralph motioned to the dog, who immediately flattened himself on the floor.

Kathleen was impressed. "Wow."

"Ralph trained him," Susan said, wondering when someone was going to say something about the loud noises that were once again funneling through the well-built home's thick walls.

The host apparently read her thoughts. "I'd better go turn down the television. One of the kids must have left it on."

Neither woman said anything, and he hurried back up the stairs. "Maybe we should leave," Kathleen suggested, when Olive Spinoza walked in the front door.

Susan and Kathleen both glanced involuntarily at the ceiling. Susan knew they had both assumed that Olive was the person making such a ruckus up there. Unlike the last time they'd seen her, Olive was well dressed and self possessed, even when another loud crash shook the room.

"She's still up there, I gather," the woman said, heading over to the bar her husband had just left and pouring herself a tiny glass of Tio Pepe. "I assume Ralph offered you something and you refused?"

Both women nodded, although Susan was hoping there would be an opportunity to change her mind. She was beginning to think that a drink sounded like a fine idea.

Kathleen stood up and walked over to pet the dog that was still immobile on the floor. "Who's up there?" she asked casually, scratching the animal behind the ears.

"Our houseguest. Shirley Arnold."

"You're kidding." It was out of Susan's mouth before she could stop it.

"You didn't know? I thought the entire town was talking about it. Just goes to show, doesn't it? We always think other people care more about our affairs than they do." Olive drained her glass and poured herself another. "Sure you don't want one?"

Susan opened her mouth, but Kathleen got there first. "Why is she here?"

"Gawd knows. I never thought Ralph was the type to take in charity cases, especially not now."

"Now? Has something changed?" Susan asked.

Olive waved her arms around the room, spraying sherry in a large circle. "What's different about now? Just take a look. Everything we've worked for is evaporating before our eyes. Of course," she added, giggling rather oddly, "I guess it was all a mirage anyway, wasn't it? How will a declaration of bankruptcy look on the bathroom walls. . . ."

"Olive. Sit down and shut up!" Ralph Spinoza roared from the top of the stairs.

It was a shock, but Susan found herself hiding a smile. Obedience training apparently worked better with dogs than with people—at least with wives. Olive said something strikingly obscene and poured herself another glass of sherry.

"My wife," Ralph announced, striding down the stairs, "has a drinking problem."

"The only problem that your wife has is her husband," Olive insisted, emptying her glass and filling it again.

Kathleen, who had seen enough domestic squabbles during her time in the police department to last a lifetime, glanced over at Susan. Susan glanced back, but both of them knew that they were probably going to find out things that they wouldn't under calmer, more ordinary circumstances.

"Why is Shirley Arnold visiting?" Susan asked.

"Shirley is our guest—" Ralph began.

"Shirley Arnold is my husband's last bit of community service. He doesn't go to town council meetings anymore. He quit the library board. He trained his own replacement for the Boy Scout council. He's even talking about giving up H.O.P.E." She shrieked at the accidental pun. "Get it? He's given up hope!"

"Olive! Pull yourself together!"

" 'Olive! Pull yourself together!' " She mimicked her husband in a whiny voice. "Olive! Give elegant parties! Olive! Lose ten pounds and get your nails done! Olive! Wear the new dress I bought you. . . ."

"Shut up!"

She did. Apparently it was a command she had been trained to obey. Lots and lots of repetition, Susan thought.

"Shirley Arnold is here trying to get her life together," Ralph began, glaring at his wife when she stifled a wild giggle. "Olive and I feel it's the least we can do for a friend."

Olive opened her mouth, but before something could come out, she chose to fill it with sherry.

"Has she been here ever since she left Bob?" Kathleen asked.

"No, she's only been our guest for a month or so," Ralph answered.

"She's—"

"I can explain, Olive."

"Why don't you?" Susan suggested.

"You've probably heard that Shirley and I have been involved romantically. . . ." He paused, and Susan and Kathleen nodded. "But I can assure you that it is not true. In fact, Shirley and my wife are the best of friends."

"We were," she said, but she said it quietly.

"Olive introduced Shirley to Bob, in fact."

Everyone in the room looked at Olive, but she didn't argue.

"When was that?" Kathleen asked.

"When was that, dear?" Ralph asked his wife, apparently forgetting that they weren't getting along. She just glared. "I think about ten or fifteen years ago," he continued quickly. "Olive and I have known Bob since we moved to Hancock. Bob and I have been, well, everyone knows that we've been involved in some of the same activities over the years—"

"You both moved to town at the same time?" Kathleen quickly interrupted.

"I think we were here before Bob Arnold," Ralph said in a manner that made Susan wonder if he thought he'd won the competition again.

"Shirley's been here longer than any of us," his wife reminded him.

Ralph nodded as though considering something of importance. "Shirley is a native. And she was very hospitable when we moved here. She introduced us around the church, and in fact, she and Olive ran the big Christmas bazaar that very year."

"And you met Bob?" Susan asked.

"No, I did." Olive was slurring her words now. "At the library."

"That's the story that they've stuck to for all these years. But of course, it's not true. Olive and Bob were lovers in college long before she met me."

His wife stopped her drinking and stared at him. "You knew?"

"Of course I knew, my dear. I made it my business to know about your past. Everything," he added in his nastiest voice.

"Not quite everything," she replied in the same tone. "I was still involved with Bob when you and I met."

"You don't really think I'd worry about a dork like that?" Ralph said, although it was obvious to all the women in the room that the last bit of information had come as a shock.

"You should have. Bob is a wonderful, intense, inventive lover. I would have married him if he hadn't dumped me."

It was apparent from the expression on Ralph Spinoza's face that he had lost the competition at last.

Susan and Kathleen had finally been allowed to go upstairs and speak with Shirley Arnold. They had found her ensconced in a large suite at the far end of a long, elegant hall. She was sitting at a delicate Chippendale desk in front of an open window through which a balcony could be seen. She turned and greeted them as they entered the room. "Is the mayhem downstairs beginning to abate?"

"Does this go on often?" Kathleen asked, sitting down on one of the two love seats that flanked the flower-filled fireplace.

"Constantly. I've been here for a while, and I can assure you that I'm not exaggerating. Although it is worse on weekends when neither of them has their job to go to. How those two produced four normal offspring is beyond me. I think it's probably an argument against the importance of parenting."

"We understand that you've known the Spinozas for a long time," Kathleen said.

"I gather you two are investigating this murder," Shirley said.

"Yes," Susan admitted. "We came here to ask the Spinozas some questions."

"I have a hard time imagining Ralph Spinoza murdering anybody—too risky. He might hire someone to murder for him. Or he might have back in the days when he had money."

"Olive said something about bankruptcy," Kathleen said.

"I'll bet she did. Money is a prominent topic in their lives these days."

"What happened?"

Shirley shrugged. "The eighties. The same thing that happened to a lot of people. They thought they were going to make money forever, more and more each year, and then it stopped. They developed bad habits: They spent everything they made each year, and then they spent everything they were going to make in the next year. Then came the cutbacks. First Olive stopped making those large real estate commissions. Houses in Hancock are still worth a lot of money, but fewer people can afford to buy them. And then Ralph's company discovered that it didn't need forty vice presidents; it could lose money just as efficiently with only fifteen or twenty."

"He's not working?"

"You're surprised? Susan Henshaw, after all I've heard about you over the years, I would never have suspected you of being naive. There are a lot of people in Hancock that are having financial problems. All these nice green lawns and large homes that look so prosperous can be symbols of massive debt. Believe me, I know all about it."

Kathleen got straight to the point. "Why?"

"I'm a bankruptcy lawyer."

"You're kidding!" It escaped from Susan before she could stop it. "I mean, that sounds interesting."

"When I got out of law school twenty-two years ago, it was anything but. It was, however, a field that was willing to hire women who had not been at the top of their classes at one of the Ivys. Now, of course, I can give people the impression that I was just well prepared for what the future would bring, if I care to do so, which I usually don't."

"Is that why you're here? You're preparing the Spinozas' bankruptcy?" Kathleen asked.

"No. I refinanced my house and rented it out. I needed a place to live temporarily, and Ralph is in no position to refuse me the use of their very luxurious guest suite."

"Why not?"

"The whole place is going to be mine any day now. I cosigned the mortgage on this house. They're going to lose it soon, and I'll be living in the master bedroom suite." She looked around. "It's even nicer than this. It has a dressing room and a whirlpool in the bath." She looked back up at the women. "I always tell people that they should never be the second signature on a loan unless they want to own the property. Loans that need a second signature are more than likely to fail."

"How did you happen to end up in this situation?" Susan asked. She knew that if she and her husband needed money, they certainly wouldn't go to a casual friend.

"Ralph asked Bob to cosign the loan he took out to buy this house."

"That was about seven or eight years ago, wasn't it?" Susan asked. "They lived over on the other side of town before that, didn't they?"

"Sure did. Bob went over the whole deal and knew immediately that they would have to be awfully lucky to keep up the payments. Bob didn't want to do it, but I saw that we'd end up with a bargain when the whole deal fell apart. So I signed the note. I have some money of my own, and I was beginning to make a decent living at that point. The bank wasn't thrilled with the prospect, but the president of that institution was cochairing some sort of fund-raising project for the local Little League, and he didn't want to turn Ralph down. Besides, if Ralph had been as smart as he thought he was, he wouldn't have gotten in this position.

There's one consolation, though. Their kids will be able to get scholarships to college now."

"I was wondering about that!" Susan exclaimed. "It surprised me that their oldest boy was going to college on a scholarship."

"Well, now you know."

"Where are your children these days?" Susan asked, remembering the young baseball players.

"Boarding school. Bob and I were not doing very well raising them, and they were happy to go. Both boys love sports, and Bob did some research and discovered a school with everything from crew to horseback riding.

"Does this have something to do with Horace Harvey's murder that I've missed?" Shirley asked.

"Probably not," Susan asked. "Detective Malarkey gave me a list of questions, and in fact, he was interested in whether or not you and Ralph were having an affair."

"I assume you've heard about Bob and Olive already?"

"It was mentioned when we were downstairs," Susan admitted.

"But there was some indication that Detective Malarkey thought that you and Ralph . . . ?" Kathleen asked gently.

"Had an affair. We did. It was duller than dull, and I ended it after about two months."

It took a few minutes for Susan and Kathleen to think of something to say after that. Finally Susan spoke. "What could cause Detective Malarkey to think that any of this has anything to do with the murder?"

"You're asking me?"

"Well, we sure don't know," Kathleen admitted.

"Bob and Ralph were both at the Inn Thursday night. I assume that's where he was murdered?"

"Yes."

"Olive and I were both in the city."

"You can prove that?"

"Oh, yes. We were on a walking tour of the herb shops of Chinatown. There were twenty people on the tour with us. I'm sure someone will be able to identify us. So it looks like only our husbands are suspects."

"Actually, they were the only ones we were considering," Susan admitted.

"Well, you can take your choice as far as I'm concerned. They're both a couple of losers. And if you arrest one, you may as well arrest the other, because without their competition, they're both dead."

"It really means that much to them?" Kathleen asked, disbelieving.

"Hard to believe, isn't it? And I'm telling the truth. Ralph is going to lose everything—his house, his cars, every dime in his pocket—and he spent most of last week worrying that Horace Harvey was going to leave his money to Q.U.I.E.T. instead of H.O.P.E. And Bob is just as bad. Ralph is always telling people that Q.U.I.E.T. was formed just to compete with H.O.P.E.—and he's right. Bob and I were still together then, and when Ralph asked him to join H.O.P.E., he went crazy. He claimed that he couldn't believe that Ralph was going to encourage more industry in Hancock, but the reality is that he could not stand the thought of Ralph being even more important. So he called all his friends and suggested that it was time to form Q.U.I.E.T."

"You're kidding."

"I'm not. Remember all those junior high school cliques that would form, dissolve, and re-form again in the 'I'm your friend, we both hate him' mode? Well, that's what all this is about."

Kathleen had been thinking. "If Horace Harvey had left all his money to H.O.P.E., would it have been possible for Ralph to get his hands on it?"

"Not a chance. We're in the middle of filing for bankruptcy. Every bit of the Spinozas' money and assets has been listed and accounted for. There is no way that any of the Harvey estate could have been skimmed off to solve Ralph and Olive's problems. If that's what you're looking at, you're going to have to look in another direction."

But Kathleen had another thought. "You grew up in Hancock. Did you know Horace Harvey before this?"

"I never met the man."

When they talked it over later, they couldn't decide whether or not Shirley Arnold had been lying.

SIXTEEN

It was going to be a long drive.

Usually the trip from Hancock, Connecticut, to Boston, Massachusetts, took between two and three hours, depending on weather and traffic conditions; at least that's what AAA reported. But AAA had not taken an angry teenager into account. Susan was beginning to think that she had personally discovered the meaning of eternity.

The day hadn't started well. Chrissy had responded to Susan's offer of breakfast with outrage. ("Don't you remember anything? I'm on a diet!") The dry cleaner had not finished Chrissy's coat, and Susan had objected to the look her daughter gave the innocent worker who reported that fact. Susan had been too busy to fill the car with gas the night before, giving her daughter a prime opportunity to comment on her mother's lack of organization. And before they had passed the boundaries of her own small town, Susan was tired of hearing what Chrissy's young man thought about anything and everything.

"Are we supposed to turn off on exit nineteen or twenty?" Susan asked her reluctant navigator.

"It's twenty," Chrissy said, finger on the map. "You're not going to go on the campus tour with me, are you?"

Susan opened her mouth and then closed it again. How could she put this tactfully? "I was planning to," she admitted quietly. "What else would I do?"

"Mother. You are trying to keep me a child. I'm going to be living on my own as an adult in just one year. I know this is going to be hard for you to adjust to, but I think you should start working on it now. I don't need you to follow me around all day."

Susan would have been furious if she hadn't realized that her daughter was trying as hard as she was to keep the conversation calm and quiet. "I suppose I can always meet you somewhere. . . ." she began.

"You could shop. Boston has wonderful stores," Chrissy leapt in enthusiastically.

"But, Chrissy, I didn't come here to shop. I . . ." Susan stopped herself before she regretted what she was going to say. "Listen, I do have some things to do today, but we're going to have to figure out where we'll meet, so why don't you let me go with you on the campus tour and then you can go off and we'll figure out where to meet later in the day."

"I knew you were going to butt in."

Susan rolled her eyes a few times before she returned her attention to the road. The dog book was in her purse, and she considered asking her daughter to read the notes Kathleen had written in the back. If she wasn't going to make any progress in family relationships, maybe she could start making some sense of the clues. "There's a book of dog names in my purse," she began.

"Good idea. Chad keeps calling her Scuzzy. That poor little puppy. I can't stand it."

"Do you have any other ideas?"

"Lady Jane. Or Colette or George . . ."

"For a female?"

"After George Sand, Mother."

"Of course." How could she be so stupid?

"Or maybe Gertrude . . ."

Gertrude? That beautiful fluffy puppy? Gertrude?

"For Gertrude Stein, of course," her daughter continued. "Or . . . I've got the perfect name: Alice B. Toklas!"

Come, Alice B. Toklas. Sit, Alice B. Toklas. Stay, Alice B. Toklas. Stop wetting on the floor, Alice B. Toklas. "Well, it's an idea," was all Susan said aloud.

It was going to be a very long drive.

* * *

"We have fish stew, oyster stew, clam chowder. Biscuits. Strawberry shortcake with whipped cream and pies."

Susan ordered, mentally thanking the registrar at the college who had recommended this tiny luncheonette. A light rain had started falling as they left the car in the visitors' lot, turning almost immediately into sleet, and Susan's feet were soaked and freezing. She looked at her watch. She was meeting her daughter for dinner in six hours, plenty of time to buy some warm boots as well as do some elementary research into Horace Harvey's background. The perky waitress returned, putting a large bowl of oyster stew in front of her, crackers and fluffy biscuits on plates at her side.

"What would you like to drink?"

"Hot tea. And would you happen to have a phone book around that I could look at for a few minutes?"

"I'll check and I'll be right back with your tea."

Susan was buttering a biscuit after tasting some of the best oyster stew she'd ever had when the girl returned.

"Here's your tea. You didn't say whether you wanted lemon or milk, so I brought both. And here are the phone books: yellow pages and white. You didn't say which you wanted, so—"

"So you brought both. Thank you so much," Susan said, pulling the large volumes within reach.

"Well, I'll leave you to your meal. Just wave if you want anything else."

"I will." Susan opened the phone book to the *H*s and began to search for Horace Harvey's past. Fifteen minutes later, she had finished her lunch and filled two more pages (left blank in the back of the puppy book for unspecified reasons) with phone numbers and addresses.

"Lemon meringue, blueberry, or sour cherry pie."

Susan resisted an urge to order a slice of each and, choosing lemon meringue, asked if there was a map of the city available.

"I don't think so, but there's a bookstore next door. They might sell them."

"Would you mind if I just ran over and checked and then had dessert when I came back?"

"No problem. The weather's so lousy that we're not going to be busy today. I'll save your seat; you go on."

The bookstore was a large one, but a salesperson as helpful as her waitress had been guided her to the right section, and Susan quickly found what she was looking for. She was paying for her purchase when she glanced up and saw a man who looked remarkably like Charles from the Hancock Inn get into a black Porsche and drive away. She returned to the small luncheonette with a smile on her face. Jed said that she was always imagining that she saw people she knew; he would be amused when she told him about this.

Susan ate her dessert and planned her afternoon. She marked the map with the location of Horace Harvey's home. She decided to start there, walking around the neighborhood if it was at all possible. Then she paid her bill, left a very generous tip, and headed back to her car. Everything would have been fine if only the people who laid out the city of Boston hadn't been quite so fond of one-way streets.

Horace Harvey had lived on Beacon Hill in an imposing brownstone house. The neighborhood, an elegant mixture of classy businesses and homes, cheered Susan. She actually found a place to park on the street and, deciding that she had nothing to lose, walked up the granite steps to the dead man's front door.

The woman who opened the door looked like Susan's idea of Mrs. Danvers from *Rebecca*. Except that Mrs. Danvers would never have worn a hot pink apron printed with the words BOSTON'S BUSY BABES in dark green italic. She might, however, have waved her dust mop at Susan and ordered her to come in.

"I thought you would never get here," the woman continued, turning and striding down the dark, maroon-carpeted hall. "Look at this place. It's not a rich man's house, it's what some deranged Hollywood director thought a rich man should live in sometime back around the turn of the century. What a dump."

Susan thanked her lucky stars, shut up, and followed, craning her neck around to see as much as she could see before she was kicked out. She trotted after the other woman into an equally dark wood-paneled library with deep red leather club chairs on either side of a massive mahogany partner's desk. Heavy fringed green velvet curtains hung at the windows, eliminating any chance beam of daylight.

"Well, there it is," the Mrs. Danvers look-alike announced, pointing her dust mop at a large safe sitting on the Oriental carpet. "Get to work."

"I . . . I have to get something from the kitchen," Susan said, thinking quickly.

"Thought it was a little strange that you weren't carrying a bag of tools. But we women can do almost anything with a hairpin and some kitchen knives, can't we? Even open a safe. Kitchen's right down the hall we were just in."

Susan hurried back into the hall. Open the safe? Who did this woman think she was? She followed the directions toward the rear of the house and, opening a green baize door, found herself in a large white-tiled kitchen, equipped with double ovens, multiple sinks, well-stocked glass-doored cupboards, and enough cutlery and crockery to feed dozens of people. The only sign of use was open cans, jars, and boxes around a small microwave oven on a scrubbed pine table. She looked around until she discovered what she was searching for: a narrow stairway leading from the kitchen.

Susan hurried up the stairs, knowing that there was a limited amount of time before someone came to find out what was taking her so long. What she found at the top of the stairs amazed her. For a second, she thought that all the furniture had been moved out. She wandered from room to room, finding them empty except for elaborate, old-fashioned window treatments, but then she discovered that one room had been furnished. The windows, like those in the rest of the house, were draped with velvet and tied back with huge satin tassels, but the room was furnished with a hideous fifties-style light maple bedroom suite.

Susan opened dresser drawers and closet doors, and discovered an extensive wardrobe of conservative business suits, shirts, shoes, and all the accessories. The room held no books, a few copies of current business magazines and newspapers, and nothing out of the ordinary—except for the cabinet across from the bed, which contained a television, VCR, and shelves of explicit heterosexual videotapes. Susan sighed. No passport. No bank records. Well, with a large library like the one downstairs, he probably had other places to keep such things.

And it was time for her to begin her career as a safe breaker. She trotted down the stairs, picking up a nutmeat pick and two knives as she passed through the kitchen, and returned to the library.

"Took you long enough, didn't it? Take a nice look around? I spent some time exploring myself," the cleaning woman admitted before Susan could protest. "Well, I'll just move out of the way and let you get to work."

Both women looked down at the large safe. Susan bit her lip and knelt down on the floor before it. Well, might as well give it the old college try. She spun the dial a few times and watched as the door slowly fell open.

"Well, look at that. You're more competent than you look, aren't you?"

Susan shut her mouth; no point in admitting her surprise.

"So aren't you going to take it?"

"Excuse me?"

"I thought you were supposed to open the safe and remove the contents to the officers down at your bank. Least that's what I was told."

Nothing ventured, nothing gained. Susan peered into the spacious interior, made even more spacious by the fact that it was completely empty.

"Well, will you look at that?"

Susan looked. And then she looked again. And then she decided that it was time to leave. She stood up and smiled at Mrs. Danvers. "I guess I'd better be going."

"No, you stay right here. I'm not going to take the blame for stealing that stuff."

"What stuff?" Susan asked quickly.

"Why, whatever stuff was in there. Stands to reason that people have safes to put things in. Why else lock them up?"

"It wasn't locked," Susan protested.

"Well, I noticed that fact myself, but no one else knows, do they now?"

"The person who unlocked it and stole the contents knows it."

The other woman peered around the room. "Well, it looks to me like no one's here but us chickens. Now, what are we going to do?"

Susan got the impression that the other woman had an idea and was waiting for Susan to ask. Susan was, in fact, willing to plead for any solution to this problem. "Maybe you have some thoughts on this subject?" she asked quietly.

"You're not from the bank, are you?"

"No. I didn't actually say that I was," Susan added, knowing that it was a technical quibble. "But I did let you believe it, and I shouldn't have," she admitted.

"You certainly did." Mrs. Danvers could not possibly have looked more intimidating. "Now, I have an idea about what we should do."

"Yes?" Susan was prepared for a long, convoluted solution to this problem.

"I think we should walk ourselves out of this house and never walk back in. I know you were here and you know I was here, but we don't really know each other, now, do we? So let's just leave and pretend this never happened."

Susan started to agree as the tall, thin, pink back of the other woman vanished down the hall. Without pausing, she grabbed her purse and headed in the opposite direction to the front door. There were narrow-paned windows on either side of the heavy door, and she noticed a black Porsche zip by as she left the house.

But it couldn't be, she reminded herself, walking down the street. She had spied a mom-and-pop grocery on the corner, and she planned to stop in and see if anyone there knew Horace Harvey. The precipitation had ended, but she was still slopping through over an inch of slush. She entered the charming old-fashioned facade on the corner and discovered that Mom and Pop were more likely to be referred to as Mother and Father, and that their clients' needs were more likely to be endive and fresh raspberries than toilet paper and canned spinach. The question was, did they know and remember Horace Harvey? She fumbled around in her purse for the photograph she had ripped from the newspaper in Martha Trumbull's hospital room.

"I wonder if you could help me?" she asked the woman standing by the cash register.

"Of course. What would you like?"

"I need some help," Susan said, suddenly realizing that she didn't know how to approach this problem. Why should people who didn't know her answer her questions? "I . . . I'm looking for information about this man." She held out the photograph. "He lived in a house just down the street."

"I think maybe I've seen him."

The man left the tower of imported sweets that he had been arranging and joined them, taking the photograph that Susan offered. "Sure," he said, returning the picture, "that's the man that cheated all those people. Humphrey or Harvey or something. Sure. He's lived in this neighborhood for a few years. At least, ever since we've owned this store. He's not a good customer, though. He comes in once in a while and buys a six-pack of domestic beer—light—or some canned tuna. It's not the type of trade that we're accustomed to or that carries a high profit margin."

"Why do you call him the man that cheated all those people?"

The couple exchanged looks, apparently puzzled about whether or not to reply, then the woman shrugged. "It's not as though he's going to be coming back in here, is it?"

"Nope. He'll be dead if any of his investment partners catch up with him," the man agreed.

Susan, who had been about to explain that Horace Harvey was dead, decided to shut up and listen.

"We just know what we read in the papers," he started slowly.

"What do the papers say?"

"They say that he had invested in a lot of businesses, successful businesses apparently.

"But there is no doubt at all that he did not share what was very considerable wealth, and he didn't make all that money sitting alone in a room, he made the money from a business that a lot of people contributed to. It's like I decided to sell this store, leave, and ignore all the work that you've done for years."

"Sure. If you can sell this place for millions, I won't mind a bit. We'll just retire to an island down in the Caribbean where it's warm and dry." His wife glanced at the gray sleet that was beginning to fall again outside their well-lit windows. "Of course, he didn't have a partner he was married to, did he?"

"He wasn't married, was he?" Susan asked.

"Nope. Never came in here with anyone either. We have a small catering business. Mostly salads, cassoulet, desserts, things like that. A lot of people in the neighborhood come to us when they're entertaining. He never did that I remember."

"I'm sure he didn't," the woman confirmed. "And I usually run that part of the business, so I'd be the one to know."

"Of course, a single businessman might do all his entertaining in restaurants—that wouldn't be all that unusual."

"Did he ever stop and chat? Just to pass the time of day?" Susan asked.

The man shook his head. "Nope. Most of the neighborhood people do, of course. He was kind of unusual like that."

"Did you get the impression that he was being a snob or something like that?"

"No. More like he was in a rush."

"That's true," his wife added. "He was always in a hurry. If he bought a paper or a magazine—always business magazines or *Barron's*, nothing fun—he'd open it and start to read while we were making change. And he was very impatient about waiting in line. It was okay if the people ahead of him were making purchases, but if they were just passing the time, chatting and the like, he'd jingle change in his pocket or clear his throat loudly. You know, to let everyone know that he was here and waiting."

"Sort of obnoxious," Susan said.

"We try not to criticize customers," the man said, "but since you said it . . ."

"Very obnoxious," his wife concluded.

The owners of the grocery shop had suggested that Susan try talking with the people at the dry cleaners around the corner; they had noticed Horace Harvey carrying shirt boxes from there when he came in. Susan walked through the door of the place claiming to be a French dry cleaner with the photograph in her hand. She only hoped that these people were as obliging as their business neighbors.

"May I help you?" A good-looking young man appeared from the rows and rows of plastic-shrouded clothing.

"I'm looking for some information," Susan began her spiel.

"We have a book for lost and problem clothing. . . ."

"No. I don't have a problem like that. Thank you. I was wondering if you could tell me something about a customer of yours. His name's Horace Harvey. I have a photograph of him," she added, passing it across the counter.

He looked at the picture and then up at Susan. "I think you need to talk to my boss," he said, turning and vanishing back into the racks of clean clothing.

Susan glanced around the immaculate shop, wondering at his reaction. Maybe she had found someone who could really help her with information about the dead man. So far, she seemed to only be adding questions.

The man who appeared in place of his employee didn't look like he was anxious to help her. In fact, he looked furious.

"What do you have to do with Horace Harvey?" he asked without preamble, waving her newspaper clipping in his hand.

Susan was startled. "I . . . I've never even met him," she protested.

"Then why are you coming in here asking me about him? Just what do you know about him and me?"

"Nothing. Really." Susan spoke quickly. She got the feeling that he would like to throw her out the door. "I know that he lived near here, and I was talking with the people that own the little grocery store on the corner. . . ."

"Philip and Frieda," he supplied their names.

"Yes," Susan agreed to establish her credentials. "Philip and Frieda. They told me that he had his laundry done here. I just thought you might be able to tell me something about him."

"Who are you? Why do you want to know?"

Susan had been hoping no one would ask. This wasn't, after all, Hancock, Connecticut, where everyone knew that helping the police investigate murders was just something she did. In Boston she was just another person asking personal questions—and apparently the news of the murder had not traveled this far north. "I'm investigating him," she said with as much courage as she could muster.

"Why?"

Susan decided she had nothing to lose by being honest. "He was going to leave money . . . a lot of money . . . to an organization in the town I come from in Connecticut. Then he was—"

"You'll never get it."

"Excuse me?"

"You'll never get a penny from that man. He'll never give a penny away. I can tell you that."

"The money wasn't coming to me," Susan said. "But how do you know that?"

"I'm not going to discuss that. I just know."

"He did come here for his dry cleaning," Susan said, hoping to get the conversation onto less emotional topics.

"Sure did. That man spent money on clothing. Maybe if you were Georgio Armani or an importer of English clothing, you'd get money from that man, but not for anything else. He spent his money on himself. And that's all I'm saying." He tossed the clipping on the counter. "I have work to do," he added, and vanished to the rear of the shop.

The young man who had helped her initially stuck his head out from between some brightly colored sweaters draped across heavy hangers, and put his finger to his lips. He didn't say anything until a loud noise indicated a door being slammed.

"He really hates that man," he said quietly.

"Do you know why?"

"Not really. I know it has something to do with his daughter—she worked for a company that Mr. Harvey invested in. Or I should say that she worked for a company before Mr. Harvey invested in it—he fired her. But that was a few months ago, before I came here."

"Then how do you know about it?"

"Mr. Harvey came in here with his cleaning right after I started working, and I was ordered to throw him out."

"And did you?"

"I asked him to leave. I'm in college right now, getting my M.S.W. I don't know anything about throwing people out."

"How did he take it?"

"Strange. He kind of smiled and said that it didn't matter. That there were a lot of cleaners. I thought it was an inappropriate response, to be honest."

"Do you know anyplace else around, any other store, that he might have patronized?"

"You've tried the bar around the corner? Ben's? You should go there. He stopped in most nights on his way home from work."

Susan was thrilled. "Around which corner?" she asked, and immediately followed his directions to an old-fashioned bar that seemed, from the outside, to have completely escaped gentrification.

Once inside, she decided that the place had escaped more than gentrification. It seemed to have avoided cleaning altogether. St. Patrick's Day decorations, so faded that they were no longer green, hung on top of metallic cardboard wishing all the customers a Merry Christmas and Happy New Year. The walls over the booths were hung with photographs of people whose reason for fame had long been forgotten. There was a long, fly-specked mirror over the chipped and sticky bar. In it she saw the reflection of Charles from the Inn. He was sitting in the rear of the room nursing a drink in a filthy, chipped glass.

SEVENTEEN

Susan had promised to meet Chrissy for dinner at a famous seafood restaurant that, to her surprise, the girl herself had chosen. She was driving around and around in smaller and smaller concentric circles trying to arrive at the place. She had left the bar without talking to anyone and continued on across town to find a willing helper on the staff of *The Boston Globe*, and she had a manila envelope stuffed with copies of clippings about Horace Harvey and his business interests. She had hoped to find the time to look at them before dinner. Now she was wondering if she was ever going to get dinner.

Finally she noticed an alley, one-way, of course, but a different way, and she slipped her car between two that had been illegally parked and headed in what she hoped was the right direction. Surprisingly enough, the restaurant's bright lights greeted her at the end of her path. She slipped her Jeep into a parking space designed for a compact and leapt out. The murder and Charles forgotten, she was a mother again, and she only hoped that Chrissy had had a successful day.

It was early, but the restaurant was crowded, and it took Susan a while to find her daughter. Chrissy was sitting alone in a large booth, capturing the complete attention of two young waiters, much to the annoyance or amusement, depending upon the priorities and personalities, of nearby diners. Susan, seeing that the girl was happy, hurried over to join her.

"Hi. Sorry I'm so late. I got into some terrible traffic."

"Hello, Mother."

Susan looked over her shoulder to see who was behind her. Chrissy had never spoken so formally before. She found no one, so, smiling, she returned her daughter's greeting. "Hi."

"I ordered some wine," Chrissy announced.

Susan opened her eyes wide, but sat down without saying a word.

"I'll just see how your order is coming along," one of the young men offered.

"Yes, I suppose we must get back to work," his companion admitted, reluctant to depart.

"Thank you." Susan dismissed them both and turned to her daughter. "How was your day? Did you like the schools?"

"I don't think it's actually a question of liking or not liking. I'm just trying to find the place where I'll fit in the best. It's a matter of the perfect match."

Susan didn't trust herself to answer that. "How did someone your age end up ordering wine?" she asked.

Chrissy shrugged. "They gave me the menu. I ordered."

Susan decided to change the subject. "Tell me about the schools. Weren't you going to meet someone from Hancock this afternoon?"

"Yes. Dorie. Remember how dorky she used to be?"

"I always thought she was a very sweet child," Susan said, damning the poor girl.

Chrissy just rolled her eyes. "She has become totally cool. Remember how she had those thick, ugly glasses? Well, she's wearing emerald green contact lenses and she had this matching stripe put in her hair. And she's thinking of getting a little green lizard tattoo put right under her left eye."

There was nothing Susan could say that wouldn't cause her daughter either to object or to interpret it as permission to go out and cover her body with multicolored tattoos, so she was relieved when the wine arrived at their table. "An entire bottle?" she asked.

"I thought we'd both had a hard day and would enjoy it."

Susan looked at the label and blinked. "I think this is a little expensive for us," she said to the waiter, thankful that it hadn't been opened. "Why don't you take it back and I'll have a Laiphroing and she'll have a Coke."

Chrissy glared at her mother and sank into an angry silence that threatened to last throughout their meal. Susan decided there was nothing to do but ignore her. That was easier to accomplish after her drink arrived and the waiter had handed out menus to hide behind.

"I had oyster stew for lunch, so I suppose I shouldn't have oysters for dinner."

Chrissy didn't comment on her mother's statement.

"I think I'll have the broiled scallops . . . or maybe fried clams. . . ."

Again, no response. It was going to be a long meal. But a good one, Susan decided. She ordered a cup of clam chowder, broiled scallops, spinach, and spoon bread. She was hungry, and it was going to be an even longer drive home if Chrissy refused to speak the entire trip. She sipped her Scotch. "I found out some interesting things today," she said blandly. She didn't expect her daughter to find them equally interesting, but she sure didn't want to spend the rest of the day with a silent, sulky teenager. "About Horace Harvey," she added, aware of the fact that Chrissy wasn't listening.

"Shh!"

Susan suppressed a grin, realizing that her daughter was eavesdropping on one of the tables behind them. "I—" she began.

"Shh! Someone's drunk back there." Chrissy insisted on her mother's silence. "He's really being obnoxious."

Susan wasn't thrilled about her daughter's interest, but she sat back and finished her drink. She was thinking that obnoxious drunks weren't as much a novelty to her as to her daughter when her clam chowder arrived.

Chrissy had ordered soup also and gave up eavesdropping in order to direct her full attention to crumbling crackers into the bowl. But after a few minutes, it was obvious that no one in the restaurant was going to be allowed to ignore the loud patron. The voice rose in the air around them.

"I've had better than this in hotel dining rooms. I don't know what he thinks he's trying to sell me." The voice was deep and hissing.

Susan noticed that most of the waiters and waitresses were positioning themselves in places where they could at least get a peek at the confrontational guest.

The voice continued, only getting louder. "What precisely is he trying to pull? I've had years and years of experience; I'm way beyond being fooled by amateurs."

The last word came out more like "armchairs" than "amateurs," and Susan glanced at her daughter. There was a puzzled look on the girl's face. "He sounds like someone we know," Chrissy whispered loudly to her mother after checking around to make sure they weren't going to be overheard.

Susan took another sip of the soup. Canned clams, and in Boston at that. If the drunk was a disgruntled gourmet, she couldn't fault his taste even if he chose to express it rather loudly.

"Let's just ignore him and eat our dinner," she suggested to her daughter.

Who was once again pretending that Susan didn't exist. Chrissy was so intent on eavesdropping that she ignored her dinner, or maybe, Susan thought, this was just another manifestation of her diet. "This is ridiculous, Chrissy," she began. "We have to finish this meal. We have a long drive ahead of us—"

"Sh."

"Chrissy!"

"Sh! He's talking about Hancock!" the girl whispered loudly.

"That's not possible," her mother insisted.

"I heard him say that back in Hancock, he's well known for his taste."

"Sure. Whatever you say. Now, would you please eat

your meal, so we can start home? Who knows what the roads are like after all the sleet that's been falling today?"

"Mother. Sh! I can't hear!"

Susan decided that she had had enough. She tossed her napkin onto the table and stood up. "Come with me," she ordered her daughter.

"What?"

"Come with me. We'll see just what's going on."

"Mother, what sort of idea is that?"

Susan ignored her daughter's obvious embarrassment and walked around the barrier that divided the two areas of the dining room. And for the second time that day, she discovered the maître d' from the Hancock Inn completely, totally, and absolutely drunk.

"Charles!"

A tall man who had been standing nearby hurried over at the word. "Madam, do you know this man?"

"I . . . Sort of," Susan admitted. Charles was obviously very drunk, but the fact that his tie was halfway in the casserole before him shocked her almost more than his inebriated state. "He comes from my hometown," she explained, "but we're not what you would call close friends."

Charles looked up at the sound of her voice. "Mrs. Henshaw. How good to see you. I think I'm going to disgrace myself and throw up."

"Mother!" Sounds of mortified embarrassment indicated her daughter's presence.

Charles lurched away from the table toward, Susan assumed, the men's room.

"We cannot tolerate this type of behavior," the man who had spoken before hinted broadly. "I would hate to have to call the police."

"I'm sure that won't be necessary," Susan assured him. "Chrissy, go get our coats. We had better take Charles home."

"We'll find your clothing and that of the gentleman. Everything will be at the door with your checks."

"We haven't even seen our food yet," Susan protested.

"It's been prepared. This unexpected turn of events is certainly not our fault."

"Then perhaps you will send one of your young men into the rest room to get our ... our friend," Susan suggested angrily.

"That won't be necessary. Your friend is currently using the ladies' room."

It had taken almost half an hour to pay both bills, collect their coats, and inspire Charles to remember exactly where he left his car. After circling the neighborhood for the underground garage where the black Porsche had been left, they agreed that Susan would drive Charles home in his car, and Chrissy would follow, driving her mother's vehicle. Luckily the rain and sleet had stopped, and the road, though wet, was no longer slippery.

Susan looked into her rearview mirror, relieved to see her daughter behind them as she traveled down the ramp to Interstate 95. Charles was dozing in the seat next to her. As she glanced in his direction, he opened one eye.

"Hi. How are you feeling?"

"Lousy. Where are we going?"

"Back to Hancock. I hope you didn't have more to do in Boston," she added, realizing for the first time just how much she had assumed when she collected him back at the restaurant.

"No. Hancock is where I belong."

They resumed their uncomfortable silence.

"I hope you don't mind me driving your car," Susan said after a while.

"No. You didn't drive to Boston, I gather."

"I did. Chrissy is driving my car. She's back there." Susan checked out the statement in the Porsche's rearview mirror.

"You brought your daughter? Are you trying to turn that sweet child into a junior detective?"

"It's been a long time since you've seen my daughter, hasn't it?" Susan answered, stepping on the brake to avoid a large tractor trailer that seemed determined to crush them.

"And what are you talking about? I was in Boston so she could visit some colleges that she might be interested in attending the year after next."

"Oh."

" 'Oh'?" Susan took her eyes off the truck and glanced at her passenger. "What exactly did you think I was doing in Boston?"

"Investigating a murder. Either following me or tracking down the nefarious past of Horace Harvey, to be exact," he answered, staring straight ahead at the road.

Susan had no idea how to reply; she said the first thing that came into her head. "What's your last name?"

"My name is Cornelius Jones. I use Charles for obvious reasons." He spoke slowly and quietly.

" 'Obvious reasons'?" Susan was beginning to feel like a parrot.

"It's classier, don't you think?"

She certainly wasn't going to argue with that. "Then it's just your professional name."

"Exactly." He bent his lips into what could almost be called a smile. "Like Madonna or Cher."

"Did your employer insist on it?"

"Pardon?" Some of the old Charles of the Inn formality returned.

"Did the person who owns the Inn insist that you be known only as Charles—" Light dawned. "You own the Inn!"

"Along with a silent partner."

"Why do you keep it a secret?"

He paused for a few moments before answering. "To be completely accurate, I don't. If anyone were to ask who owns the Inn, I tell them."

"Has anyone?"

"Only one or two people from town who were interested in the Inn as an investment. Mr. Spinoza was interested last year. And maybe one or two others since I remodeled. But I'm not in any position to add partners, even it I wanted to, which I don't."

"Then you've owned the Inn for a long time?"

"About twelve years. I bought it when it was just a rather ordinary inn, one of many colonial inns in Connecticut, and I've turned it into a showplace."

Susan agreed, but she didn't say anything, and he continued.

"I had very little extra money when I began. I spent where it made sense: I hired one of the best chefs from C.I.A., found professional waiters and waitresses, invested in the beginnings of a credible wine cellar. There was no money left for a classy maître d'. Most of the inns like mine have women greeters wearing hideous colonial costumes. I wanted to avoid that particular image, but I couldn't afford what I wanted. So after trying two or three people unsuccessfully, I took over the job myself. And it's worked. I can oversee everything, greet guests, and set a certain tone for the Inn. And, I must admit, I find that I enjoy it."

"To many people, you *are* the Inn, Charles."

"Thank you," he answered simply. "I appreciate you saying that. I . . . I came very close to making a complete mess of my life," he said quietly. "I'm an alcoholic, as you may have guessed today, and my life was completely out of control for years. But I stopped drinking, completed a degree in hotel and restaurant management, came to Connecticut, found the Inn and the money to finance it, and everything was fine until recently."

"What happened recently? Or do you mean the murder?"

"It began with the burglary, actually. You see, I fall off the wagon sometimes—rarely, though, only twice in the past five years until these last few weeks—and I had done so the night we were burgled. Apparently I was passed out in the office upstairs while the cash register was broken into in the bar."

"Really?"

"Yes. If I hadn't passed out, I would have been long gone, the alarm system would have been set, and whoever broke in would have been caught before they actually got inside. Unfortunately, I started drinking after the main dinner rush, continued through closing up, and wound up on the second floor unconscious when the window was broken and the Inn was robbed."

"But you weren't drinking the night of the murder," Susan said, hating, in this case, to pry.

"I'm afraid that I did have a few after everyone had left. It was very late by then—probably two or three o'clock in the morning."

Susan checked again for her daughter. "It was strange running into you tonight," she commented as casually as she could.

"Yes. It was," Charles agreed. He was silent a moment before continuing. "I came to Boston to check out a chef at that restaurant. I'm looking for someone to take over the lunchtime trade. The woman who is head chef on that shift now just told me that she's pregnant. Naturally I am not going to hire the person who prepared dinner tonight. I don't know how much of your meal you ate before coming to my rescue, but even completely drunk, I can tell a decent meal from a poor one."

"It wasn't very good," was all Susan said. She was, in fact, very hungry. And she couldn't decide whether or not to mention that she had seen Charles earlier in the day at the sleazy bar near Horace Harvey's house. If he didn't mention it himself, it didn't mean anything incriminating, she reminded herself. He might merely be embarrassed to admit how early in the day he had begun to drink. Except that he had apparently been very honest about his alcoholism, and why start to lie now, even if only by omission? "Did you come all the way to Boston just to eat a dinner prepared by a chef you might be interested in hiring?" she asked.

"I always eat more than one meal prepared by someone I'm thinking of hiring," was Charles's rather oblique answer.

"There's a rest area ahead," he continued. "I wonder if we might stop?"

"Of course," Susan answered eagerly. "I just hope Chrissy is paying attention and follows us." She flicked on the turn signal and was relieved to see her daughter follow her lead and change lanes.

It was easy to find a spot in the large lot in front of the fast-food chain that seemed to be their only option on the road. Chrissy pulled Susan's car up beside the Porsche, and all three of them headed for the brightly lit building.

"I'm starving," Chrissy whispered.

"I thought I'd head to the ladies' room while there's a chance," her mother replied, digging around in her large purse. "Here's a twenty. Get what you want and pick up a small black coffee in a large cup for me to take on the road. I'd hate to spill coffee all over that car."

Charles (and Susan knew she wasn't going to be able to think of him without using the name he had chosen for himself) had headed straight for the men's room, but he was waiting near the front door when Susan left the rest room. "Are you feeling better? Do you want to stop and get something to eat?"

"No. Nothing." He looked awful standing there in the bright light.

"Why don't I just see what's keeping Chrissy and meet you in the car?" Susan suggested.

Charles nodded, smiled his crooked smile, and pushed open the swinging door. Seven or eight rowdy children, apparently thinking that this was a courtesy designed expressly for their convenience, swarmed noisily into the building before he could make his escape. Susan headed off to find her daughter.

Chrissy was still in line, waiting to choose between French fries, hamburgers, hot dogs, and golden onion rings—all of which shared the distinction of being cooked at least twenty-four hours previously. She waved to her mother, the standard irritated look on her face. Susan slid through the line, explaining to everyone who would listen that she was joining her daughter, not cutting in.

"I was afraid you'd driven off without waiting for me to follow," Chrissy said by way of greeting.

"Why would you think that?" Susan was looking at the counters of food, realizing that she was very hungry.

"A black Porsche just drove by the window. I've been staring at that car for fifty miles; I'd know it anywhere."

"What! Oh, no! Come on!" Susan grabbed her daughter's arm.

"No. I'm starving. I haven't eaten all day. And if that was Charles, what good is it going to do anybody if you dash out of here after him? You're not going to catch up, are you? You'll just get back to Hancock a few minutes earlier, and he might not even be going there. For all you know, he turned around and headed straight back to Boston—or to San Francisco, for that matter. And we're both hungry."

Susan paused for a moment. "You're right. I wasn't thinking. Just let me make a few phone calls. Order me some dinner and we can at least take the time to sit down and eat."

"I'll look for a table near the phones," Chrissy agreed as Susan pushed her way out of line. She was glad she was never going to be forced to ask any of these people for a favor; she was not winning friends and influencing people today.

She did run out to the parking lot to assure herself that Charles had vanished before finding the phones and giving Kathleen a call. Kathleen was bathing her son, but she assured Susan that she would put the child to bed early, leave her husband in charge, and go over to the Inn to be there if Charles returned. Jed and Chad were in the city at a Mets game, but Susan left a short message on her own answering machine and hurried back to her daughter. Chrissy had actually found a nearby booth, and Susan slid in across from her and looked down at the meal awaiting her.

"Thanks." She picked up her coffee cup and tasted the bitter brew.

Chrissy noticed her frown. "There wasn't a lot of choice," she explained.

"I know. It was nice of you to get this for me."

"I thought the hot dogs looked safer than the hamburgers. Sometimes it's better to have a few preservatives, you know?"

"Definitely."

They ate their dinners in a companionable silence that was rare for them these days, and they were back on the road in less than half an hour. Chrissy had asked to drive, and Susan sat back in the passenger's seat and tried to appear calm. Her daughter, despite a tendency to trim the side mirrors from any car she drove, was really a very good driver, and Susan was sure that she would feel relaxed as her passenger in about ten or twenty years.

"I'm thinking about going into art therapy," Chrissy surprised her by speaking up.

"What an interesting idea." It was Susan's standard answer to either of her children's plans for their futures. It wasn't an inspired response, but it was safe.

"Yes. It's really almost impossible to make a living as an artist, and I think I'd like to do something that would give me contact with people." Chrissy was repeating something that her parents had been suggesting for a long time, and Susan held her breath waiting for the kick. And it came. "Of course, maybe I shouldn't even bother with a formal education. Four years is a long time to wait to start living real life."

Susan knew whose words she was hearing this time, and she was determined to shut up about it all. "Why did you miss lunch?" she asked, aiming for neutral ground.

"That's exactly what I mean. I was so busy looking at schools that I didn't even get time to eat lunch. And if I decide to go to college, it will be even worse. Artists shouldn't live like that. I should be sitting in a small bistro near the Bois de Boulogne and absorbing life, not driving down this dreadful, bourgeois ... What's going on?"

"It's okay," her mother cried out. "There's something wrong with the car. Just pull over to the shoulder of the road and put on your flashers. Slowly, don't skid in the slush. You're fine."

It took almost as long to say this as to do it, and, in fact, they actually were fine by the time Chrissy had stopped the car. "I don't know where the flashers are," she said, her voice trembling.

Susan wasn't sure that she did either. "I think . . ." She reached out and twisted a knob that she had always wondered about on the edge of the steering wheel. Happily, for her reputation in her daughter's eyes, it worked, and the gentle click, click of the system seemed to soothe them both.

"What are we going to do?" Chrissy asked.

"I don't know." Susan appreciated that she had been returned to her position of authority by this crisis.

"There's someone stopping. Do you think they want to help us?"

Susan, recognizing the underlying fear in her daughter's voice, opened the door and got out of the car to greet the person who would turn out to be either a good samaritan or evil incarnate.

"You ran out of gas?" Kathleen was sitting across from Susan in the bar of the Hancock Inn. Jed and Chad were still in the city, Chrissy had hurried from the car into the arms of her boyfriend, and Charles had not been seen. Susan was on her second Scotch.

"You don't have to rub it in," Susan insisted. "If that nice man hadn't stopped and helped us right away, who knows what might have happened? Of course, Chrissy is torn between blaming herself and being mad at me for not filling up when we got to Boston. What a day. I'm completely exhausted."

"Maybe you should go home to bed."

"I'd like to talk with Charles first."

"From what you've told me, you're not sure that he's planning to come back here tonight."

"He always locks up," Susan said.

"He's been doing things a little differently these days," Kathleen said. "And that might not be just because he's been drinking."

Susan leaned closer to her friend. "Do you think he had something to do with this murder?"

"You're asking if I think he's our murderer. And I think it's a serious possibility, don't you?"

"Of course not!"

"Susan, think about what you've just been telling me. He was in that bar near Horace Harvey's house—you don't really think that could just be a coincidence, do you?"

"I don't know that it isn't. And you don't know that it is," she added quickly. "Just because you want to prove that Tillie isn't the murderer, you jump on anyone else as a possible suspect."

"Susan, I'm not doing that. And you're not being real objective here either, are you? You said that Charles asked you if you were trying to turn your daughter into a junior investigator, didn't you? Why would he automatically think that you were in Boston looking into Horace Harvey's life unless that's what he was doing?"

Susan frowned, but she didn't have time to think of an appropriate answer. Their waitress had just put a note on the table between them. Susan reached out, picked it up, and read it, then looked up at Kathleen.

"He wants to see us in his office upstairs."

She didn't have to identify the writer.

EIGHTEEN

CHARLES STARTED HIS EXPLANATION BY APOLOGIZING FOR leaving Susan at the highway restaurant. "It wasn't what I was planning to do when I asked you to stop, I can assure you, but, of course, that's no excuse," he said very quietly.

"Why did you leave?" Kathleen was not gentle, and Susan tried to resist glaring at her friend.

"I didn't know what else to do. I didn't want to answer any questions, I didn't want to explain anything. I just wanted to get back in my car and forget everything that's happened in the past few weeks."

"So you left," Susan said, nodding.

"Yes. I left."

"And you came right back here?" Kathleen asked.

"Yes. I arrived here a few minutes before Mrs. Henshaw. I saw her drive in, as a matter of fact."

Susan didn't dare look at Kathleen. They both knew that Susan had eaten in the restaurant, that she had run out of gas, that it had taken her a lot of extra time to return home. The question, of course, was what had Charles done with all that extra time? She waited for Kathleen to speak, but when she did, the question was not the one she expected.

"Why did Susan see you near Horace Harvey's house earlier in the day? It couldn't possibly have been a coincidence that you chose that bar."

"It's time to explain, isn't it?" Charles asked sadly.

Kathleen wasn't going to allow for any possible misinterpretation of her answer. "Yes."

He surprised them both with the way he began. "I understand that you've been running around town and asking questions about Horace Harvey's past, about the time he spent growing up in Hancock. I teach a class in hospitality at the Senior Center one afternoon a week, and I went in to set up my equipment for this week's lecture (I'm doing a display of napkin folding and floral napkin rings—it's a little formal for my taste, but the elderly ladies love it), and everyone there was talking about it."

"No one seemed to know very much. Horace Harvey managed to grow up without making a very big impression on this town."

"Well, years later, he made a big impression on me."

"He's your backer in the Inn!" Susan guessed.

"Exactly."

"That's some coincidence," Kathleen muttered.

"It's no coincidence. I grew up in Hancock. He grew up in Hancock. . . ."

"But you're much younger," Susan protested.

"Not that much. Although I didn't know him, hadn't even heard of him until I was looking for money to open the Inn. Because of my background, I couldn't get money from conventional sources." He turned to Kathleen and explained about his drinking problem before continuing. "So a man at a bank in town mentioned a venture capitalist with money to invest and who believed in the future of Hancock. That's exactly how it was put to me—believed in the future of Hancock."

"And that was Horace Harvey?"

"Yes. I didn't actually meet him at that time. I had a broker negotiating for the purchase of the Inn from the family that had owned it for generations—literally. Horace Harvey did his research well, however. He even visited the Inn, and he was the person who suggested that the modernization should take place almost immediately after I gained possession."

"And he loaned you the money to make that possible, too?"

"Yes."

"So you owed him a considerable amount of money," Kathleen said slowly.

"Yes."

"That's why you let him take over the Inn last Thursday night on such short notice," Susan said, trying to connect all the small pieces of the story that were flying around.

"That's why I've let him do a lot of things," Charles answered bitterly.

"Like what?" Kathleen asked. "Has he tried to interfere in the way you've wanted to run the Inn? Things like that?"

"No. I've been completely autonomous in every way except financially. Horace Harvey didn't care about anything except the money, but the money, he cared about completely. And he got it coming and going."

"What do you mean?"

"He took a cut of everything. Every financial transaction went through him or a company that he had interests in; everything the Inn did, he got a piece of."

"Like what?" Susan asked, knowing that her knowledge of financial matters was infinitesimal.

"Like food, furniture, insurance. Everything! Let me explain. I think the first I realized what was going on was when I had to get insurance. I had to do that before I could actually hold a mortgage on the Inn. My financial agreement stipulates that I have fire insurance, theft, liability, accident, all the traditional things. What's different is that it stipulates that I purchase them through a specific insurance broker. . . ."

"One that Horace Harvey had an interest in?" Susan guessed.

"Exactly. And everything is like that. I buy all my alcohol from a supplier that he stipulated, the construction on the Inn was done by a company that he has an interest in—as well as the landscaping. He even picked out the plowing service that I use to keep the parking lots and the driveway clear in the winter."

"And this has something to do with why you were in Boston looking for a new chef. Horace Harvey had some control over who you hired?"

"No. Nothing to do with personnel, only businesses and corporations. Many of my employees are union—and I've encouraged that—and there was never any suggestion that he was involved in anything like skimming off the top of benefit programs or things like that. That would be illegal, and I've never gotten the feeling that he was doing anything absolutely illegal.

"No, I was using the fact that I need a new chef as an excuse to be in Boston today. I actually called to see if there was anyone there. When a woman answered, I said I was from Harvey's bank and that we were sending someone over to open his safe and collect his papers. Of course, I was drinking to get up my nerve, and I'm afraid the alcohol became more interesting than the papers. It was foolish, I know that. . . ."

"Go on."

"Yes, please," Susan urged more gently than her friend. She still didn't know who had actually opened and removed the contents of the safe.

"I had met with Mr. Harvey at his home once or twice. I was trying to get him to release me from my original agreement. . . ."

"Why?"

"Because it cost so much. Not just in interest on the original loan, but because I didn't have the option of looking around for the best deals when it came to everything else. I have, over the years, begun to understand the term 'highway robbery.' Every dollar that I must spend ends being a dollar fifty. And the fifty goes to that man."

"So why couldn't you just refinance?" Susan wondered.

"There's a prepayment penalty in my contract that makes it financially undesirable, to say the least."

"Is that all?" Kathleen asked.

Charles looked at the two women and didn't speak for a moment.

"Does it have something to do with your drinking?" Susan asked gently, hating the fact that they must continue to pry.

"Yes. I told you that I fell asleep here the night of the robbery."

Susan nodded.

"I did the same thing years ago, back when I was managing an inn. It was a small place in the foothills in Colorado. I was working there for the summer in college. I was interested in pursuing a career in restaurant management, but I was more interested in drinking. So one night after the last guest had gone, I sat down and started on a bottle of Scotch. A few hours later I woke up in the middle of a fire. The bar had a large fireplace that we kept going on cool summer evenings. I had fallen asleep without properly smothering the fire, and apparently a log had rolled out and caught the rug and the inn itself on fire. I got out, but the building was old and wood, and it burned to the ground before the firemen from the surrounding communities could control the blaze."

"Were you prosecuted?" Kathleen asked.

"No. I should have been, of course, but the owner was afraid that his insurance company wouldn't pay off the benefits if it looked like anything but an accident. There were people who knew it was my fault, of course, but it was a small town and it was kept hushed up."

"Not so hushed up that Horace Harvey couldn't find out about it years later," Kathleen guessed.

"Right. Horace Harvey had extraordinary sources. I couldn't get a standard mortgage because I was just out of school, had no real practical experience owning an inn, and I had more than a few DWI arrests and two convictions, but he found out about this fire in Colorado. He offered me the money that I wanted, but I had to accept his terms."

"Or else he wouldn't give you the money," Susan concluded.

"Or else he would make the fire public knowledge, and I would never be trusted by any investor in the entire world—or any insurance company for that matter. You can stop drinking, but you can't erase the past."

"You hated him," Kathleen said.

"I hated him. But I didn't kill him. But I can't prove it.

In fact, I think I may have been the last person to see him alive."

"Except for the murderer," Susan reminded him.

"Yes. Of course. Except for the murderer."

"Where was he when you saw him?" Kathleen asked.

"In the wine cellar. Where he was found."

"How long before he was discovered?" Susan asked.

"About ten, maybe fifteen minutes . . . Oh, I wasn't drinking then," he insisted, perhaps thinking that he saw skepticism on their faces.

"How did he happen to be down there?"

"He had asked me to meet him there. He said that he had something important to tell me."

"When was this?" Kathleen was trying to get her facts straight.

"He was in and out of the Inn an awful lot that Thursday. But I think he told me to meet him in the wine cellar at eight o'clock when he came in to have lunch—around noon."

"Why?"

"Why what?"

"Why did he want to meet you there? He must have given a reason."

"Not actually." Charles sighed and looked at Kathleen. "Let me think for a moment. It's obvious that you want me to be as accurate as possible."

"Definitely."

"It might help us a lot," Susan added. "Could you tell us everything you remember about that day?"

"No," Kathleen protested. "Tell us everything you remember about how you found out Horace Harvey was coming to town, how he contacted you about using the Inn for his meeting . . . how often you've seen him over the years since you borrowed the money from him, in fact."

Charles frowned at the desk before him and then, slowly, began his tale.

"I have seen Horace Harvey . . ." He paused. "I guess you could say infrequently over the years. Never more than once a year, sometimes less."

"And how long has this been going on?"

"Ten, eleven years." He continued when he saw that there were going to be no more questions. "As I was saying, usually I saw him less than once a year. I realized how successful the Inn was going to be about six years ago, and I went to see him once or twice after that, hoping he would allow me to pay off my mortgage and end the rest of my obligations to him. But after the first time, I knew that it was hopeless. I just didn't see how I could stop trying. And he came to see me a few times. I remember once he wanted to explain to me that I was going to need a large increase in my fire insurance because I had enclosed the porch—at his suggestion, I should add."

"Then he made good suggestions?" Susan asked.

"Always. He was a fine businessman. Except, of course, he wanted to keep most of the profits himself."

"Were his deals legal?" Susan asked the question she had been wondering about all evening.

"I doubt if people who had something to hide, probably something only quasi-legal, were going to worry about that," Kathleen said. "Right?"

Charles nodded. "I know that's true in my case."

"So go on. About last week."

"Well, Mr. Harvey came to the Inn on Sunday morning, for breakfast with some members of the chamber of commerce, I believe. I was . . . well, I was shocked to see him. That was when he chose to inform me that he was going to require full use of the Inn later in the week. He said that he'd call me with all the details."

"He said this in private?"

"No. He said it in front of his guests."

"So he didn't hide the fact that he had had previous contact with you."

Charles stopped and thought for a moment before answering. "He did actually. The mayor introduced us and he nodded then, but he didn't acknowledge that the introduction was unnecessary, and later he just announced his plans. If anyone who was with him thought anything, they probably assumed that he just treated everyone like that."

"But I understood that it was very unusual for the Inn to be turned over to a private party on a Thursday evening," Susan said, remembering the conversation she'd had with the waitress.

"Not unusual. Unheard-of. But, of course, I had no choice."

"Did the mayor or anyone else say anything about it?"

"No. I listened in to the conversation. I don't usually, of course, but I was so shocked to see Harvey. And seeing him with some of the most important people in Hancock . . . well, it worried me. I seated them in the booth at the rear of the room where it's possible to listen from the corner of the bar. Horace Harvey was telling everybody about his plan to leave money to a deserving group in Hancock. They were, naturally, thrilled. I don't think they were thinking about much else."

"So when did you see Harvey after that?"

Susan admired the way Kathleen stuck to the point.

"He called that night, right around the time I was closing the Inn, and explained that I should just . . . I believe his exact words were that I should follow his lead. And he hung up without another word."

Susan had the feeling that Charles was lying, but about what? "You did see him later in the week? Before Thursday night?"

"He came in Thursday at lunch and explained exactly what he wanted done that night, what he wanted the decorations to look like, what food and drink were to be served."

"Short notice," Susan commented.

"Yes. But, of course, he knew that I had no choice but to do exactly what he wanted."

"When did he set up the meeting in the wine cellar?" Kathleen asked.

"At that time. He ended the conversation by announcing that he wanted to see me in the wine cellar at eight o'clock that evening and that he would have something to tell me that I would find very interesting."

"That's all he said?" Susan asked.

"How did he know that the Inn even has a wine cellar?" Kathleen asked. "I've been going there for years, and I had no idea that there was an actual cellar."

"Horace Harvey knew every detail of the Inn. He had approved of every addition and every piece of the remodeling. He probably had a very good idea of exactly how many cases of Château Lafitte I had down there." Charles frowned.

"Did you see him between the time of his call and when he showed up in the wine cellar Thursday night?"

"No. I was very busy getting everything ready. . . ."

Susan wondered if he had started drinking then, but she didn't feel comfortable asking. Kathleen apparently had no such problem.

"No. I told Mrs. Henshaw that I was drinking the night of the burglary, but I was completely sober from that night until after the murder. I blame myself for that incident, and I certainly was not planning on a repeat performance any time soon."

"And you didn't see Horace Harvey until eight o'clock in the wine cellar."

"Oh, no. I saw him as soon as he arrived at the Inn. That was around six-thirty, I believe."

"Tell us about that," Susan suggested.

"It wasn't at all unusual. I did the same thing I would have done with anyone who was holding an event here. I escorted him around the floor to make sure there were no last-minute changes or adjustments that he wanted made, I took him to the kitchen to oversee the food that was being prepared. We must have spent about half an hour together."

"And did he want any changes?"

"None. He was almost complimentary."

"And did you go to the wine cellar to pick out wines or liquors?"

"No. He had requested that wine be served and that liquors be available for those who desired them, but all that had been brought up and was already behind the bar. That's our regular routine for any large event. In fact, that's what we do on an ordinary day. There's always a selection of house wines brought up from the cellar in the morning."

"So usually the wine cellar is empty?"

"Not so that someone could depend on it. The bartender, myself, and one or two of the waiters go down to bring up various bottles. No one spends much time down there, but there is a fair amount of traffic."

"But that night things were different. You said that everything was already behind the bar, and since the Inn was closed to regular customers . . ." Susan began.

"Yes. I wouldn't expect there to be many reasons to visit the cellar," Charles agreed. "But there was no guarantee that it would be empty. The order was for people to be given what they wanted. So if there was an order for something unusual, an old brandy, for instance, or grappa, someone would have gone down to get it."

"There's a large and very expensive collection of wine there. Don't you keep the place locked?" Kathleen asked.

"It's locked when the Inn is closed, and it is connected to our alarm system, of course, but I've never seen any reason to worry about it. Our customers don't steal from us, and it would be very inconvenient if we didn't have easy access throughout our business day."

"How do you keep track of what wine or liquor is taken from the room?"

"There is a book on a table near the door. Each bottle that is removed is written down. Later that night, after we close up, the daily information in that book is transferred into our computer records—usually by the bartender, but if he's too busy, I do it myself," he added before Kathleen could ask. He leaned across his desk, flipped on the computer, and showed both women how the system worked before continuing.

"And do you have the records for that Thursday?"

"I have to admit that no one did anything that evening. I thought there were more important things to worry about at the time, and I did have a drink or two after it was all over."

"So tell us about how you met Horace Harvey in the

wine cellar," Susan requested quickly. "What happened? Was he on time? What did he have to say to you?"

"We were both on time. He was already present when I arrived. . . ."

"Did that surprise you?"

"Not really. I had been busy making last-minute arrangements, so I hadn't been following his every move, but he had been greeting people who came early. . . ."

"Did a lot of people come early?" Kathleen asked.

For the first time in their conversation, Charles chuckled. "Yes. In fact, I think everyone came early, everyone who ran a committee or was close to someone who ran a committee. I think most of them either wanted to do some last-minute convincing or else hoped to find out exactly which group the money was going to before it was revealed to everyone else. Horace Harvey was very, very busy for the hour or so before he met me."

"So all the other suspects were present when you went to meet him in the cellar," Kathleen said. "Ralph Spinoza, Bob Arnold, Alissa Anthony, Honey Bradshaw, Pat Taylor, Tillie Greenleaf—and maybe Ethan Trumbull."

"I suppose so. Yes."

"So what happened when you met him?" Susan asked.

"I walked down to the cellar and he was already there—I told you that. He was looking around rather casually, in fact. Pulling out bottles, reading the labels, and then putting them back. I asked him to stop doing that. On some of the older wines, it stirs up the sediment. But he just ignored me and continued. I . . . I waited to see what he had to say to me."

"You must have been angry," Kathleen suggested.

"Furious," he agreed. "I would have liked to kill him, just like you're thinking. And what he said made me even more furious."

"What?"

"Well, he finally stopped slamming around the wine after pointing out that, in fact, it could be said that he owned those bottles as much as anybody."

"And then?"

"Then he said that something that was going to happen at the Inn that night would change my life more than the lives of any one of the people running one of those damn committees, and then he said that he wanted to see me back there at eleven o'clock that night. And that was all."

"All? You didn't respond?" Kathleen asked quickly.

"No. I didn't say anything. I just turned around and left the room and walked up the steps, and that's the last time I saw him alive."

"Did you take anything with you?" Susan asked suddenly.

"I . . . Yes. I took the jeroboam of champagne. It was the first thing that I reached out and grabbed. But I didn't take it from the room. I realized what I'd done and I put it down. I think on the desk near the door."

"The desk where the checkout book is kept?"

"Yes. I don't know why I did it. I wasn't thinking. It didn't make any sense, but it was . . . 'distressing' is the best word, I guess. I knew that the worst place for me to be then was around all that alcohol. So I came back upstairs and greeted guests."

"And you didn't go back downstairs until after Horace Harvey was dead?"

"No, but he must have been killed almost immediately. It was only about ten or fifteen minutes later that I heard the scream and joined everyone else downstairs."

Kathleen seemed to have run out of questions, so Susan spoke up. "Could we go see the wine cellar?"

"Now?"

"Yes, if it's not a problem."

"Of course not. Just follow me."

They did, trailing him down the elegant stairway to the main floor of the Inn and then down the narrow curving steps that led to the cellar. As Charles had said, the room was not locked, and they gathered together on the very spot where Horace Harvey's body had lain.

"The temperature is controlled," Kathleen said, peering at a thermometer hanging on the wall. Susan was busy walking around the tall shelves of bottles that jutted out into the room and bending over to peer into large wooden bins full of cardboard cases.

"Those are for ale and beer. They're fairly new and not nearly full. Drinking imported beers and those made at the smaller breweries in this country is becoming more and more popular, so we had these built a few months ago. Before that, we were always falling over the cases lying around on the floor."

Susan opened some of the boxes he was speaking about. "There's room for someone to hide in one of these," she said slowly.

"I guess there is," Charles agreed as Susan and Kathleen exchanged looks.

"It is possible that the murderer was here while you were talking with Horace Harvey," Susan explained. "It's certainly too bad that everything was so confused that night and that there's no way of being absolutely sure who wasn't on the first floor after you returned upstairs."

"Even people we saw upstairs during that time could have been here, climbed out of that box, killed Horace Harvey, and walked upstairs and mingled with the crowd until the body was discovered," Kathleen said. "This murder is not going to be solved using a nice, orderly process of elimination."

"No, it's going to be solved by finding out exactly how the murderer got Horace Harvey and the clues together in the wine cellar at the Inn on Thursday night."

NINETEEN

"He's lying," Kathleen said, getting back into the car.

"I know. He lied about the time he got back here. Without breaking the speed limit, he would have been back in Hancock at least an hour before me," Susan agreed.

"It would be interesting to know where he was and what he was doing during that time."

"True."

"You don't believe he did it, do you?" Kathleen asked.

"Not any more than you want to think Tillie did it—although I don't want to believe that either," Susan added quickly.

"Too bad we can't be sure of hating the guilty person, isn't it?"

"Or at least disliking them. If only it could be Alissa or Ralph Spinoza. I don't suppose either of them did it, but . . . This is absurd," Susan ended.

"Doesn't that story about the champagne bottle strike you as a little odd? Picking it up and putting it down by the doorway, so that it would be waiting conveniently for the murderer to come in, pick it up, and then use it to smash Horace Harvey's skull?"

Susan thought for a moment before answering. "It doesn't fit in with what I've been thinking. Not at all. Because this murder couldn't have been a spur-of-the-moment decision after all."

Kathleen nodded. "You're thinking about the French lilac, right?"

"All those clues. They couldn't have been rounded up at the last moment. Someone collected all that stuff and then went down to the wine cellar, murdered Horace Harvey, distributed their collection of evidence, and got away before the body was discovered. Which was probably almost no time at all. The person who killed Horace Harvey planned to kill Horace Harvey."

"But how did the murderer know that Harvey would be in the wine cellar when he was?"

"Maybe it wasn't necessary for him to be in the wine cellar. Maybe all that was necessary was for him to be alone."

"But, Susan, where else was he sure of being alone at the Inn that night? There's no place but the wine cellar. The offices are on the second floor between the rest rooms. People are always coming and going. And you've spent a lot of time around that place. It's two hundred years old; the floors roll and the doors don't fit perfectly. There's no guaranteed privacy anywhere . . . except for the wine cellar."

"So," Susan said, "how did the murderer know that Horace Harvey was going to be in the wine cellar?"

"They must have agreed to meet there," Kathleen said. "And when you think about it, you'll realize what I'm saying."

"That Charles is the person who asked Horace Harvey to meet him in the wine cellar. . . ." Susan said slowly.

"And therefore must be the murderer."

Susan didn't say anything for a long while. "Somehow it just doesn't feel right to me."

"Susan . . ."

"I know. I know. But we don't have any evidence, do we? You just think Charles is lying, and unless someone can prove that he is, there's no evidence against him."

"I wonder what sort of evidence James Malarkey has collected," Kathleen said.

"I do, too. You know, maybe we should just stop in and see Betsy. She works the overnight shift, so she'll be there."

"What a good idea," Kathleen said.

It took them only a few minutes to get to the municipal

center. Susan went in while Kathleen waited in the car. That way, if Susan was kicked out, Kathleen could come back later.

It had been a long day, and Susan was yawning as she entered the brightly lit building. But her first look at Betsy perked her up considerably. The girl was wearing a long gauzy skirt, tunic top, tights, and three or four scarves, all in the bright jewel tones that suited her admirably. The bank of police monitors was quiet, and notebooks covered the table where she sat.

"Hi, Mrs. Henshaw. Is everything okay?"

Susan glanced around. The door leading to the hallway where the offices were located was closed, and they were alone. "Yes. I'm here to talk to you, in fact. If you have a minute or two?"

"Sure do," Betsy replied with the cheerfulness that Susan was beginning to think of as habitual with her. "Are you still investigating the murder?"

"Yes, I—"

"Great! You should see the stuff I have here." Betsy pulled a large straw bag decorated with blowsy silk flowers from under her desk. "Take this, but don't tell anyone where you got it. I sure don't want my aunt to lose her job because I copied all this."

"I—"

"Don't thank me. Ethan said I should do it. Oh, listen to that damn thing," she added as illegible squawks blared out from the equipment behind her. "See you. Ethan's waiting at his aunt's house!" She waved and turned her back on Susan.

Susan would have asked why Ethan expected her to need him, but the door to the coffee room was opening and she didn't want to see anyone. She grabbed the bag and hurried out the door.

"Are you planning on a trip to the beach?" Kathleen asked as Susan got back into the car.

"Betsy gave it to me. That girl's a wonder. She looks like a flibbertigibbet, but she comes up with the most amazing information. And this is it." Susan scrounged through the bag. "I don't believe it! She copied everything. All the notes taken at all the interviews . . . It even looks like she copied someone's private notes on the case. These couldn't be James Malarkey's notes . . . but they are. Look. They match the memos on his imprinted memo paper!" Susan looked up from her work and at Kathleen. "He travels with his own personalized memo pads?"

"Seems like it." Kathleen had been sitting quietly in the driver's seat. "Do you want to go over to your house to read them? Or we could go home. . . ."

"No." Susan stopped her. "Betsy said that Ethan is waiting for us at his aunt's house. I don't know what it means or why he would want to see us, but . . ."

"But if he's waiting for us, we may as well go see him, don't you think?"

"I do."

Susan continued to examine the bag of materials, and by the time they had driven to the Trumbull house, she was more impressed than ever. "Incredible," she said, opening the door of the car.

"I assume you're not talking about me," Ethan said, with a courtly bow.

"We're talking about Betsy's research," Susan explained.

"She did it! She's some woman, isn't she?"

"We're impressed," Susan agreed, following him into the house.

"Did you ask her to collect all this stuff for a reason?" Kathleen asked, looking around the home.

"That's right," Susan agreed. "How did she know that we were going to want it?"

"I suppose she assumed that you had spoken with my aunt again," he explained as they all settled down in the room that had so impressed Susan the day before yesterday. "Her aunt has just gained mobility and she was wheeling her way around the floor yesterday, and we introduced them to each other. They started comparing notes about the murder. They've both been following the investigation in the local papers, and Betsy's aunt is very interested. She's been working as a dispatcher for almost twenty years, and apparently she thinks that the police department is going about this investigation in the completely wrong way. And she's been having a lot of visitors who work down at the department, and she claims that they're not all that happy with the way the investigation is going either. So she suggested that Betsy copy the relevant material and bring it to her."

"But you were going to do that, weren't you?"

"Yes. Betsy has to go back to school to take an exam tomorrow" (Susan remembered the books spread out on the desk) "and so I said I'd take everything in to her aunt. She probably just assumed that you were picking this stuff up to bring to me."

"Then we aren't actually supposed to be going through all this," Kathleen said.

Susan pulled the bag closer to her. "You're not going to get this away from me now," she insisted. "At least not until I've looked at it."

"I couldn't agree with you more," Ethan said. "Pass me a pile."

Susan handed each of her companions a pile of papers, and they all settled down to read. They were busy for over an hour, exchanging papers, making short comments, and passing around a bottle of Pinot Gris that Ethan had offered.

Ethan finished first, but he waited for the women before saying anything, refilling everyone's wineglass and fussing a little with the couch cushions.

Kathleen spoke first. "I don't see it," she announced.

Susan and Ethan both nodded. "You mean that this looks like a normal police investigation," Susan said.

"Exactly. It's not an inspired investigation. It's almost textbook. The right people were interviewed. The right questions were asked. The notes appear to be complete. Actually, this is a good murder investigation file."

"Why did you say it wasn't inspired?" Ethan asked.

"Well, it follows all the rules, but there's nothing extra, nothing that's personal. Except that's probably the wrong word. Let me explain. Brett Fortestque is our chief of police, and if he ran an investigation, a lot of the results would look just like this."

"But not all of it," Ethan guessed.

"No way. He would talk with people that he knows here in town, he would use people like Susan, and he would record their impressions and instincts. Of course, everyone works that part of the investigation differently, but everyone does have their own way of augmenting the normal channels of information."

"But James Malarkey isn't from Hancock. He doesn't have any sources like that here," Ethan protested.

"That could account for it. Or he could just be keeping those notes in a different place than the rest of this information."

Ethan shook his head. "Betsy said that she got it all. Apparently Detective Malarkey had everything together this morning for some reason."

"Probably to hand it over to the district attorney," Kathleen said grimly. "And his case is still pushing for Tillie's arrest." She sighed. "Well, it's late. I suppose we'd better be going." Being the closest to the bag, she started to scoop up everything and stuff it in.

"This reminds me of all the stuff you carried to my house on Thursday afternoon. Remember? All the records of H.E.C. Of course, all the research about the organizations was included in his investigation. . . ."

"Susan, what are you thinking about?"

"Is she all right?" Ethan asked, leaning forward. Susan was staring at the pile in front of her with her mouth open.

"I think we're about to hear a revelation. And the solution to this murder," Kathleen said.

Susan shook her head. "I may know who did it. It's the only person who could have done it, who would have had a reason to do it, but there's one thing I just don't understand."

Her companions waited until she spoke again.

"It's exactly what we were saying this morning," she said to Kathleen. "Why the wine cellar at the Inn?"

* * *

Susan was perched on a stool at her kitchen counter. Laid out before her were the case notes, which she had promised to bring to Betsy's aunt first thing in the morning, the information that Kathleen seemed as unlikely to sort as every other secretary at the H.E.C., the envelopes of clippings from the newspaper morgue in Boston, and *Lovely Names for the Puppy You Love*. At her feet lay the nameless puppy that she loved just a little bit less after discovering that it had consumed one corner of her handmade Italian kitchen cabinets.

Susan had reread the police file, skimmed H.E.C.'s records, and was busy examining the scribbles she and Kathleen had made in the back of the dog book. She was sure there must be a clue here. But where? She got up and stole an empty notebook from her son's backpack, which was waiting on the floor by the back door (making a mental note to ask him about the grade on the top paper in the pack), poured a large mug of the Kona-blend coffee she had made, and started to scribble.

It was almost two A.M. when she sat back to study the results of her work. She had organized the material three times into three different piles, and she still didn't see how she was going to prove what she was sure must be true.

"Aren't you going to come to bed?"

Susan looked up at her husband in the doorway. "Hi. Want something to drink? Some herb tea?"

"Sue, I hope that's decaf you're drinking." Jed stared at his wife. "It isn't, is it?"

"Jed, I have to figure this out before it drives me crazy. Go back to bed. I can sleep once this is all over."

"You're not doing this because you think Tillie Greenleaf has been accused falsely anymore, are you?"

"No. I think I know who did it; I just can't prove it." She told her husband the name of her favorite suspect.

"You're kidding," he responded. "Let me see all the stuff you've been writing."

Susan was glad for the help. "Look. I've organized everything I know in three different ways." She pushed a pile of papers across the counter toward her husband. "This is the list of suspects—the people that the police consider to be suspects."

Jed read down the list. "Alissa Anthony. Bob Arnold. Honey Bradshaw. Tillie Greenleaf. Ralph Spinoza. Patty Taylor. Ethan Trumbull. Why is Charles dash dash the Hancock Inn in parentheses?"

"Because it all has to hinge on the Inn. I'll explain that in a minute. Let's talk about the police suspects first. These people all run one of the organizations that hoped to benefit from the death of Horace Harvey. And clues to all of them were left on the body: the lilac, the playbill from the little theater, the marijuana, the pipe from the archaeological site, the minutes of the meeting of H.O.P.E. and Q.U.I.E.T., the design of the new playground that P.A.P. wanted to build down by the duck pond."

"Which just goes to show that the murderer came prepared to plant the clues, right?"

"Exactly!"

"These things aren't big. They would have fit easily into a coat or jacket pocket, so I don't see that they're so significant," Jed suggested.

"Except that they prove that the murderer knew exactly which organizations Harvey was considering."

"True. Didn't most people?"

"Doesn't prove anything, does it?" Susan asked.

"Nope."

Susan crumpled up the page. "Okay, second thought. This is, as far as I can tell, a time frame for the night of the murder. Listen: When the day sheet came out at the Inn on Thursday morning, there was no mention of the affair that night."

"The day sheet?"

Susan explained about the organization that Charles had devised for his business.

"He sounds like a fabulous manager," Jed commented. "Of course, we should have known that. The Inn is very well run."

"Yes. So Horace Harvey had not bothered to confirm his plans for Thursday night by late the evening before when the sheet was drawn up. But he had invited everyone that he planned to entertain that night, and the murderer had to have some notice to collect the clues."

"Are you sure?"

"Definitely. The French lilac must have been stolen from Tillie Greenleaf's greenhouse during the night. Her husband said that he was working where he could see the building for most of the day Thursday. It isn't likely that the murderer would have taken the risk of being seen."

"Is this why you're eliminating Charles? Because he didn't know about the party until late that morning?"

"I hadn't thought of it that way, but you're right." She wrote a note to herself in the margin before continuing. "Okay, so sometime right after noon on Thursday, Charles found out that the Inn was going to be taken over that evening, and he issued instructions to his staff. He also found out at lunchtime that he was to meet Horace Harvey in the wine cellar at eight o'clock that night."

"And who else knew about that?"

"Good question . . ."

"In fact, that's an argument against Charles's innocence, isn't it?"

"It is unless Harvey didn't just ask to meet Charles. What if he had set up appointments with other people? The murderer, to be more specific."

"Can you prove that?" Jed asked.

"No, damn it." She took a large gulp of coffee. "But I'll be able to before tomorrow night."

Jed looked startled. "What's happening tomorrow night?"

"The police are going to arrest Horace Harvey's murderer."

TWENTY

IT WAS POSSIBLE THAT THERE HAD NEVER BEFORE BEEN SO many people in the Inn's wine cellar at one time.

"You called everyone here to disclose the name of the murderer? You've spent too much time watching television, Susan."

"Why don't you just sit down and wait till everyone gets here, Honey? Then we'll see what Susan has come up with," Kathleen suggested.

"That's right, you're not all that different from the rest of us. Just a little more vocal," Alissa said, calling the kettle black.

"There's an empty seat here," Patty Taylor said, pulling her coat off the folding chair beside the one she was sitting on.

"You probably have things to do. . . ." Susan began to the teacher.

"Not me. I found out Monday morning that I'd gotten the Woman's World job. I'm doing what I'm paid for, but I took today off. I have two personal days coming to me . . . not that that's important now." Patty looked a little embarrassed by her own volubility.

"Congratulations," Kathleen said.

Both Alissa and Honey scowled at her smile. "Are we ever going to get on with this? It's a little chilly in here," Honey said, pulling her cashmere sweater just a little closer to her pearl drop earrings.

"It's a wine cellar, for heaven's sake!" Ralph Spinoza exploded. He was leaning heavily against one of the wooden shelves holding cases of wine, and Susan hoped they were secured tightly. "Did you expect it to be warm?"

"Only a drunk like you would know about that, dear." Honey dripped false sweetness.

Susan was amazed. Evidently Ralph's drinking problem was well known.

"Well, at least I didn't have to turn to Harvey in my hour of need back in high school."

Damn! Susan had been hoping that they could deal with the past only as it had to do directly with the murder. She didn't see any reason to hurt people who had done stupid things, made mistakes, and then gotten on with their lives. She believed that the innocent had a right to privacy.

"Yeah, Honey thinks it's a big secret, but Shirl once did a bankruptcy for a group medical practice and found out all about it," Ralph continued. "She told me one time when we were . . . well, when we were feeling relaxed and talking. I guess you don't tell the story of your illegal abortion in high school when you're reminiscing about your charmed youth, do you, Honey?"

"You are a disgusting drunk, Ralph Spinoza, and you are certainly no gentleman. Of course, why would you be? You've spent most of your adult life pretending to be someone you're not, haven't you?" Honey spit back. "You weren't a student activist at Berkeley in the sixties, you went to a community college in Nebraska, where you barely passed most of your courses for the two years that you bothered to attend until you joined the coast guard to avoid the draft. It was lucky for you, of course, since you happened to meet two rich kids whose parents were happy to give their sons' friends a start in life when you all finally got out—probably hoping that you would be quiet about some of their sons' more disgusting habits. . . ."

"That is not true!" he roared. "And how do you know where I went to school?"

"Kept it a secret, did you?" Honey countered.

"My ex-wife and your ex-girlfriend hired a private detective to investigate your past back when she was thinking about cosigning your mortgage. Recently she's begun divulging some of your secrets," Bob Arnold said very quietly.

"Why? Is that woman trying to ruin my life?" Ralph cried, putting his head in his hands.

"I believe so," admitted Bob. "She's like that, you know."

Everyone in the room shifted uncomfortably in their chairs.

"Maybe we should get back to the murder," Tillie Greenleaf suggested.

"We're waiting for someone," Susan admitted as James Malarkey and two of his detectives walked in the door. "Now we're ready," she said, nodding at the three men. Two of them nodded back.

"I hope you're not wasting our time," James Malarkey said. "We're pretty busy. We have a murder investigation going on, you know."

Susan ground her teeth, thinking that the wrong people were always murdered. On the other hand, she reminded herself, she hadn't known Horace Harvey.

"Well," she began. "I'm not quite sure how to start." It wasn't true, but she hoped that it would buy her some time. She looked around the room. Charles and Ethan were sitting together on the large bin that she suspected had hidden the murderer last Thursday night. Honey was glaring at Ralph from across the room, and Patty was sitting next to her, looking . . . well, *perky* was the only word Susan could think of. She was sure the young woman would be a wonderful adventure guide. Alissa was perched on a tall stool with her fabulous hair flying out to the four winds. Bob Arnold was by her side, looking, surprisingly, bored. Tillie was standing against the back wall of the cellar; she looked angry. Betsy walked in the door, a newspaper in her hand.

"Well, it looks as if we're ready to go, doesn't it?" Susan said as she watched Betsy smile shyly at Ethan.

"It's about time," Honey announced, and Susan had the feeling that everyone in the room agreed with her.

"Okay." Susan took a deep breath and began. "This

didn't start last week, last month, or, for that matter, in the last decade. This began over thirty years ago when a young man that no one liked found that he could gain some control over his life and the lives of other people if he loaned them money.

"Hancock is a community of commuters, and there aren't many around who grew up here, but those that did don't have a very clear memory of Horace Harvey. He wasn't on any of the school teams, he wasn't an outstanding student except in math, he was almost completely forgettable ... except to the students who, for one reason or another, were forced to borrow money from him."

"Like me," Honey said bitterly. "I suppose I may as well explain since everyone knows about it now." She glared at Ralph Spinoza and continued. "I got pregnant my freshman year of high school. I was stupid, but that's another story. I didn't want anyone to know and I was desperate. Abortions were illegal back then, but I had heard that there was a doctor in Bridgeport who would perform them—for two hundred dollars." She sniffed. "I pay more than that for a simple dress now, but at that time it might as well have been twelve million dollars. I had absolutely no idea how to raise it. I had money in my savings account, of course, but I was afraid that my parents would find out if I withdrew it. And then I heard about Horace Harvey.

"I was a junior varsity cheerleader, and we sometimes practiced with the varsity team. In the locker room after a practice, I heard one of the older girls talking about needing money, probably for a reason similar to mine, and one of them told the other to go to Horace Harvey for cash, that he would always loan it. Well, I got out of there and started my search for this savior. I asked everyone I knew and finally tracked him down in the chem lab the next morning.

"He was there, leaning over a Bunsen burner, with greasy hair and an intense look on his face. I remember being so relieved to see him that I just dashed up and blurted out that I needed two hundred dollars." She leaned back and looked around the room. "You know, I remember exactly the expression he had on his face when he heard my words. What a slime. He smiled a sickly smile and said fine, but that I would have to pay it back with interest."

"Sex!" Alissa guessed, sounding thrilled at the real life drama.

"Ha! Cash was all he was interested in. I paid him one hundred percent interest before I was done."

"Did you sign something?" Bob Arnold asked.

"No. He knew that I would never tell anyone that I had been pregnant. I took the money, promised to pay what he asked, and went to Bridgeport. The abortion worked, but an infection afterwards left me sterile—and emotionally as well as physically exhausted. But I had no choice but to find a job, because I had promised to pay that man back before he left for college at the end of summer. I lied about my age and was hired to work off the books at a fast-food place out on the highway. The one that burned down three years ago, remember? I was thrilled by that fire."

"But you did manage to pay him back?" Kathleen asked.

"Yes. And I had to pretend that I was making much less money than I was to hide what had happened from my parents. That whole summer was a nightmare. It was all I could think of when I heard that Harvey was coming back to town."

"And what happened the first time you met?" Susan asked.

"Well, he looked so different, so well dressed and all that, I could hardly believe it was him at first. But it was all a facade. It didn't take any time at all to see that he was still the same man, still trying to be powerful because he had money."

"Did he remember you?" Susan asked.

"Probably, but he didn't say anything about it, if that's what you're wondering. The mayor brought him to our meeting last Monday. It was a breakfast meeting at the home of one of our newest members, and she wasn't very organized, so I was busy making sure everything was being taken care of when he arrived. In fact, I didn't notice him until I had served myself."

"Did he ever mention what had taken place between you two in high school?" Susan asked.

"Never. We were never alone together. I was dreading that, but it didn't happen. Later, I thought that perhaps he had been avoiding it, that as long as other people were around, no one would talk about the past, and he didn't want that any more than I did."

"So you're claiming that you didn't kill him," Alissa summed up.

"Of course I didn't. I knew I'd be suspected if anyone knew about the abortion—which is why I lied to you and claimed to be in the ladies' room when it happened. But why would I kill him? What did I have to gain by that?"

"She wouldn't admit it if she had," Ralph reminded those present.

"Shirley Arnold grew up in Hancock," Honey said.

"But she wasn't here the night of the murder," Susan said.

Ralph jumped in quickly. "But Bob was. Maybe he murdered Harvey because of something in his ex-wife's past."

"You're more likely to be defending her honor than I am right now," Bob argued. "Besides, let's face it, Shirl is more likely to have been involved in the same business as Harvey was than to have needed his services. You should know that."

"I don't think we need to discuss things that have nothing to do with the murder," Ralph said pompously.

"No, you wouldn't, would you?" Bob said, and Susan got the impression that he felt he had won a battle at last.

"Well," Susan said, "to continue the story. Horace Harvey left Hancock and became very successful doing exactly what he had been doing since he was in high school. Lending out money. But over the years, and after an education, he became more sophisticated. He still loaned money to people in his old hometown. In fact, he was the silent partner of Charles in the Hancock Inn." She paused and waited for the exclamations of surprise to cease. "And he still asked for more in return than any reasonable person or bank would." She hoped that she wouldn't be forced to say any more. She didn't want to drag Charles's dirty laundry through the mud.

"So there he was, living in Boston as though he was a rich man. Only it was all a facade—an expensive facade. He had the money to buy the big house and even to decorate it where it showed." Susan remembered that second floor with the expensive window treatments that neither opened nor closed because no one actually lived in those rooms. "But he still hung out in a cheap corner bar, and he had no social life that anyone could detect. He was a rich venture capitalist who had made no impact on anyone who didn't need his money or who stood in the way of him making more." She remembered the dry cleaner's daughter and wondered how many others had suffered the same fate. "And so, I think, he decided to show off, to become the rich benefactor of the town where he had grown up. In fact, when he came to visit Ethan's aunt in the hospital, she said she felt like he was a famous millionaire condescending to toss her a dime.

"So he came back to town to show off his success, to flaunt it in everyone's face, the prodigal son returned. And, as Martha Trumbull pointed out, he didn't do what almost any normal person would have done. He didn't announce that he was going to leave his money to the League of Women Voters, the County Historical Society, the Red Cross, or an organization like that—and he would have gotten lots of publicity from any of those groups. Instead he chose to do exactly the same thing he'd always done: make everyone uncomfortable.

"He chose small civic organizations that were run by individuals. And he looked at them carefully; he asked to see the parks, he visited the place that Alissa is hoping to turn into a theater—"

"That Alissa is *going* to turn into a theater," Alissa insisted loudly.

Susan ignored the interruption. "He ate a lot of food, went to lots of meetings, talked to a lot of people."

"So that he could decide which group needed the

money," Detective Malarkey said sourly. "It would be nice if you had called us here to tell us something new."

"If you'll just wait," Susan suggested, looking over at Kathleen, who smiled and nodded. "Although, in fact, you come in here, too. I got involved in this investigation because Kathleen was so sure that you had arrested the wrong person."

"Anyone who knows Tillie Greenleaf would know that she's not a murderer," Kathleen insisted.

"I thought I would just check into things, the way that I normally do. I guess you could say that my method of investigating is more intuitive than organized. And it would have been like that this time if you hadn't given me a list of questions to ask all the suspects. The questions were entirely personal. I was surprised by that and thought you were just trying to waste my time, but I did what you wanted. It gave me a certain authority to say that I was asking questions for the acting chief of police—an authority that I lacked with Brett out of town."

"We're thrilled to hear how important you were to this investigation," Alissa said sarcastically.

"I think this is all very interesting," Pat Taylor insisted. "And you're being rather rude, aren't you?"

Alissa narrowed her eyes, folded her arms across her chest, and scowled. But she shut up.

"Well, I asked all your questions, and I found out a few things that seemed significant and a lot of things that didn't. And then I went to Boston to visit colleges with my daughter. And I found out a lot about Horace Harvey, a lot about Charles, and a whole lot about why you didn't want me to go there. Although I didn't understand that at the time."

"What happened?" Pat asked. "Besides the college interviews. Chris told me all about them."

"Well, I found the answers to a lot of questions in Boston, and then more answers when I spoke with Charles here that night, but I still didn't understand one thing: Why did the murder take place here?"

"In the wine cellar or in the Inn?" Honey asked.

"Both," Susan explained. "But I should have understood

right away. Because Charles told me that he met Horace Harvey here at eight o'clock Thursday night. Harvey had insisted on the meeting."

"So Charles is the murderer? Not a chance," Alissa insisted. "I know about character. That man is not a murderer. Besides, you're saying that Charles murdered Horace Harvey and then admitted that he met him here at about the time we all knew the murder was committed. He's not stupid, for heaven's sake. No one would play it that way. Too risky—and the audience wouldn't believe it."

"No, but I think the murderer was here already," Susan said, and then explained her thoughts about the large trunk that Ethan and Charles were sitting upon. They both moved rather nervously. Susan walked over and opened the bin. There was ample room inside for even the largest man.

"So do you want to explain how it happened that Horace Harvey called a meeting with Charles that the murderer just happened to attend?" James Malarkey asked sarcastically. "And the murderer just happened to show up with a collection of clues to lead us to all the organizations that Horace Harvey was thinking about endowing?"

"That had me stuck, too," Susan admitted. "It looks like the murderer just took advantage of happening to be in the right place at the right time—which I couldn't believe. The clues indicate that this murder was planned. Someone showed up in this place planning a murder. And the only person who could have done that—"

"He didn't! I know he didn't!" The young waitress who had slipped the note in Susan's hand insisted, appearing at the door.

"She's right. I didn't." Charles spoke quietly, smiling at the young woman.

"I know. It was Horace Harvey who planned the murder. It was Horace Harvey who brought the clues here. Of course, he wasn't planning to be the victim."

The room was silent, and the footsteps in the doorway attracted universal attention. Susan had a hard time not crying out with relief when she saw Brett Fortesque there. He had three uniformed men standing behind him.

"You see," Susan continued more calmly, "Horace Harvey came here hoping to impress the citizens of Hancock with how successful, brilliant, and rich he had become. He certainly didn't want anyone to know about the slimy methods he had employed to make that money. And James Malarkey knew all about that. Didn't you?"

Susan looked the detective straight in the eyes, amazed at how quickly Brett and his men surrounded him. There were a few busy minutes while Hancock's acting police chief was arrested, frisked, read his rights, and led off in handcuffs before she could continue.

"You are going to explain, aren't you?" Ralph still sounded aggressive, but Susan thought she heard relief in there someplace.

"Please." Charles sounded exhausted.

"You said it yourself," Susan began to Charles. "You said that Horace Harvey had 'extraordinary sources'—your exact words. And James Malarkey was one of them. James Malarkey was a private investigator, and he worked for Horace Harvey for years. You see, someone had to do the research on the people whose businesses Harvey was going to invest in. James Malarkey was that man. Betsy." Susan held out her hand, and Betsy put the newspaper she had been carrying into it. "When I was visiting Martha Trumbull in the hospital, Ethan came in with this paper. He said that there was information about James Malarkey's background in the article about the murder. If only I had seen this sooner, I might have made the connection. As it was, Betsy's aunt did—and she called me last night and read the proper quotation.

"Let me see . . . 'Before becoming an officer in the Connecticut State Police Department, James Malarkey was a private investigator in Boston, specializing in research for private industry.' " She looked up. "Turns out that he worked almost entirely for Horace Harvey for fifteen years. Fifteen years of digging into personal secrets and tragedies that Harvey could turn into money."

"You're saying that Horace Harvey brought the pipe, the marijuana, the lilac, and everything else that was found on his body down here with him?" Ethan asked. He had moved over to Betsy, and Susan was glad to see that they were holding hands.

"Yes. He was going to kill James Malarkey. It had to be done, otherwise he couldn't appear as this benevolent community benefactor. And he was going to try to pin the murder on one of the groups in competition for his money. There was no other reason to get everyone here, was there?"

Kathleen looked at her and nodded slowly. "This accounts for the double murder weapons, doesn't it?"

"Yes. I think that probably James Malarkey's appearance surprised Horace Harvey, and there was a fight. Harvey was hit over the head with the jeroboam of champagne and then, to finish him off, strangled with his own belt. The fact that it was a full money belt was just Malarkey's good luck."

"And he found the clues in Harvey's pocket. . . ." Ethan began.

"And used them in probably the same way that Harvey was planning to—on a different corpse, of course."

"Wow!" Pat Taylor exclaimed.

"There is one question that no one has answered," Tillie Greenleaf said, breaking the silence that followed Pat's comment.

"What?" Kathleen asked.

"Who did Horace Harvey leave his money to? Or wasn't he planning to make a will at all? Was this whole thing a sham that ended in a murder?"

"I don't think so. Brett . . . Chief Fortesque . . . has that information," Susan said, looking at the door. "He was planning on coming back. . . ." She smiled. "There he is."

"Yes. Here I am!" Brett smiled and sat down, too accustomed to living with his own good looks to preen over the attention he was getting from all the women in the room.

"We were wondering about Horace Harvey's will," Kathleen said. "Have you had a chance to look at it yet?"

"Sure have. And from what I understand about this case, it's not going to make anyone here very happy: The entire estate, worth a couple of million dollars, is going to go to the Hancock Library to form a Horace Harvey collection." Brett looked around the room to see how his audience was taking this disappointment. To his and Susan's amazement, everyone seemed perfectly content with this information.

"Well, that's that," Ralph declared, standing up and stretching out his back. "Guess it's time to get this show on the road. I don't suppose you need a ride, do you?" he offered Honey Bradshaw.

"I'd rather die first." She scowled. "And I have my Mercedes, of course. You know," she added, turning to Tillie Greenleaf, "we should probably make some suggestions about that new collection. There are so many marvelous gardening books coming out these days. . . ."

Tillie smiled. "You're right. And there are classics in reprint that the entire town could benefit from." She smiled at Kathleen and Susan, and followed F.O.P.P.'s leader from the room.

"Do you have time to get lunch before we go to the hospital?" Ethan asked Betsy.

"I suppose so, but we should call and tell the aunts the news—they'll be waiting," she reminded him.

"Okay, there's a phone upstairs next to the men's room," Ethan agreed, making way for her to leave ahead of him.

"One of the librarians has been very active in my group," Alissa Anthony was explaining to Bob Arnold. "I think she'll be very interested in hearing what I have to contribute about the selection of materials in the new collection. I think I'll stop there on the way home."

"Good idea. I would love to have a modem connection into the . . ." Bob Arnold said, following her up the stairs.

" 'Bye." Pat Taylor stood uncertainly in the doorway. "It's strange, isn't it?" she added. "They don't seem to care so much about whether they got the money or not—it's more like they just didn't want someone else to get it." She shook her head in dismay. " 'Bye," she repeated, and left.

"She's right, isn't she?" Charles asked.

"Oh, I think they'll continue to try getting a piece of that particular pie—by the selection of books added to the library, if nothing else," Susan said. "How are you doing?" she asked Charles, who was staring at the floor.

"Okay. I'm just glad it's all over," he said.

"Well, I have one question," Brett announced.

"What's that?" Susan asked.

"Did you realize just how risky it was to accuse an armed man of murder in a room full of people?"

TWENTY-ONE

Susan and Kathleen were squatting on the grass in one of Hancock's parks, tossing a red rubber ball back and forth between themselves and Bananas. The puppy chewed a twig, keeping a close eye on the action.

"It was the lies that made everything so difficult to figure out," Susan was saying.

"That's true in any murder investigation, isn't it?" Kathleen asked, laughing at how seriously her son was working to catch the ball.

"But these people weren't lying to hide their guilt. They had other reasons. Like Ralph Spinoza."

"What about him?"

"Well, the first time I talked to him, he tried hard to convince me that Bob Arnold couldn't be guilty—he was willing to consider anyone other than Bob. And that was because he was afraid of upsetting Shirley. He needed her help to straighten out his financial affairs. And that made sense after Shirley explained the situation."

"I have to admit that I really thought it was Charles."

"You were supposed to. Horace Harvey had invited Charles to the wine cellar, planning to murder James Malarkey and then blame the murder on Charles as the last person who had seen Malarkey alive. Of course, Malarkey just followed the plan. When he went to the Inn earlier to investigate the burglary, he recognized the place and Charles as a concern that he had researched years ago. And knowing about Charles's past, he knew just how vulnerable he would be in a murder investigation."

"Good at thinking on his feet, wasn't he?" Kathleen asked.

"Sure was. He certainly wouldn't have met Horace Harvey if he had known that Harvey planned to kill him, and the murder itself must have been self-defense. But once he had killed Harvey, he took advantage of every aspect of the situation, both the clues and Charles's past."

"I stopped in to see Brett this morning," Kathleen said, getting up to retrieve the ball her son had accidentally tossed over his head.

The retriever, living up to its breed's reputation, beat her to it, and Kathleen had to work to get the ball from the dog's mouth, much to her son's delight.

"Is Brett still criticizing me for last night?" Susan asked, getting up to help her friend.

"You have to admit, it could have been very dangerous," Kathleen said.

"You're right. I just didn't think about the fact that he was armed. It was stupid."

"Well, Brett had copies of the papers from the safe in Boston—the police department up there faxed them out overnight—and there were complete records of all Harvey's financial transactions from Honey Bradshaw on."

"He really wasn't a nice man," Susan said.

"At least the library will benefit from his death," Kathleen reminded her, looking down at the dog. "Should she be eating those flowers?"

Susan leapt to protect a bed of pansies from her pet. "Come on, Clue, Tillie Greenleaf and H.E.C. will ban you from the park if you eat their flowers."

"Clue?"

"The family has finally decided on a name. They announced it over breakfast this morning. They named this sweet little thing Clue in honor of me. Or, to be more exact, they filled out her papers, mailed them in, and registered her as 'Susan Hasn't Got a Clue.' "

"Maybe the American Kennel Club already has a dog registered under that name and they won't allow it," Kathleen suggested.

The puppy crawled up in Susan's lap, leaving muddy paw prints on her slacks and drooling petals on her linen shirt. Susan scratched the soft golden head. "We can only hope."